Christian Jacq is one of France's leading Egyptologists. He is the author of the internationally bestselling *Ramses* series, which has been translated into twenty-four languages and sold more than six million copies worldwide. He is also the author of the stand-alone novel *The Black Pharaoh*.

Also by Christian Jacq:

Ramses: The Son of the Light
Ramses: The Temple of a Million Years
Ramses: The Battle of Kadesh
Ramses: The Lady of Abu Simbel
Ramses: Under the Western Acacia
The Black Pharaoh
The Stone of Light: Nefer the Silent
The Stone of Light: The Wise Woman
The Stone of Light: Paneb the Ardent
The Stone of Light: The Place of Truth

The Living Wisdom of Ancient Egypt

About the Translator

Sue Dyson is a prolific author of both fiction and non-fiction, including over thirty novels, both contemporary and historical. She has also translated a wide variety of French fiction.

The Queen of Freedom Trilogy

The Flaming Sword

Christian Jacq

Translated by Sue Dyson

SIMON &
SCHUSTER

LONDON • SYDNEY • NEW YORK • TOKYO • SINGAPORE • TORONTO

First published in France by XO Editions under the title
L'Épée Flamboyante, 2002
First published in Great Britain by Simon & Schuster UK Ltd, 2003
A Viacom company

1 3 5 7 9 10 8 6 4 2

Simon & Schuster UK Ltd
Africa House
64–78 Kingsway
London WC2B 6AH

www.simonsays.co.uk

Simon & Schuster Australia
Sydney

A CIP catalogue record for this book is available
from the British Library

HB ISBN 0-7432-3079-5
TPB ISBN 0-7432-3943-1

Typeset in Times by SX Composing DTP, Rayleigh, Essex
Printed and bound in Great Britain by
The Bath Press

I dedicate this book to all those men and women who have devoted their lives to freedom, by fighting against occupation, totalitarian regimes and inquisitions of every kind.

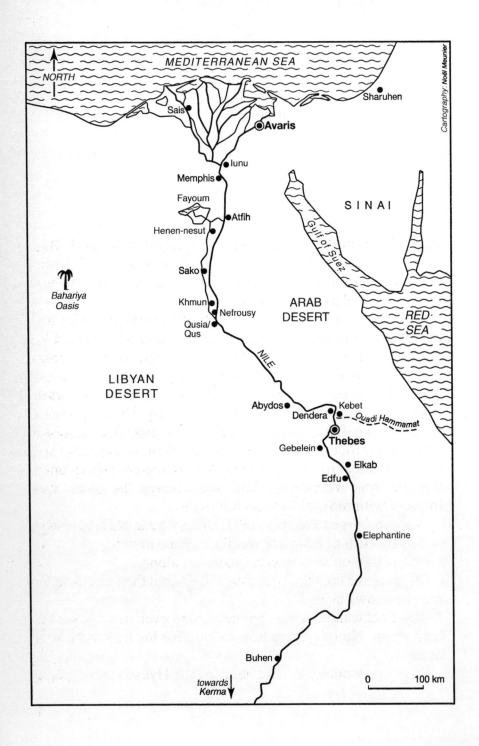

NORTH

MEDITERRANEAN SEA

Sharuhen

Sais

◉**Avaris**

Iunu

Memphis

Fayoum

Atfih

SINAI

Henen-nesut

Gulf of Suez

Sako

ARAB
DESERT

Khmun

Nefrousy

RED
SEA

Qusia/
Qus

NILE

Bahariya
Oasis

LIBYAN
DESERT

Abydos

Kebet

Dendera

Ouadi Hammamat

◉**Thebes**

Gebelein

Elkab

Edfu

Elephantine

Buhen

towards
Kerma

0   100 km

1

Prisoner number 1790 collapsed, face down in the mud. Big-Feet had lost the will to live. After all these years in the death-camp at Sharuhen, in Canaan, the last of his strength had finally drained away.

Sharuhen was the rearward base of the Hyksos, who had occupied Egypt for more than a century and who had set up their capital at Avaris, in the Delta. Their supreme commander, Emperor Apophis, was not content merely to use his army and security forces to impose a reign of terror. Approving a tempting idea dreamt up by High Treasurer Khamudi, his faithful right-hand man, he had set up a prison camp at the foot of the fortress of Sharuhen, in a marshy and unhealthy area. In winter the winds were ice-cold, in summer the sun was mercilessly hot, and always the place was infested with mosquitoes and horseflies.

'Get up,' urged Prisoner 2501, a thirty-year-old scribe who had lost a fifth of his body weight in three months.

'I can't go on any longer. Leave me alone.'

'If you give up, Big-Feet, you'll die – and then you'll never see your cows again.'

Big-Feet wanted to die, but he wanted even more to see his herd again. No one knew how to care for his beasts the way he did.

Like many others, he had believed the Hyksos' lies. 'Come

and graze your scrawny animals on the lush Northern grasslands,' they had said. 'Once they are in good health again, you shall return home.' In fact, the Hyksos had stolen the herds, killed any herdsmen who protested, and thrown the others into the death-camp at Sharuhen.

Big-Feet would never forgive them for separating him from his cows. He could have borne extra work, forced labour, arduous marches through the flooded lands, a pitiful recompense, but not that.

Prisoner 1790 clambered to his feet.

Like his companions in misfortune, he had suffered the horrible ordeal of being branded with his prison number, all the other prisoners being forced to watch. Anyone who turned away or closed his eyes was executed on the spot.

Big-Feet could still feel the appalling pain of the red-hot copper branding-iron. The louder the victim screamed, the longer the torture lasted. Several of the wounded had died from infection, because at Sharuhen there were neither doctors nor nurses, and no one was given the slightest care. Had he not been strong, naturally lean and accustomed to getting by on little food, the herdsman would have died long ago. At Sharuhen, big eaters lasted only a few months.

'Here, have a little stale bread.'

Big-Feet did not refuse the sumptuous gift offered by his friend, who had been sent to the camp for keeping a hymn to Pharaoh Senusret in his house. Denounced by a neighbour, the scribe had been condemned as a dangerous conspirator and deported immediately. Emperor Apophis, the self-proclaimed pharaoh, did not permit references to Egypt's glorious past.

A frail little girl approached the two men. 'You haven't got anything to eat, have you? I am so hungry.'

Big-Feet was ashamed to have swallowed the scrap of bread so quickly. 'Didn't the guards give you your rations today?' he asked.

'They forgot me.'

'Didn't your mother ask them?'

'She died last night.'

The child turned and went back to her mother's corpse. No one could do anything for her. If someone took her under their wing, she would be snatched away instantly and thrown to the whims of the mercenaries at the fortress.

'There's another convoy arriving,' said the scribe.

The heavy wooden gate of the camp swung open, and the new prisoners straggled in. A tall woman with enormous hands was hitting some of the old men with a club, even though they could scarcely walk. One of them collapsed, his skull fractured. The others tried to hurry, in the hope of escaping the blows, but the Hyksos torturers did not spare a single one.

Eventually, astonished still to be alive, the strongest of the new arrivals got up very slowly, afraid of yet more torments. But their torturers were content to sneer at them.

'Welcome to Sharuhen!' shouted the lady Aberia. 'Here, you will at last learn obedience. The living shall bury the dead and then clean up this camp. It's a real pigsty!' No worse insult could be uttered by a Hyksos, for they never ate pork.

Big-Feet and the scribe hurried to obey. Aberia liked the prisoners to prove their goodwill; any lack of enthusiasm for the task in hand led to torture.

They dug shallow ditches with their bare hands and threw in the bodies, unable to perform even the most perfunctory funerary rite. As always, Big-Feet addressed a silent prayer to the goddess Hathor, who welcomed the souls of the righteous into her bosom and whose incarnation was a cow, the most beautiful of all creatures.

'Tomorrow is the night of the new moon,' announced Aberia with a cruel smile as she left the camp.

An old man who had arrived with the latest convoy came over to Big-Feet and asked, 'May we speak?'

3

'Now that she has gone, yes.'

'Why is that she-devil so preoccupied with the moon?'

'Because each time it is reborn she chooses a prisoner and slowly strangles him or her in front of the others.'

Shoulders slumping, the old man sat down between prisoners 1790 and 2501. 'What are those numbers on your arms?'

'Our prison numbers,' replied the scribe. 'First thing tomorrow, you and all the new prisoners will be branded.'

'You mean . . . more than two thousand unfortunates have been deported here?'

'Many more,' said Big-Feet. 'A lot of prisoners died or were tortured to death before they could be reduced to a number.'

The old man clenched his fists. 'We must keep hope alive,' he declared with unexpected vigour.

'Why?' asked the scribe in a cynical tone,

'Because the Hyksos are getting more and more worried. In the Delta towns and at Memphis, resistance is being organized.'

'The emperor's security guards will root it out.'

'They have more than enough work on their hands, believe me.'

'There are too many informants,' said the scribe. 'No one slips through the net.'

'With my own hands I killed a papyrus-seller who had denounced a woman to the Hyksos militia because she refused to sleep with him. He was young and much stronger than I am, but I found the strength I needed to kill that monster – and I don't regret it. Little by little, the people of Egypt are coming to understand that bowing the knee to the enemy leads only to slaughter. What the emperor wants is to wipe out all us Egyptians and replace us with Hyksos. They steal our goods, our lands, our houses, and they want to destroy our souls, too.'

4

'That's what they're trying to do in this camp,' said the scribe, his voice faltering.

'Apophis forgets that Egypt has a real reason to hope,' blazed the old man.

Big-Feet's heart beat a little faster.

'The Queen of Freedom,' went on the old man, 'she's our hope. She will never give up the fight against Apophis.'

'The Theban troops failed to capture Avaris,' the scribe reminded him, 'and Pharaoh Kamose is dead. Queen Ahhotep is in mourning and has gone to ground in her city. Sooner or later, the Hyksos will seize Thebes.'

'You're wrong, I tell you! Queen Ahhotep has already worked a lot of miracles. She'll never give up.'

'That's nothing but a myth. No one will ever defeat the Hyksos – and no one will get us out of this camp alive. The Thebans don't even know it exists.'

'Well, I believe in her,' said Big-Feet. 'The Queen of Freedom will enable me to see my cows again.'

'In the meantime,' advised Prisoner 2501, 'we'd better get on with cleaning the prison, or we'll be flogged.'

Four of the new arrivals died during the night. Big-Feet had just finished burying them the next morning, when Aberia stepped through the gates of the camp.

'Come on, quickly,' he told the old man. 'We must line up.'

'I can't. I have a terrible pain in my chest.'

'If you aren't on your feet, Aberia will beat you to death.'

'I shan't give her the pleasure . . . Whatever else you do, my friend, hold on to hope.' The old man's voice faded, and his death-rattle sounded. His heart had given out.

Big-Feet ran to join the others, who were drawn up in orderly ranks in front of Aberia. She was a good head taller than most of the prisoners.

'The time has come for some entertainment,' she

announced, 'and I know you are eager to know the number of the lucky prisoner chosen to be the hero of our little celebration.'

She stared greedily at each prisoner in turn. Here, Aberia held the power of life and death. As if she were not satisfied, she walked back up the rows, then halted before a man who was still young, a man who could not help shaking from head to foot.

'You, Prisoner 2501.'

2

Bathed in the bright light of dawn, the beautiful thirty-nine-year-old Queen Ahhotep raised her hands towards the Hidden God in a gesture of worship.

'My heart inclines unto your gaze. Because of you, we are satisfied without food and our thirst is quenched without drink. You are father to those who have no mother, and husband to the widow. How sweet it is to gaze upon your mystery! It tastes of life, it is as a delicate fabric to those who robe themselves in it, it is a fruit swollen with sunshine.'

The queen had gone alone to the east of Karnak, and was celebrating the resurrection of the light, which had defeated the darkness.

That defeat sometimes seemed merely an illusion, when the provinces of upper Egypt still groaned under the Hyksos emperor's yoke. After losing her husband and her elder son, who had fought valiantly against the occupying power, Ahhotep, who held the office of Wife of God, now felt only one love, the love of freedom. Yet freedom seemed out of reach because of the enemy army's superiority.

She was well aware of the courage and determination with which the Theban troops had fought their way to Avaris, the Emperor of Darkness's capital. But their advance had been halted by that impregnable fortress, and they had been forced to beat a retreat.

After the death of Pharaoh Kamose, a worthy successor to his father Seqen, the Regent Queen had withdrawn to Thebes, to regain her strength in silence. Within the enclosure of the beautiful but modest temple, she had meditated under the protection of Amon and Osiris. Amon, the lord of Thebes, the creator of the good wind, the keeper of the secret of the origins of life, whose shrine would not open willingly until the day total victory was won over the Hyksos. Osiris, who had been murdered, then brought back to life, the judge of the afterlife, master of the brotherhood of those who were 'of just voice', a brotherhood which now included Seqen and Kamose.

Seqen had died in battle, lured into an ambush. And Kamose, just when he was preparing to launch a new assault on Avaris, had been poisoned and had come back to Thebes to die, his mother by his side as he gazed upon the Peak of the West. In both cases, one person had been responsible: a Hyksos spy who had infiltrated the Theban headquarters. Twice he had struck a lethal blow.

Yet the men who surrounded Ahhotep were above suspicion, for they had all proved their bravery and risked their lives, each one fighting the Hyksos in his own way. Qaris, the palace's head steward, was a specialist in gathering information, while Heray, officially the Overseer of Granaries, was an excellent minister for the economy. Emheb, the Governor of Edfu, had held the front at Qis during a desperate time, and had been wounded more than once. The scribe Neshi, Bearer of the Royal Seal, was so devoted to Kamose that he had offered his resignation, which the queen had refused; while the superbly skilled archer Ahmes, son of Abana, was a great killer of Hyksos officers. Then there were the Afghan and Moustache, two rebels who had been appointed to lead elite regiments and had been decorated for their deeds; and Moon, commander of the war-fleet, who was exceptionally skilful and whose courage never failed.

How could she imagine, even for a moment, that one of

them could be a spy in the pay of the Emperor of Darkness? All the evidence suggested that she must look elsewhere and remain constantly on the alert. Despite his diabolical cunning, the spy would eventually give himself away, and when that happened Ahhotep must strike with all the speed and decisiveness of the royal cobra.

The Wife of God walked alongside the little sacred lake from which, each morning, the pharaoh should have drawn fresh water derived from the Nun, the ocean of energy. This was needed in order to proceed to the purification ceremonies and so create a new dynamic energy, vital for all forms of existence from the star to the stone.

But young Pharaoh Kamose had died at the age of twenty, and his successor, his brother, Ahmose, was only ten. For the second time, Ahhotep had had to become Regent Queen and steer the ship of state. Although still far from defeated, the emperor was not going to triumph. It was for the Queen of Freedom to prove to him that he would never reign over the Two Lands.

Ahhotep's huge dog, Young Laughter, came bounding up and greeted his mistress with obvious joy. Forgetting how heavy he was, he reared up and put his two enormous front paws on the queen's shoulders, almost knocking her over. After licking her cheeks thoroughly, the dog led the way as Ahhotep headed for the palace at the large military base north of Thebes.*

Here, deep in the desert, young King Seqen had trained the first soldiers of the army of liberation, in notably harsh conditions; later a barracks, houses, a fortress, a small royal palace, a school, an infirmary and shrines had been built. And here the recruits learnt their trade as soldiers, under the command of rigorous instructors who hid nothing of the terrifying battles that awaited them.

*On the site of Deir el-Ballas.

At the entrance to the palace, Young Laughter halted and sniffed the air. More than once, just like his father Old Laughter, he had used his keen sense of smell to detect danger and so save Ahhotep, who was careful not to ignore his warnings.

Qaris appeared in the doorway. A plump fellow, with round cheeks and an air of imperturbable calm, he was the very embodiment of good humour. Even at the height of Hyksos oppression, he had unhesitatingly acted as a contact between the few existing rebels and collated all the information, at constant risk of being denounced and condemned to death.

'Majesty, I was not expecting you so soon,' he said. 'The cleaners are still at their work, and I have not had time to supervise the meal.'

With smiling eyes, Laughter calmly licked the steward's hand.

'Summon the officials to the council chamber,' said Ahhotep.

In the centre of the chamber stood Qaris's masterpiece, a model of Egypt showing those parts of the country which had been liberated and those which were still occupied by the Hyksos. When Ahhotep had first seen the model, only Thebes had enjoyed relative autonomy. Today, thanks to the achievements of Seqen and Kamose, the Hyksos controlled only the Delta, and their Nubian ally, the King of Kerma, remained lurking in his far-off realm of the Great South.

It was true that the 'Balance of the Two Lands', Memphis, which acted as a crossing-point and fulcrum between Upper and Lower Egypt, had been liberated, but how long could it stay free? The troops led by the Hyksos commander, Jannas, would not be content to defend Avaris for ever, and would soon launch an offensive.

The officials bowed before the Regent Queen. Their long faces betrayed their anxiety and discouragement.

10

Neshi, the thin, shaven-headed Bearer of the Royal Seal, whose responsibilities included supplying the army with food and weapons, afforded his colleagues some relief by breaking the silence.

'The news is not good, Majesty. If we wish to defend Memphis, which would be particularly difficult, we shall have to mass the greater part of our troops there. If we are defeated, the road to Thebes will lie wide open.' Ordinarily so incisive, Neshi seemed crushed beneath the weight of reality.

'What do you think, Emheb?' asked the queen.

That big, stout-hearted man had just returned from Memphis; he looked as impressive as ever, with his bull-neck, broad shoulders and generous girth. Because he had fought for so long in the front line, he had the authority to speak his mind, and many considered his opinions conclusive.

Emheb expressed himself with his customary candour. 'Either we attack Avaris again, and break Jannas's back, or we must establish a defensive line against which his men will come to grief. The first solution seems much too risky to me, so I would advocate the second. But in that case Memphis would be a very bad choice. Except during the annual flood, the Hyksos could use their heavy weapons, their chariots and horses, and we wouldn't have time to build walls round the city.'

'That means we have no choice but to abandon the city to its fate,' concluded the queen.

The officials hung their heads.

'Have weapons delivered to the Memphis garrison,' ordered Ahhotep, 'and use carrier-pigeons to keep us informed of the situation as it develops. We shall establish our line of defence at Faiyum, three days' march to the south of Memphis, at the place renamed the Port of Kamose in honour of my son. Neshi is to set up a military camp there immediately, and the artificers must build stone platforms. Commander Moon will regroup

11

the majority of our warships there, and Governor Emheb will take whatever measures are necessary to halt a Hyksos chariot attack. And instruct our boatyards to redouble their efforts – we urgently need more warships.'

Everyone agreed with the queen's decisions.

The members of the council were dispersing when an officer of the guard rushed into the chamber. 'Majesty,' he panted, 'something very serious has happened. Hundreds of soldiers have just deserted.'

3

In a terrible rage, Emperor Apophis replaced the Red Crown of Lower Egypt in the strongroom of the citadel at Avaris, from which it would never again emerge. Once again, he had tried to put it on; once again, it had caused unbearable pain in his head and burnt his fingers.

Rejecting this emblem of an age of rebellion, the lord of the Hyksos climbed slowly to the top of the citadel's highest tower, which loomed over a capital city which had been transformed into one gigantic military camp.

The seventy-year-old emperor was a tall man, with a prominent nose, flabby cheeks, a pot belly and thick legs. His ugliness was so frightening that he used it as a weapon to intimidate those he addressed.

From round his neck he removed a gold chain on which hung three amulets embodying life, prosperity and health. Gullible people believed they gave him the power to know the secrets of heaven and earth, but now, at a time of total war against the Thebans and their damned queen, he could no longer bear to wear these worthless trinkets. The Emperor of Darkness broke all three amulets and flung the pieces over the battlements.

His nerves soothed, he gazed down upon his realm, mighty Avaris, the greatest city in the world, which he had established in the north-east of the Delta, on the eastern bank of the branch of the Nile that the Egyptians called 'the Waters of Ra'.

Ra, the divine Light. Many years had passed since the Hyksos had replaced the Light with armed force, so perfectly symbolized by the thick walls, battlements and crenellated towers of the seemingly impregnable fortress.

Since the abortive assault by Pharaoh Kamose, who had been poisoned by Apophis's spy, the emperor had left his lair only once, to go to the Temple of Set, lord of storms and cosmic disturbances, and faithful protector of Apophis. He who was nourished by the violence of Set could never be defeated.

Formerly a hive of activity, the trading-port at Avaris now housed only a few cargo-vessels, which were closely guarded by the war-fleet. No one had forgotten the exploits of Kamose's troops, who had seized three hundred boats filled with valuable cargo and carried them off to Thebes.

This slump in trade with the empire's vassals would not last long; as soon as the Theban rebellion had been crushed, enormous quantities of gold, silver, lapis-lazuli, precious woods, oil, wine and other goods would once again reach the Hyksos capital. The wealth of the emperor and his inner circle would continue to grow, even faster than before.

Apophis loathed sunshine and fresh air, so he went back into his palace, which had been built inside the fortress. Small openings allowed only the minimum amount of light to enter.

Using the team of painters he had brought over from Minoa, the emperor had had the walls decorated with frescoes of the kind popular in Knossos, the capital of the Great Isle. Apophis had destroyed numerous masterpieces of the Middle Kingdom, and boasted of having eradicated all traces of Egyptian art from his city. Each day, in his council chamber, he gazed admiringly at the Minoan landscapes, labyrinths, winged griffins, yellow-skinned dancers, or acrobats jumping over the horns of a bull.

Once he had conquered Upper Egypt and razed Thebes to the ground, the emperor would have vast numbers of immigrants brought in, and would wipe out every last vestige of the Egyptian population. The old land of the pharaohs would become a true Hyksos province, from which the very notion of Ma'at, the frail goddess of truth, justice and harmony, would disappear.

Apophis liked to wander around the citadel for hours on end, dreaming of the vast extent of his empire, the largest ever created, which stretched from Nubia to the Mycenean islands, by way of Canaan and Anatolia. Any fools who tried to rebel were ruthlessly massacred. The Hyksos army tortured the ringleaders and their families, and burnt down not just their houses but their villages, too.

And, thus, Hyksos order reigned.

Only Queen Ahhotep still dared defy that order. Though he had initially regarded her as a madwoman and a mere schemer, the emperor had been forced to admit that she was a formidable adversary. Her ridiculous army of peasants had become battle-hardened over the years, and the intrepid Kamose had even succeeded in leading it up to the walls of the citadel of Avaris itself.

Fortunately, that amazing feat had done no more than scratch the surface of Hyksos power. The Thebans had had to withdraw, and were no longer in a position to retake the offensive, but they excelled in the art of laying traps because of their perfect knowledge of the terrain. So the emperor was taking care not to act hastily, particularly since he must resolve an annoying dispute between his two most senior officials, High Treasurer Khamudi and Commander Jannas.

Khamudi was depraved, cruel, and ready to do anything to increase his own wealth, but faithfully carried out the emperor's decisions. Jannas, the commander-in-chief of the Hyksos forces, was the hero who had saved Avaris, and his popularity continued to grow.

To please his senior officers, Apophis ought to have sacrificed Khamudi; but doing so would have made Jannas far too powerful – many soldiers already regarded him as the future leader of the Hyksos.

Nourished by the strength of Set, Apophis would continue to reign for a long time. Fortunately, Jannas was a true soldier, who scrupulously obeyed orders and would never consider plotting against the emperor. Kamudi must be brought to understand that the commander guaranteed the empire's safety, and that he, Khamudi, would have to be content with his many privileges.

The emperor did not pay a visit to his wife, the lady Tany – he had not granted her the title of Empress, for real power could not be divided. Tany was an Egyptian woman of modest origins, who had sent many prosperous ladies to torture and death by denouncing them as rebels. She had been so terrified by the sight of Egyptian soldiers, during Kamose's attack, that she had taken to her bed.

When Apophis emerged from his apartments, he was greeted by Khamudi, who bowed very low.

The High Treasurer had black hair plastered to his round head, rather bulging eyes, a heavy frame, and plump hands and feet. He was a man of large appetites, a lover of fine wines and of young Egyptian women, upon whom he inflicted the most hideous tortures in the company of his wife, Yima, who was as perverted as himself. He hid none of his perversions or financial misappropriations from the emperor, and did nothing without his master's consent.

'All is ready, Majesty.'

Khamudi was also the commander of Apophis's personal bodyguard. He had selected Cypriot and Libyan pirates who would instantly kill anyone who made the slightest threatening gesture towards the emperor. Dressed in tunics with floral motifs, these dogs of war with their tattooed arms and plaited hair formed an impregnable wall around the lord of the

Hyksos whenever he appeared in the streets of his capital. Generously paid, they could afford any woman they wanted. Since his abolition of the courts of law, Apophis was the only judge in Egypt, and he never punished his servants.

The procession crossed the palace burial-ground, where Hyksos officers killed in battle had been laid in makeshift tombs, along with their weapons. Because of the lack of space and the number of bodies to be buried, the emperor had taken a decision which horrified the Egyptians. Instead of creating a new burial-ground, he decreed that the dead were to be buried in gardens and even inside houses – it would have been stupid to waste space on mortal remains which would soon be reduced to bones.

'Have there been any protests against my burial policy?' enquired Apophis, in his hoarse, chilling voice.

'A few,' replied Khamudi, in honeyed tones, 'but I have done what was necessary. Sharuhen is full at the moment, so it was necessary to open another one at Tjaru.* The rebels have been sent there.'

'Excellent, Khamudi.'

Commander Jannas's appearance was deceptive. Of medium height and almost frail-looking, slow of speech and movement, he habitually wore a mushroom-shaped, striped headdress. Those who had thought him no danger, however, were no longer of this world.

After he, too, had bowed before the emperor, the commander attended the brief funeral ceremonies for his men, who had died of the wounds they received during fierce fighting with the Egyptians in the trading-port of Avaris. Jannas could boast of having beaten off Kamose's attack, but Queen Ahhotep remained a real danger.

---

*Tjaru-Sileh, in the Delta, on the isthmus formed between the lakes of Ballah and Menezaleh.

Amid general indifference, more than a hundred donkeys had their throats slit and were thrown into the ditches with the soldiers' bodies.

Then the emperor inspected the security arrangements put in place by Jannas to prevent a future Theban attack from the river having any chance of success. 'Good work, Commander,' he said.

'Majesty, when are we to go back on the offensive?'

'Just obey my orders, Jannas.'

4

In less than a day, the rumour had spread all over the military base at Thebes. Queen Ahhotep was going to withdraw once and for all into the temple at Karnak, Pharaoh Ahmose had abdicated, and the army of liberation was to lay down its arms. Before long, the Hyksos hordes would sweep down upon the city of Amon and slaughter anyone who tried to resist.

Flat-Nose was the first to desert, followed immediately by Lively, an officer who had fought at Avaris and who knew the enemy's savagery. Convinced by their explanations, hundreds of footsoldiers had made up their minds to leave the base as quickly as possible. A lone officer tried to remind the men of their duty, but his voice was lost in a chorus of shouts and he had had to step aside to avoid being trampled to death.

'We must warn our comrades at the fortress,' said Lively.

The guards joined the crowd of fleeing soldiers, who were soon followed by the majority of the troops billeted in the building.

'Which way are we going?' asked Flat-Nose

'Not north,' replied Lively. 'We'd come up against the regiments led by the Afghan and Moustache.'

'So what? They may be the best, but they surely don't want to die any more than we do.'

'There'd be bound to be a fight. I'm going to head south.'

In a state of utter confusion, the deserters dispersed. Led by Flat-Nose, a howling mob marched northwards.

Beautifully shaped feet, long, elegant legs, a shapely bottom and a back made for caresses . . . After Queen Ahhotep, She-Cat was the most beautiful woman in the world. And he, Moustache, had the insane good fortune to make love with her! When he met her, during the Nubian campaign, he had fallen for her instantly, but had decided against a lasting relationship, which was incompatible with his life as a soldier. But She-Cat had hidden on the boat as it left for Egypt, and Moustache had not had the courage to resist her.

The beautiful Nubian had not been content simply to become a wonderful wife. A specialist in potions, drugs and talismans, she tended wounded soldiers, had saved many lives, and had been appointed head of the battlefield medical service. She-Cat was regarded as a heroine of the war of liberation.

Moustache kissed her neck tenderly as they reclined on their bed.

'The meeting of the Great Council is taking for ever,' she complained.

'What does that matter? The queen is wasting her time trying to persuade her officials. As usual they'll disagree with her decisions, and as usual she'll implement them anyway. Anyway, shouldn't you be thinking about something else?'

Someone hammered furiously at the bedroom door.

'Oh no!' protested Moustache. 'Surely I'm entitled to just one hour's privacy.'

'Open up, quickly,' demanded the Afghan, his voice filled with urgency.

'What is it now?'

'Some sort of riot,' said the Afghan, a sturdy, bearded man who wore a turban. 'A mass of soldiers are deserting, and they're trying to get our men to join them.'

'They'll never do it!' roared Moustache, suddenly very sober. 'Our fellows won't behave like cowards!'

But Moustache was wrong. Convinced the rumours were the truth, the men of the elite regiments were allowing themselves to be swept away by the tide.

The Afghan tried to stop a man as he fled, but Moustache caught his arm and said warningly, 'They're like madmen. We can't hold them back.'

'What about the ones who are heading for the palace?'

'Surely they won't attack the queen?'

Carried away, Flat-Nose and more than two hundred deserters were marching on the palace at the military base, set on looting it.

'There may only be two of us,' declared the Afghan, 'but we're not going to let them do that.'

'It is vital that you do not go out, Majesty,' urged Neshi. 'Our soldiers have lost their minds! We should leave the palace by the back entrance and take refuge in the desert.'

Qaris agreed. If the queen's personal bodyguard confronted the horde, it would be a massacre, and Ahhotep would not escape the fury of her own troops.

'Leave the camp, all of you, and return to Thebes to protect my mother and my son,' ordered Ahhotep.

'But what about you, Majesty?' asked Neshi anxiously.

'Do not argue.'

'But, Majesty, we cannot simply abandon you!'

'The only thing that matters is Ahmose's safety. Go back to Thebes – you must not waste a single moment.'

The queen's tone was so imperious that her officials and guards could offer no further resistance.

Placing a fine gold diadem atop her brown hair, the green-eyed, majestic queen went out to confront the rioters, who were so astounded to see her that they halted.

Taking advantage of this moment's vacillation, Moustache

and the Afghan positioned themselves on either side of the queen. Even with their bare hands, they would kill a good number of attackers.

Flat-Nose stepped forward. 'People said you were withdrawing into the temple, Majesty. But you're here . . . No, you can't be – you must be a ghost!'

'Why did you listen to the rumours?'

'Because the Hyksos are coming and we no longer have a leader.'

'I am Regent Queen, and I am in command of the army. No attack forces have been detected, and if an attack were launched we should halt it.'

'Are you really . . . real?'

'Touch my hand, and you will know I am.'

Flat-Nose hesitated. Fighting the Hyksos frightened him, but he had a minuscule chance of emerging from that alive. On the other hand, touching the Wife of God would be such an insult that he would be struck down dead.

So he bowed lower and lower, until his flat nose touched the ground. All his comrades followed suit.

'You were lied to,' declared Ahhotep, 'and you have behaved like frightened children. I shall therefore overlook this incident. Every man is to return to his post.'

The soldiers got to their feet and cheered the Queen of Freedom. Never again would they give credence to rumours.

But the crisis was not yet over. Full of alarm, Neshi came hurrying up. 'Majesty, deserters led by Lively are trying to seize boats and leave the base.'

Followed by Moustache, the Afghan and the soldiers who had been won back to the cause, the queen hurried to the landing-stage. There, the war-fleet archers commanded by Ahmes were facing Lively's supporters, and the incident was threatening to turn into a major disaster.

'The queen!' shouted a deserter. 'The queen is alive!'

Alone and unarmed, Ahhotep stepped between the two sides.

Lively knew he had committed an unpardonable crime. By spreading false rumours and inciting many soldiers to flee, he had condemned himself to death. He drew his sword.

'I am sorry, Majesty,' he said, 'but I have no choice. I need a boat so I can get away, and I'll kill anyone who tries to stop me.'

'Keep your sword for fighting the enemy and liberating your country.'

Lively gaped at her. 'Majesty, do you mean . . .? But surely you cannot pardon a deserter?'

'I need you. I need you all if we are to defeat the Emperor of Darkness. If we had started killing one another we would have given him victory, but I have destroyed that curse. Let us once more become one soul, and from now on you must trust no one's word but mine.'

Lively sheathed his sword. Under Ahhotep's bright gaze, her soldiers became brothers once more.

5

'Commander Jannas, an unauthorized cargo-boat is coming this way along the northern canal.'

'Intercept it.'

This could hardly be a trick on the part of Ahhotep, but since the attack on Avaris Jannas had taken even the most minor incident seriously. All river access to the capital was guarded day and night, and the smallest vessel strictly controlled. At the slightest hint of danger, the archers were under orders to fire. It was better to make a mistake than to put the capital at risk.

Jannas was a perfectionist, who inspected several warships each day and checked their weapons himself. Each ship had to be permanently ready for combat. Either the Egyptian fleet would try to launch a new offensive, or Jannas would receive orders to leave for the south and destroy the Thebans. Either way, he must ensure that victory was certain.

During his short break at midday, while he was eating a frugal meal of grilled mullet and lentils aboard his flagship, his assistant came in to warn him that High Treasurer Khamudi had arrived.

'He is very upset and demands to see you immediately, sir.'

'Tell him to wait. I am finishing my lunch.'

Jannas took his time. Khamudi had humiliated him before

the attack on Avaris, so he would return the favour. Here, on the flagship, the High Treasurer, a mere civilian, could rant and rage as much as he liked. No sailor would let him into the commander's cabin.

Unusually for him, Jannas ate some pomegranates and figs, which he decided were to his taste; in certain circumstances, he appreciated sweetness. Then he washed his hands, put on his striped headdress and stepped out on to the bridge, where Khamudi was pacing up and down.

Red-faced with anger, the High Treasurer rushed towards Jannas, who raised a hand and halted him in his tracks.

'No sudden movements on my ship, Khamudi. Here, everything is regulated and precise.'

'Do you know what you have just done, Commander?'

'After a morning's inspections, I had lunch. Any other questions?'

'You have intercepted a boat which belongs to me!'

'The one on the northern canal? It was not on my list of vessels authorized to enter the trading-port.'

'Shall we go into your cabin? No one must hear us.'

Jannas nodded. Given Khamudi's agitated state, the conversation promised to be interesting.

'I'd like to accept that the boat belongs to you, Khamudi, but why did its Cypriot captain not say so?'

'Because his mission is highly confidential – as is his cargo, which ought to have been delivered directly to me.'

'You seem to have forgotten that we are at war and that I am required to inspect all goods entering Avaris.'

'Not these goods,' said Khamudi. 'Return them to me and we'll say no more about it.'

'I'd like to, but I can't. Supposing you've been tricked? Unknown to you, your vessel might be bringing dangerous goods into the capital, or even weapons for the rebels.'

The High Treasurer turned purple. 'How dare you accuse me of such a thing!'

'I am not accusing you of anything. I am simply afraid someone might have taken advantage of your good faith, which is why I must know the nature of the cargo you were expecting.'

'Do you expect me to believe you haven't examined it?'

Jannas pretended to think. 'I had no choice, I'm afraid, but I was puzzled by what was found. I'd be glad to hear your version of the facts.'

Khamudi was boiling with rage. 'It's a drug, Commander, and all the officials and senior officers use it.'

'I do not.'

'Everyone has his own own form of amusement. In times like this, many people find the drug indispensable, and I have to ensure they have access to that little pleasure. Moreover, I have the full agreement of the emperor, who would be extremely unhappy to learn that you were impinging on my territory.'

'Nothing could be further from my thoughts, High Treasurer.'

'Then have that cargo delivered to me immediately.'

'Since everything is now out in the open, that is indeed what I shall do. To prevent any more incidents like this, kindly see to it that your next delivery conforms with security regulations.'

Khamudi slammed the door of the cabin behind him.

Feeling relaxed, Jannas allowed himself a cup of lukewarm beer. He had known for a long time about Khamudi's lucrative traffic in drugs, and in fact he thought it an excellent idea, because such things soothed people's anxieties.

The important thing was that the High Treasurer now realized he was not the only master after the emperor. From now on, all trade would have to be approved by Jannas. No detail would escape him, and Khamudi's influence would start to wane.

*

At the end of a trying day, the sun's burning heat was at last on the wane: soon it would sink swiftly in the west. Indifferent to this magnificent sight, Jannas was angrily reprimanding the commander of a vessel whose crew discipline was poor. There would be no second warning. One more mistake and the culprit would end up in the emperor's labyrinth, from which no one had ever emerged alive.

An officer of the river guards came up and saluted. 'Commander, there is a small problem.'

'What sort of problem?'

'We have arrested a suspect in a storehouse at the trading-port. He claims to have important information for you, and refuses to speak to anyone else.'

'Very well. We'll go and hear what he has to say.'

The drugs had been unloaded and delivered to Khamudi, and the dock-workers were now carrying heavy jars of lamp-oil destined for the palace, where the lamps burned night and day. A cargo-vessel laden with copper could wait until the following day. Mined by forced labourers with a limited life-expectancy, the metal would be used to manufacture weapons.

Jannas had authorized only a single access canal, the others being blocked by floating barrages. If Ahhotep applied the same strategy as her dead son Kamose, she would meet with crushing failure.

But what insane plan could this incredibly stubborn queen come up with now? The death of a husband and a son should have been enough to break any woman, yet she doggedly went on believing in a victory she knew was impossible. Even the summary execution of civilians and the destruction of entire villages had not persuaded her to give up her madness.

'This way, Commander.'

Two guards were on duty in front of the storehouse, which was old and ought to have been demolished. Inside were broken packing-cases and old rags.

Sitting with his back to a wall was an unshaven young man with manacles on his wrists.

'Are you Commander Jannas?' The prisoner spoke haltingly and his eyes were unfocused.

'I am indeed.'

'I want to speak with you alone.'

'Why?'

'It concerns the emperor's safety.'

The commander gestured to the guards to leave. 'Now talk.'

Quick as a cat, the man leapt up, seized Jannas by the throat, and tried to throttle him. He was so much bigger and heavier that Jannas seemed bound to die. But the commander had lost none of his fighter's reflexes. Unsheathing his dagger, he plunged it into his attacker's belly. The man screamed with pain and let go.

After freeing himself, Jannas cut the man's throat.

'Probably drugged,' he concluded. 'A drug-addict sent by Khamudi to kill me.'

6

Despite the years of war and the seeming inevitability that it would crumble into ruin, the modest city of Thebes had actually grown. Here and there small white houses had been built for newly married couples. Defying destiny, they gave birth to children who would perhaps be the future of Egypt.

At Ahhotep's insistence, the most beautiful room in the hastily rebuilt royal palace was the large bedchamber belonging to her mother, Teti the Small. Teti was very old and increasingly fragile, but she still painted her face and dressed with great care. Although she had been deeply affected by the deaths of her son-in-law and elder grandson, she had taken charge of bringing up the younger boy. Mingling strictness and gentleness, alternating games and teaching, she passed on to ten-year-old Ahmose the honey of ancient wisdom. True, he must learn how to fight, to handle the bow and the sword; but he must also be able to write beautiful hieroglyphs so that he might become an exemplary scribe.

His brother's death had abruptly matured the boy, and in any case ten was the age at which a person became fully responsible for his actions. Far from minimizing the ordeal he faced, his grandmother always spoke to him as to an adult whose path would be strewn with obstacles.

Today, Ahhotep found Teti sitting by the window of her bedchamber, watching the birds flying around in the garden.

'How do you feel today, Mother?'

'A bit more tired than yesterday, but I am so proud of you! I understand that you have put an end to some sort of rebellion by our soldiers.'

'They had been misled by malicious rumours. In future, Neshi will give them official information each week, and I shall take action myself whenever necessary.'

Teti took her daughter's hand tenderly. 'Without you, Ahhotep, Egypt would no longer exist.'

'Without you, I would have been nothing but a feeble would-be rebel. Through the way you conducted yourself, you taught me everything. And you are the one who is preparing Ahmose for the harsh battles that await him.'

'Although he is astonishingly mature, he is still only a child. He is as careful and measured as Kamose was lively and enthusiastic. He needs time to assimilate an idea. It would be best not to overwhelm him and to let him grow at his own pace, but will you be able to do that?'

Ahhotep shared her mother's view. It did indeed depend upon whether the Hyksos precipitated events by unleashing a general offensive.

Qaris brought Teti some honey-cakes and fresh carob juice. 'The doctor would like to examine you, Majesty.'

'There's no need for that,' protested the old lady. 'Just order me a good dinner.'

Seeing Qaris's troubled expression, Ahhotep said goodbye to her mother and left the room with the steward.

Once outside, Qaris said quietly, 'The High Priest of Karnak has just died, Majesty. Your mother is bound to hear about it soon, and, as they liked each other and were the same age, I'm worried that the news may upset her.'

'You may be right, Qaris. What else?

'The High Priest's assistant, who considers himself the natural successor, is not the man for this situation.'

'Why not?'

'He is ambitious by nature, his heart is not generous, and he has confused the service of the gods with the forging of his own career.'

Ahhotep had rarely known Qaris be so critical: he usually tended to minimize people's faults.

'Majesty,' he went on, 'you must be able to trust the High Priest of Amon implicitly. When you leave to fight again, it is he who will ensure that the link with the Invisible here in Thebes is maintained. This man will not fulfil that vital function, but will think only of ways to increase his own worldly power.'

'Then whom do you suggest as a candidate?'

'I cannot think of anyone, Majesty, and I have faith in the clear-sightedness of the Wife of God.'

'With your experience, Qaris, you yourself would make a perfect High Priest.'

'Oh no, Majesty! My place is here, in the palace.'

'Summon all the priests, scribes and administrators to the open-air courtyard of the Temple of Karnak.'

'Including Heray?'

Ahhotep smiled. 'No, because I shall never find a better minister for the economy.'

When the Wife of God entered the courtyard, all eyes turned towards her.

The High Priest's assistant came forward. 'The inventory of this temple's possessions is at your disposal, Majesty, as are the documents concerning its management.'

'Before consulting them, I must pay homage to the late High Priest.'

'He rests in his official residence. May I escort you there?'

'I know where it is.'

The assistant frowned.

The queen walked slowly past the men Qaris had selected. One of them impressed her: he was contemplative, and had a serious expression, although he could not be much more than thirty years old.

'What is your office?' she asked him.

'I am a bearer of offerings, Majesty.'

'Do you know the words of the gods?'

'Between carrying out my duties, I study the hieroglyphic texts.'

'What do you know of Amon?'

'He is the sculptor who sculpted himself, the creator of eternity whose perfect act was the birth of the Light. He is the One who remains all by creating multiplicity. His true name is secret for ever, for he is life itself. His right eye is the day, his left eye the night. A good shepherd, he is also the ship's pilot. Master of the silent ones, he brings the gods into the world.'

'These words lead us nowhere,' protested the assistant. 'Karnak has need of a serious administrator, not a thinker lost in abstractions.'

'It is for the Wife of God to choose the new High Priest, is it not?

'Indeed, Majesty, but I beg you to think deeply. I worked for many years at my superior's side, and he did not appoint me at random.'

'Then why did he not name you explicitly as his successor?'

The assistant looked embarrassed. 'Illness had weakened him greatly . . . but no one could doubt his intention. And Djehuty, the offerings-bearer, is not the man to replace him.'

'Djehuty . . . the name of the god Thoth, master of the sacred language on which we base our civilization. Surely that is a sign from heaven.'

The assistant stared, open-mouthed.

'Write your name upon a piece of papyrus and Djehuty shall do the same,' commanded the queen. 'I shall place both in the innermost shrine of the goddess Mut, and she shall take the decision.'

As soon as the funeral vigil was over, under the protection of Isis, the High Priest's mummification began. After meditating before the mortal remains of her faithful servant and speaking the words of glorification, Ahhotep entered the shrine of Mut, opened the innermost chamber and withdrew the papyri. Then she returned to the great courtyard.

The assistant's fists were clenched, whereas Djehuty seemed strangely calm.

'One of the papyri was burnt by Mut's fire,' she revealed, throwing the charred fragments to the ground. 'The other is intact.'

'We must accept the will of the Invisible,' said the assistant, who had recognized the piece of papyrus in Ahhotep's hand.

She showed it to him. The name that had been preserved was Djehuty's.

7

With his mother, Young Prince Ahmose crossed the threshold of the temple at Karnak. He was tall and thin, with eyes which radiated depth and seriousness. For a long time he gazed at the central gateway, which was built of pink granite, then he went on towards a square-pillared portico whose austere beauty made his heart swell. This accorded with his view that all beings must behave righteously when confronted by the vagaries of destiny. And he marvelled at the second portico, whose pillars were gigantic statues of Osiris standing with his arms crossed over his chest and the sceptres of judgement and resurrection in his hands.

Before each statue stood a priest of Amon.

'Look carefully at the priests, my son,' said Ahhotep, 'and choose the one you believe capable of fulfilling the office of High Priest.'

'What does the office involve?'

'Serving the hidden principle by celebrating the rites daily, so that he will consent not to leave this earth.'

Ahmose looked deep into the eyes of each priest in turn, without arrogance and without haste. He allowed his mother's words to enter his soul and tried to determine whether the man he was looking at matched up to them.

'I choose this one,' said the prince firmly, looking into Djehuty's eyes.

The High Priest's assistant prostrated himself before the queen. 'Forgive my vanity, Majesty. I shall obey Djehuty and do my utmost to accomplish the tasks he entrusts to me.'

After enthroning the new High Priest by handing him the Staff of the Word and slipping a gold ring on to the middle finger of his right hand, the queen took Ahmose to the east of the temple.

On an altar facing the shrine of Amon lay the Sword of Light, which had been borne by Pharaohs Seqen and Kamose.

'The door of this shrine will not consent to open until the Hyksos are defeated once and for all,' Ahhotep told him. 'Until that happens much blood and many tears must be shed, and you must know how to wield this weapon unfalteringly. Do you feel capable of so doing, Ahmose?'

The prince approached the altar, touched the hilt and ran his finger along the blade. 'The Sword of Amon is too heavy for me now. But when my arm is strong enough, I shall wield it.'

'You are only ten years old, and you have lost your father and your brother, who both died to liberate Egypt. Despite their courage, that task is a long way from being achieved. Do you agree to continue it, despite the danger to your life?'

'To live without freedom is worse than death.'

'Egypt cannot survive without the presence of a pharaoh, Ahmose, and destiny has chosen you to hold this supreme office, as you have just proved. Until you are truly capable of fulfilling it, I shall continue my duties as Regent Queen.'

'Why don't you become Pharaoh, Mother? I shall never be able to equal you.'

'When my task is done, when Egypt can breathe freely, she will need a great king, young and steeped in the spirit of Ma'at, to rebuild a world in harmony with the creative powers. So the energy of government must quicken your heart.'

Ahhotep and her son made their way towards the new High Priest, Djehuty.

'Prepare for the coronation ceremonies,' the queen told him.

At the very moment Ahhotep spoke those words, Emperor Apophis was seized with a violent sickness as he rested in his bedchamber, whose many lamps burned day and night. His lips and ankles swelled, his throat tightened, and he could not breathe.

'There will never be any king but me,' he muttered, with such venom that his strength returned.

Seizing his dagger, whose hilt was inlaid with a silver lotus and whose triangular blade was made of copper, he plunged it into the wall, stabbing through a palm-tree the Minoan painter had drawn.

'Everything belongs to me, even this picture.'

The emperor opened the door of his bedchamber. Outside stood two guards.

'Send for the High Treasurer and have the bearers prepare my travelling-chair.'

'How do you feel, Majesty?'

'Send for the High Treasurer, then take me to the Temple of Set. And hurry.'

Khamudi had to abandon his calculations of the profits from drug sales, and run to the palace. As soon as he arrived, he helped Apophis into the magnificent travelling-chair that had been used by the pharaohs of the time of Amenemhat III. Twenty sturdy fellows lifted it and set a quick pace while taking care not to jolt the lord of the Hyksos. Fifty soldiers ensured his safety and Khamudi, who was a lover of the good life, found it difficult to keep up.

As the procession went through the streets, the few passers-by darted aside. Women and children rushed back into their homes. But one little boy dropped his wooden toy, a toy crocodile with moving jaws, right in the procession's path. He let go of his mother's hand to retrieve it.

'Stop!' ordered the emperor.

Wide-eyed with astonishment and curiosity, the child gazed up at the soldiers with their black helmets and breastplates. If Apophis had not spoken, he would have been trampled underfoot. He hugged his wooden crocodile to his chest.

'Bring him, Khamudi.'

As Khamudi picked the child up, the child's mother rushed towards the soldiers, frantic with worry. 'He is my son! Don't hurt him!'

At a sign from the emperor, the procession recommenced its forward march. The little boy did not see an officer slit his mother's throat.

The priests of Set and of Hadad, the Syrian storm-god, ceaselessly chanted words of conjuration to hold back the heavens' anger. Since early morning, strange clouds had menaced Avaris. A furious wind from the south was shaking the oak trees around the main altar, making them moan. The waters of the nearby canal were whipped up into furious waves.

'The emperor has arrived!' exclaimed a priest.

The chair was gently set down. Apophis got to his feet with difficulty; he was very pale and short of breath.

'This bad weather is abnormal, Majesty, and we are very worried,' confessed the High Priest of Set.

'You and your colleagues are to leave. Continue to recite the incantations.' Apophis's hoarse voice and icy gaze were even more terrifying than usual, and the priests hurried away.

The emperor gazed up at the enraged sky, as if he alone could decipher its message. 'Bring the child here, Khamudi.'

The High Treasurer led the little boy, still holding his toy, to the altar.

'I must regenerate myself,' said Apophis, 'because Ahhotep has just devised a new way of attacking me. Her plans must not come to fruition. To prevent them doing so, Set demands a sacrifice which will give me back my health, a sacrifice which will unleash a monstrous storm against Thebes. Lay the child on the altar.'

The High Treasurer realized what his master intended. 'Majesty, would you like me to do this myself?'

'Since it is I who shall henceforth possess his breath, only I can take it from his body.'

Ignoring the child's screams and tears, Khamudi broke his toy and forced him down upon the altar. The emperor unsheathed his dagger.

8

Teti the Small was awoken by a peal of thunder. As if she had regained her youth and energy, the old lady leapt out of bed, donned a dark blue tunic and hurried down the corridor to Ahhotep's bedchamber.

The door opened before she had time to knock, and Ahhotep stood there.

'Did you hear it, Mother?' she asked.

Zigzags of lightning criss-crossed the dawn skies.

'I cannot remember a storm like it,' said Teti.

'This is not normal,' said Ahhotep. 'There is only one possible explanation: the Emperor has unleashed the fury of Set.'

'Then it will be impossible to celebrate the coronation ceremony, won't it?'

'You are right. It will be impossible.'

Even the heaviest sleepers had been jolted out of their sleep. Everyone in the palace was worried, and Qaris could not calm their fears.

Ahhotep hurried to her son's bedchamber. He was standing at a window, gazing out at the furious heavens.

'Are the gods angry with me?' he asked soberly.

'No, it isn't that. The Emperor of Darkness has realized what we intend to do, and wishes to prevent you from ascending the throne of the living.'*

Torrential rain pelted down on Thebes, and darkness hid the sun.

'This is the blackness of hell!' cried one serving-woman, while another, who was even more frightened, ran away, her arms flailing.

'Light all the lamps,' the queen ordered Qaris.

The steward's face fell. 'The oil will not burn, Majesty.'

An enormous crash made the whole household jump. The raging wind had just blown the roof off the nearby barracks, sending it smashing down on to a granary.

In utter panic, the Thebans emerged from their houses and ran about in all directions. The dogs howled, all except Laughter, who did not leave his mistress's side. The walls of a house on the outskirts of the city collapsed, killing the children of the family as they huddled in their bedroom.

'We're all going to die!' predicted a blind man.

Then the Nile's fury was in turn unleashed.

A boat carrying fishermen, who were trying to head south, was lifted up by a wave and capsized. Although they were excellent swimmers, all five men drowned. In the port, the boats disintegrated as they bumped into each other. Even the warship that had brought Ahhotep from the military base to Thebes could not withstand the storm. Her masts fell on to the sailors on guard, and her captain was crushed by the bar of a steering-oar which had become uncontrollable. In less than a quarter of an hour, the ship had sunk.

And still the thunderbolts kept coming. A ball of flame set a carpenter's workshop alight, and the fire spread to the neighbouring houses. The wind fanned the flames, negating the efforts of the water-bearers.

*These cosmic disturbances are recorded on a limestone stele 1.80 metres tall and 1.10 metres wide, which was exhibited in the temple at Karnak.

40

Ahhotep watched the disaster, powerless. Soon, Thebes would be no more than a ruin, as would the military base. By using the power of Set, Apophis was reducing twenty years' work to nothing.

Without a war-fleet, and with only a few hundred soldiers left, all the queen would be able to do was beg for mercy from the tyrant, who would have the survivors of the cataclysm executed. It would be better to die in battle. Ahhotep decided that she would hide her son in the desert with a few faithful followers, and then confront Apophis alone. She would have no weapon save the flint dagger she had wielded as a young girl, when she became the first person to rebel against the invaders.

Twenty years of struggle, suffering and hope, twenty years in which she had known love and times of intense happiness, twenty years fighting oppression, were now ending in a defeat from which Egypt could not recover.

She called her son to her and told him, 'You must prepare to leave Thebes.'

'I want to stay with you.'

'You cannot. Set's fury will not abate until Thebes is destroyed, and you must survive. One day you shall take up the struggle again.'

'What about you, Mother? What will you do?'

'Gather together all the soldiers who can still fight, and attack Avaris.'

The boy was indomitable. 'But that would be suicidal, wouldn't it?'

'Apophis must believe that his victory is total. If I were dead and you had died at Thebes, he would have nothing more to fear. You will have to begin from nothing, Ahmose, as I did myself. Above all, never give up. And if death interrupts your work, may your *ka* inspire another heart.'

Ahmose rushed into his mother's arms, and she hugged him for a long time.

'Think only of righteousness and the respect of Ma'at, my son; those are the only forces the emperor shall never wield.'

The storm grew even more ferocious. Many houses had been destroyed and there were countless deaths and injuries. The wadis had turned into torrents, carrying along stones and debris. On the western bank of the Nile, the ancient burial-grounds had been invaded by rivers of mud.

'Hurry, Qaris,' commanded the queen. 'You must leave with my son for the eastern desert. Heray shall go with you, if you can find him.'

'Majesty, you should—'

'I shall stay here with my mother.'

Ahhotep kissed Ahmose one last time and entrusted him to the steward, in the hope that they would escape from the storm.

When she turned round, the queen found she had unexpected company: Way-Finder, a huge grey donkey with a white belly and muzzle, large nostrils and enormous ears. He was gazing at the queen with his bright, intelligent eyes.

'What are you trying to tell me?'

The donkey turned and moved away, Ahhotep following closely. When she left the palace, the queen was soaked within seconds. Way-Finder lifted his head and pointed his muzzle at the inky-black clouds which were still zigzagged with lightning.

'Yes, we must try,' she said, stroking him.

She ran to the palace shrine, which housed a gold sceptre whose head was shaped like the beast of Set. The embodiment of power, it had been entrusted to the queen by Mut.

And another creature of Set, the donkey, had just opened up a possible way: since the emperor had petitioned the god of storms, why should she not do the same?

Ahhotep climbed up to the palace roof and raised the gold sceptre to the heavens.

'You who command the lightning, unveil yourself! What

have you to fear from me? I wield your symbol. I possess this light, which does not destroy but illuminates the earth. Obey me, Set, or you shall no longer be worshipped. No, the Emperor of Darkness is not your only master. Why do you rise up against your country and against your brother Horus, the Pharaoh of Egypt? Show your true face, and may your energy enter your sceptre.'

The clouds parted, and in the northerly part of the sky appeared the shape of a bull's hoof,* in which resided the mysterious force that humans could never master. And another bolt of lightning, more violent and more intense than the others, flashed out from the depths of the heavens and entered the golden sceptre, which the Queen of Freedom gripped with a firm hand.

*The Great Bear, believed to be the seat of Set's power.

9

Apophis's howl of rage echoed through the citadel, chilling the blood of all who heard it.

An atrocious pain had just seared through the emperor's flesh: a burning sensation, signifying that the fire of Set was turning against him.

Above Set's temple black clouds were gathering from all four corners of the sky, faster than a galloping horse. Lightning forked from them, striking the priests' houses and the avenue of oak-trees leading to the altar. The branches caught fire, and the wind whipped up the flames.

The rain fell on Avaris in such violent torrents that the soldiers took refuge in their guard-posts and barracks, covering their heads with their hands in an attempt to escape Set's wrath.

'We are cursed!' cried Tany, the emperor's wife, standing on her bed, her lips flecked with foam.

Two serving-women forced her to lie down, but she went on, 'It's the Thebans – they're coming back! I see Queen Ahhotep, with a sword . . . Waves are submerging the capital, fire is destroying the citadel.'

While Tany raved in her delirium, the emperor slowly climbed the stairs to the top of the highest tower.

Ignoring the deluge, he pointed his dagger at the inky sky and bellowed, 'You are my ally, Set, and you must strike down my enemies!'

There was an even more blinding flash than before and, with an ear-splitting roar, lightning struck the tower.

Since his narrow escape from the assassination attempt, Jannas had ensured that he was guarded closely night and day. Khamudi would not get another chance of a surprise attack.

The commander had not been surprised to learn that his enemy had taken precisely the same protective measures. Khamudi knew Jannas knew who had been responsible for the attack, and feared that he would be killed. A struggle to the death had begun between the two men.

His assistant came in bowed. 'Commander, the Supreme Council meeting is to go ahead,' he confirmed.

'Is there any news of the emperor?'

'Some say he was killed by a thunderbolt, some say he is on his deathbed, and some claim he has lost the power of speech. Commander . . .'

'What is it now?'

'The majority of the Hyksos are ready to acknowledge you as their leader.'

'You are forgetting Khamudi.'

'He has his supporters, it is true, but they are far fewer than yours. As soon as necessary . . .'

'Let us see what the Supreme Council says,' decided Jannas.

Despite the Minoan paintings, with their brilliant colours, the council chamber was cold and sinister. All the great dignitaries of the empire were present, and Jannas and Khamudi were face to face, next to the emperor's modest pinewood throne.

Everyone was nervous. When the palace doctors officially announced Apophis's death, or his inability to rule, what would happen? Some thought Khamudi would use his position as High Treasurer as an excuse to take temporary power which he could later make permanent, but Jannas, the commander of the armed forces, would never accept that solution. Only a bloodbath could resolve the inevitable conflict between the two claimants to power, and in that game the commander would be the stronger man.

For that reason, Khamudi, who was suffering from an itch that salves could not soothe, did not look as confident as usual. Although he had bought with him as many loyal senior officers as possible, he feared that he might not emerge from the citadel alive.

Suddenly, Apophis appeared. Dressed in a dark brown cloak, he walked heavily to his throne, staring icily at each of the dignitaries, and sat down.

Everyone felt guilty for having doubted him, and Khamudi's smile returned.

'Set has inflicted terrible damage on Thebes,' declared Apophis, in his harsh, chilling voice. 'The city has been half destroyed; Ahhotep's army has been decimated, and her war-fleet wiped out.'

'Majesty,' asked Jannas, 'will you give me the order to attack the rebels in order to deal them a death blow, and bring back their queen to you, dead or alive?'

'All in good time, Commander. First, you should know that my protector, Set, has made me into a new Horus. In official documents, I am from now on to be called "He who Pacifies the Two Lands". Next, Set has revealed to me the reasons for his anger with Avaris. This city, my capital, is harbouring traitors, plotters and faint-hearts who dare to criticize and disapprove of my decisions. I am therefore going to eliminate this rottenness. And then, Commander Jannas, we shall deal with Ahhotep.'

The harem at Avaris was a hell. The most beautiful young women of the former Egyptian aristocracy were imprisoned there. At any time of the night or day, they must satisfy the lusts of the empire's dignitaries. If one of them tried to kill herself, her family were tortured and deported. Yet some of the women clung to survival, reminding themselves that, a while ago, a plot conceived in the harem had almost succeeded. And people said that the emperor was on his deathbed. Perhaps his successor would be less inhuman.

Dreaming of a less cruel fate, a magnificent brown-haired girl of twenty opened the door of the room where she and her companions put on their face-paint while waiting for visitors.

Her cry of terror stuck in her throat, for the Hyksos officer who stood there smashed her skull with a blow from his club.

'Kill all these vermin,' he ordered his men, who were clad in helmets and breastplates as though about to go into battle. 'The emperor has decided to close this harem, where there are murmurings against him.'

The murderers regretted not being able to enjoy these beautiful girls before killing them, but Apophis's orders had been strict.

The grey donkey with the gentle eyes died without understanding what it was being punished for, its heart pierced by a dagger. This was the hundredth donkey sacrificed to appease the god's fury.

The High Priest of Set hastily changed his blood-spattered robe when he saw Khamudi heading towards him at the head of a squad of men.

'Follow us, High Priest,' ordered Khamudi.

'But I still have animals to kill and—'

'Follow us.'

'Where are you taking me?'

'The emperor wants to see you.'

'The emperor? I must wash, and—'

'That is not necessary. And you know how much the emperor dislikes being kept waiting.'

Christian Jacq

Apophis was sitting in state on the platform that over-
looked his two favourite entertainments: on one side the
labyrinth, on the other the arena where a fighting-bull pawed
the ground. Since the start of the purge, he had spent several
hours each day watching the deaths of the men and women he
had condemned. Some were gored and trampled, others were
torn to pieces as they fell into one of the labyrinth's many
traps.

The High Priest prostrated himself at the emperor's feet.
'We pay continual homage to Set, Majesty. Your orders are
being faithfully carried out.'

'I am glad to hear it. But during the storm you began to
doubt me, didn't you?'

'Not for one single moment, Majesty.'

'You are a bad liar. Because of your high office, I shall
allow you a choice: the labyrinth or the bull.'

'Majesty, my obedience is unswerving, and I assure you
that—'

'You doubted me,' cut in Apophis. 'That is treason, a
crime which merits death.'

'No, Majesty! Have pity!'

Exasperated by the condemned man's sobs, the emperor
kicked him hard and he fell into the arena.

The High Priest ran from the monstrous bull, but it soon
caught him and ran him through with a single toss of its horns.

The emperor was more interested in his next victim, a
palace cook. The insolent woman had dared to say that
Apophis was gravely ill. That one would end her days in the
labyrinth. She would be followed by soldiers, traders and
government officials who had also doubted Apophis's
greatness. As for the Egyptian suspects, they were all to be
sent to Tjaru and Sharuhen, the operation being overseen by
the remarkably skilled and efficient Aberia.

All this would take time, but eventually Avaris would be
purged.

10

Crowned with the sun-disc, its eyes aflame, the statue of Mut gazed upon Queen Ahhotep. The queen had just given thanks to her for protecting the Temple of Karnak during the devastating storm, from which Thebes was recovering only with great difficulty.

As soon as the lightning had been imprisoned in the gold sceptre, the clouds had dispersed, it had stopped raining and the wind had dropped. Little by little, the sky became calm again, once more lit by a triumphant sun.

Heray had organized groups of volunteers to clear up the aftermath of the cataclysm. The only effective weapon in the face of misfortune was unity. A daily manifestation of Ma'at, it gave back hope to the victims and increased tenfold the effectiveness of those who helped them.

The legends surrounding the queen, who was already the subject of a thousand tales, was now embellished by her ability to appease the violent Set and capture his fire. Ahhotep herself paid no heed to people's extravagant praise, for she was waiting in desperate anxiety to learn the judgement of Mut. Would the Wife of Amon, who was at once Father and Mother, Life and Death, accept that young Ahmose should become Pharaoh? Without the goddess's assent, even miracles would be useless.

'You, Mut,' she prayed, 'have always shown me the path

to follow. Ahmose is not only my son, he is also the future Pharaoh. If it were not so, I would have sought someone else to take on that office. I am convinced that Set's fury was unleashed by the Emperor of Darkness in order to prevent the coronation, not because Ahmose is incapable of reigning over the Two Lands. But perhaps I am wrong . . . Your eyes can see through the darkness, and you have never lied to me. Is Ahmose to ascend the throne of the living?'

The statue inclined its head in assent.

Ahhotep was conferring with Heray, Qaris and Neshi about the damage the storm had wreaked.

As Heray lowered his considerable bulk on to a sturdy low chair, she saw that he seemed to have lost his usual cheerfulness.

'Majesty, the damage is extensive,' he said. 'It will take many months to repair everything and build all the houses we need – and then there are all the temporary shelters we must provide straight away.'

'The Treasury will help those who have suffered most,' Ahhotep promised.

'Unfortunately there have been many deaths, including a lot of children.'

'Each is to be ritually buried, and I shall appoint *ka* priests to bring them back to life each day.'

'In addition, Majesty,' said Qaris, 'the military base has been seriously damaged. Despite the sailors' best efforts, more than half the war-fleet was destroyed.'

'The carpenters must begin work at once and take on as many apprentices as possible. Until enough boats have been built, there will be no holidays – but pay will be doubled.'

Neshi said worriedly, 'Majesty, it is pointless to ignore the truth. If the Hyksos attack now, we shall be wiped out.'

'First they must get past the obstacle of the troops we have massed around Faiyum.'

'You know very well, Majesty, that our men could not hold off a mass offensive. And rebuilding our forces will take time – a lot of time.'

'Everything you have all said is true,' said Ahhotep. 'But the most urgent matter of all is the coronation of the new pharaoh.'

For a few days, Thebes decided to forget its wounds, not to think about the probable Hyksos attack, and to devote itself to the coronation ceremonies, the secret part of which would take place within the Temple of Karnak. The new High Priest, Djehuty, and the Wife of God presided over the proper conduct of the rites, which saw Ahmose purified by Horus and Thoth, then proclaimed King of Upper and Lower Egypt by the vulture- and cobra-goddesses.

His first act as pharaoh was to offer a statuette of Ma'at to Amon, the Hidden One, and to swear that all his life he would observe righteousness and justice so that the links between the divine and the human should not be broken.

After being acclaimed king, Ahmose emerged from the temple to go and meet his people. He was preceded by bearers of signs symbolizing all the provinces of Egypt, which he was to unify.

'Ahmose is he who brings together the Twofold Land,' proclaimed Ahhotep, 'the son of Amon-Ra brought forth from his being, the inheritor to whom the Creator has given his throne, his true representative on earth. Courageous, and free of all falsehood, he endows us with the breath of life, radiates royalty, firmly establishes Ma'at and spreads joy. He supports the heavens and steers the ship of state.'

Late that night, while the full moon shone directly above the temple and the city still echoed with the sounds of celebration, the ten-year-old boy thought back over every word his mother had spoken. Caught between fear and pride, he had come to realize that his life would never be like that of other men and that, little by little, the office of king would take over his entire being.

Having destroyed or defaced all the palace's Egyptian stelae and statuettes, Apophis was taking full advantage of Minos's paintings. And he had just summoned the Minoan artist, plunging Windswept into anguish. The empress's beautiful young sister was a formidable seductress and a veritable man-eater, who lured into her bed any dignitaries suspected of not agreeing unreservedly with Apophis's policies. After obtaining their bedroom confidences, Windswept denounced them, and the traitors were condemned to the labyrinth.

But her whole life had been turned upside-down when she fell passionately in love with Minos. Although she continued to play her role as a spy, she was being torn in half, because she knew the Minoan's terrible secret: willing to do absolutely anything in order to return home, he was plotting against the emperor.

Windswept had almost told Apophis the truth, but that would have meant condemning the man she adored to a terrible death. For the first time in her life, she had decided not to obey the emperor.

When Apophis looked at her, she felt as thought she were imprisoned in a spider's web, struggling helplessly. Surely he would eventually realize the truth and then, at the moment of his choosing, devour his prey, both Windswept and Minos.

The young woman paced up and down her bedchamber. At the moment, she knew, the emperor was talking to Minos. In her torment, she feared the worst. Apophis might have her beloved tortured, or deport him, or fling him into the labyrinth . . . And then it would be her turn. Her brother, so much older than she, had always frightened her, although she was one of the few people, if not the only one, who could talk to him with a certain lack of respect. But Windswept was under no illusions: the day she ceased to be useful to Apophis, he would throw her to his officers or, worse, to the two women who hated her most, the 'empress' Tany and Yima, the High Treasurer's wife.

Windswept would not be able to justify her silence. As a conspirator, Minos ought to have been executed. And she could not hope to gain the slightest mercy from the emperor by talking to him about love.

It was impossible to imagine life without Minos. In the cruel, perverse world she inhabited, he was the embodiment of innocence and true love, free of dark shadows and calculation. A painter of genius, a sincere lover, he gave her a happiness she had not dared to hope for.

Whatever the consequences, she would protect Minos. But was he still alive?

Windswept disdained the drug that was circulating in the capital and making a fortune for Khamudi, that pretentious upstart whose greed was equalled only by his cruelty. He was just as depraved as his half-mad wife, their favourite form of entertainment being to inflict appalling tortures on young slaves. But he was still the emperor's right-hand man.

The bedchamber door opened.

'Minos,' cried Windswept in passionate relief, 'there you are, at last! But you look so pale. What did Apophis want?'

'Griffins – he wants me to paint griffins on either side of his throne, like the ones in the palace at Knossos. That will make him invulnerable.'

Almost physically sick, the painter could not admit to his mistress that he had thought his last hour had come.

Even in the arms of Windswept, who gave herself to him with such fervour, the Minoan still felt impaled by Apophis's icy stare.

He knew. The emperor knew, and was toying with his prey. The griffins would probably be Minos's last work.

11

Minos was working on the griffins, determined to beat all records for slowness. As long as the work remained unfinished, his life would be safe and he might perhaps find a way of killing the emperor. Despite the difference in their ages, he doubted that he would be able to kill Apophis with his bare hands. He would need a dagger, but no one, not even Windswept, could come before the lord of the Hyksos without being searched.

Suddenly, a gust of icy breath sent a shiver down his spine.

'Your work is not going very quickly, Minos, and the months are passing,' commented the emperor in his cruel, rasping voice. As usual, he had appeared like a demon emerging from the shadows. No one ever heard him coming.

'Majesty, if I hurry I might spoil the work.'

'I need these griffins very quickly, my young friend. Above all, they must inspire fear and their gaze must be terrifying.'

Despite Jannas's repeated requests, Apophis would not launch an offensive until the two griffins were in a fit state to defend his throne. The commander was fuming with impatience, and saying that they should not give Ahhotep time to build up her forces again, but that was too short-term a view. The emperor knew it would take several years for the damage inflicted on the Thebans to be put right. As soon as his griffins' eyes blazed forth destruction, as soon as his power was beyond the reach of conspiracy, and the purge was complete, Apophis would settle the matter of the queen and the rebels once and for all.

Minos dared not turn round.

'Do you understand me clearly, my young friend?

'Yes. Oh yes, Majesty!'

Apophis turned and moved off down the corridor that led to the council chamber.

Khamudi greeted him on the threshold, in a state of great agitation. 'My lord, there's a message, a message from your informant.'

The Hyksos spy had not been in touch for a long time, probably because he had had great difficulty in sending the papyrus, which was written in a code to which only the emperor had the key.

As he read the words, Apophis's face expressed such hatred that even Khamudi was awed by it.

'That damned Ahhotep! She has dared to have her son – a boy of ten – crowned, and has presented him to the people as Pharaoh! Both of them are to be utterly destroyed. But first of all we shall sow discord in their ranks.'

Khamudi suddenly doubled up in pain, his hands clutching his belly. 'Forgive me, Majesty, it is a bladder-stone. I do not think I shall be able to attend the council meeting.'

'Summon the doctor and have it removed. We have a great deal of work ahead of us.'

Khamudi's wife, Yima, paced up and down, biting her nails, while she waited for the doctor. Without her husband, she was lost. If, as some people whispered, his malady was the result of a curse laid on him by Apophis, the unlucky man had no chance. After his death, Yima was sure she would lose most of her wealth, because it would be requisitioned by the palace. True, she could plead her cause to the lady

Tany, but Tany was bedridden and cared about nothing but herself.

'The doctor has arrived,' her door-keeper informed her at last.

The doctor was a Canaanite, as Tany was, a skilled man reputed to be able to treat a case like Khamudi's. Meanwhile, the High Treasurer moaned and groaned in agony.

'My husband is a very important man,' said Yima haughtily. 'You must take great care of him.'

'Everyone knows of the High Treasurer's eminent status, my lady. Have faith in my method.'

'Does it really work?'

'Yes. But it will be painful.'

'I have a drug which will kill the pain.'

Yima fed her husband a potion made from poppies. Ordinarily, he took only a little to improve his love-making, but this time the dose sent him into a deep sleep.

The doctor took from his bag a tube made out of cartilage, and slid it up the patient's urethra, as far as the neck of the bladder. Khamudi did not react.

The surgeon slid a finger into the patient's anus, located the stone and pushed it towards the bladder's neck. Then he blew with all his strength into the other end of the tube to dilate it, and breathed in suddenly to make the stone pass through. Attaching another tube to the one he was using, he brought the stone down into the patient's penis and removed it by hand.

Khamudi's mind was still hazy when he entered the emperor's office, where Apophis was putting the finishing touches to a hieroglyphic text.

'Ah, Khamudi. How do you feel, my friend?'

'Better, Majesty, just tired and feeling a bit sick.'

'You'll soon recover. There is no better remedy than hard work, and that is precisely what I am planning to give you.'

Khamudi longed for a few days' rest, but one did not question the emperor's orders – especially not when facing an adversary as alarming as Jannas.

'Have we plenty of scarabs?' asked Apophis.

'We have them in all sizes and several materials, from stone to porcelain.'

'I shall need thousands, and I require them to be inscribed with the utmost speed. Here is the message. It is to be sent out into every single region.'

In Middle Egypt, at the Port of Kamose, which had been renamed thus in honour of the dead pharaoh, Governor Emheb was consolidating his military defences day by day, and the work was going well, thanks to the enthusiasm of his veteran soldiers. Soon he would have to hold the front line again, and he was glad that fighting alongside him again would be the great archer and ship's captain Ahmes, son of Abana. The two of them could always keep their men in good heart, even in the most difficult conditions.

The big man often thought of his home, Edfu, to the south of Thebes; he knew he would probably never see it again. Luck had favoured him during the fighting at Qis, but he had called upon luck so often that it was bound to abandon him eventually. When he learnt that Thebes had been terribly damaged by the storm, he could not help wondering if the age of Ahhotep was in danger of ending in disaster.

Without reinforcements, how could Emheb possibly fight off a major Hyksos offensive? The emperor was taking his time, enabling Jannas to prepare an enormous army whose first action would be to raze Memphis to the ground. Then, as it moved along, it would destroy the pockets of resistance, the largest of which was at the Port of Kamose, before finally thundering down on Thebes, which would be utterly defenceless.

Emheb's musings were interrupted by the arrival of

Ahmes, who said, 'Governor, our allies in Memphis have just sent us these messages put out by the emperor.'

He showed Emheb ten porcelain and cornelian scarabs. They all bore the same inscription, written in coarse hieroglyphs and containing mistakes which no experienced scribe would have made.

'We must send them to the Regent Queen at once,' advised Emheb. 'This attack could be our death-blow.'

12

In the name of Emperor Apophis, King of Upper and Lower Egypt, let this be made known to all inhabitants of the Two Lands: the thunderbolt of Set has struck Thebes, the rebel city. Its palace has been destroyed, Queen Ahhotep and her son Ahmose, the puppet pharaoh, have perished in the ruins. The rebel army no longer exists. The survivors have deserted. Let every man submit to Apophis. Anyone who disobeys him will be severely punished.

'We must make sure no one sees these scarabs,' said Neshi furiously.

'It's too late,' lamented Ahhotep.

'They might cause a general collapse,' agonized Qaris. 'Here, at Thebes, you can easily prove that these are simply more of the emperor's lies and half-truths, but in other places . . . Our soldiers will lay down their arms at Memphis, and perhaps even at the Port of Kamose.'

'We still have a way of fighting back,' said Ahhotep. 'I shall immediately write a short message for our scribes to copy on to small pieces of papyrus. These will be entrusted to Rascal and his fellow carrier-pigeons.'

Rascal, an exceptional and much-honoured bird, was the undisputed leader of the pigeons, and could cover vast distances in a single flight. Wounded during a dangerous mission, he had recovered completely and spent happy evenings with Laughter, telling tales of his adventures as a tireless warrior.

Although able to navigate using the earth's magnetism, the pigeons were at risk from from birds of prey and enemy arrows, but Rascal's flock had learnt to be cunning, making full use of their acute eyesight. There was also another, more treacherous danger. Ahhotep believed that the Hyksos spy had previously poisoned one of the birds to sever communications between her and Kamose. Since then, soldiers had kept a constant watch on the pigeon-loft.

Rascal and his comrades took to the skies in a great flapping of wings, some heading south, the others north, to spread the message from Queen Ahhotep.

'Don't move,' Ahmes warned two soldiers with bundles on their shoulders, who were preparing to desert.

'You can kill only one of us with one arrow,' retorted the younger of them.

'Be careful,' disagreed his comrade. 'He will have fired a second shot before you can get near him.'

'I have no wish to kill Egyptian soldiers,' said Ahmes, 'but I hate cowards. If you take one more step it will be your last, because I'll cripple you and you'll never walk again.'

'Haven't you heard the news? The queen is dead, there is no more pharaoh, no more Thebes, no more army of liberation. We have to get away before the Hyksos arrive.'

'The emperor is a liar.'

'Then why doesn't the queen come?'

Ahmed's attention was caught by the sound of wings, but he kept on aiming at the deserters. The pigeon landed, and he recognized it: Rascal, with a message attached to his leg.

'We're going to wake up Governor Emheb,' he said. 'And you can lead the way.'

The two men took one look at Ahmes's resolute face and decided to obey.

The governor was not sleeping. He, too, recognized Rascal, who greeted him with bright, intelligent eyes. After gently stroking the bird's head, he unrolled the tiny papyrus bearing the royal seal, looked through it quickly, then read it aloud:

> *Year two of the reign of Pharaoh Ahmose, the third day of the first month of the second season.*
>
> *The vile Apophis, Emperor of Darkness and usurper, continues to send out scarabs bearing lies and false information. Queen Ahhotep, Wife of God and Regent Queen of the kingdom, is extremely well, as is her loving son, the Pharaoh of Upper and Lower Egypt, Ahmose. At Thebes, the rites are conducted in respect of Amon, god of victories, and the army of liberation continues to prepare to strike down the invaders and re-establish the reign of Ma'at.*

The two deserters listened, open-mouthed.

'I told you so,' said Ahmes.

'All right, we made a stupid mistake,' admitted the older man. 'But we can forget about it, can't we?'

'It is for Governor Emheb to decide what your punishment will be.'

Ahmes's bow remained drawn, the arrow ready to fly. And Emheb had a hard, fiery expression which did not augur well. He went round behind the two soldiers, and kicked them both hard in the backside.

'That will be enough this time,' he decreed. 'But if you ever do anything so stupid again, I shall let Ahmes deal with you.'

The war of words lasted several months. At Memphis, after

the initial panic, the senior rebel officers managed to restore and maintain order among their troops.

Everywhere, inundated with Hyksos scarabs contradicting the papyri brought by the carrier-pigeons, the citizens and peasants constantly gathered to discuss them. At the beginning of year three of Ahmose's reign, they came to their conclusion: the emperor was lying. Officers arriving from Thebes confirmed to the leaders of the liberated provinces that Queen Ahhotep was continuing the fight and that young Pharaoh Ahmose was every bit as determined as his father and brother had been.

With a little luck, the news might spread to Avaris and the Delta.

'I've worked all day and I'm exhausted,' complained Minos.

'I'll cure your tiredness,' promised Windswept, as she washed her lover's firm young body with scented water.

Minos quickly forgot the hours spent perfecting every tiny detail of the griffins, in accordance with the emperor's very precise demands, and eagerly caressed the beautiful woman's perfect form.

Together they attained pleasure, a dazzling new height which calmed Windswept's anguish and gave Minos back hope. But, once their ecstasy had passed, reality once more stared them in the face. Never could Windswept confess to her lover that she had spied upon him and that she knew his intentions. Never could Minos admit to his mistress that he wanted to kill the emperor. Convinced that Apophis had unmasked him and was toying with his prey, the painter was afraid he might not survive once he had finished his griffins.

'The palace talks of nothing but your new masterpiece,' said Windswept, 'yet no one has seen it. The throne room has been out of bounds for such a long time.'

'Apophis won't use the monsters until he thinks they're perfect. He's in a terrible hurry, yet he makes me amend my work so that it matches his vision exactly. They're terrifying, Windswept – I hardly dare look at them! All that's needed is a little more intensity in their eyes, and I shall have finished. And then the emperor will bring them to life with his destructive magic.'

'Why are you so afraid, my love?'

'When you see the griffins, you'll understand.'

'Surely you don't think Apophis will choose you as their first victim?'

'He's quite capable of doing that.' The painter stepped away from his mistress. 'Do you know that Avaris is filled with strange rumours claiming Queen Ahhotep and her son are still alive?'

'Don't pay any attention to gossip.'

'I want to return to Minoa with you, Windswept. We could marry there, we could have children and we could live happily and simply.'

'Yes, simply . . .'

'King Minos the Great loves artists – he himself gave me permission to bear his name. We'd have a beautiful house, near Knossos, in a sunny valley. My work's nearly finished, so you must speak to the emperor and ask him to let us leave.'

13

Khamudi had to abstain from all sexual activities while he was convalescing, which his wife considered was taking far too long. So Yima simpered in the palace corridors, in search of a man who was both attractive and sufficiently discreet never to reveal their brief liaison.

She stepped out in front of the handsome Minos as he was returning to his apartments. 'Have you finished your masterpiece?' she asked, with a winning smile.

'That is for the emperor to decide.'

'People talk of nothing but you and your extraordinary talent. I should like to know you better.'

'My work takes up all my time, my lady.'

She wiggled her hips, rubbing herself against him.

'One must also know how to enjoy oneself, don't you think? I'm sure you deserve better than the arms of just one woman.'

Cornered in the narrow passageway, the Minoan did not know how to escape this ever-more-demanding blonde.

'Keep away from Minos!' commanded Windswept's icy voice.

Yima's smile did not slip. 'Ah, here is our beautiful princess! So the rumours are true: you still haven't tired of him.'

Windswept slapped Yima, who squealed like a frightened little girl.

'Go back to your husband, and never again set your eyes on Minos – or I'll tear them out.'

The lady Tany could not bear either daylight or the darkness of night. She had had ten lamps arranged around her bed, so that their flames might reassure her.

With the windows covered by heavy curtains, which let not even the smallest ray of sunshine through, the emperor's wife felt safe. Never again would she dare to gaze out at the canals of Avaris, which the Egyptians had used to launch an attack against the city.

Each evening, Tany took a sleeping-draught made from crushed lotus-seeds, hoping not to be awoken by the nightmare that maddened her: an extraordinarily beautiful woman was destroying Apophis's army, burning the emperor with her gaze, dismantling the citadel, and reducing the empress to the status of a slave forced to kiss the feet and hands of her servants.

Tany howled in terror; her night-robe was soaked with sweat. Her maids came running in and soothed her, propping her up with cushions and rubbing soothing ointments into her skin.

'Majesty,' one of them informed her, 'the lady Yima would like to see you.'

'That dear, sweet friend. Send her in.'

Khamudi's wife bowed before Tany. The empress was the ugliest woman in the capital and, despite all the ointments, she stank. But Yima needed her. Although the frightful Tany no longer left her bedchamber, she still exerted a certain influence, and Yima intended to make good use of it.

'Majesty, how are you feeling today?'

'As dreadful as ever, alas! I shall never get better.'

'Do not say that, my lady,' purred Yima. 'I am quite sure you will.'

'How kind you are, my faithful friend. But you look upset. What is the matter?'

'I dare not burden Your Majesty with my petty worries.'

'Dare, I beg you!'

Yima put on the look of a sulky child. 'I have been insulted and dragged lower than the dirt.'

'Who can have done such a thing?'

'Someone very important, Majesty – I cannot reveal that person's name, even to you.'

'Do not annoy me, Yima.'

'I am so embarrassed . . .'

'Tell me what's in your heart, my sweet friend.'

Yima lowered her eyes. 'It was the painter, Minos. He may look like a shy boy, but in fact he's a vile, disgusting goat! Never has a man treated me like that.'

'You mean . . . ?'

Yima nodded.

Tany kissed her on the forehead. 'My poor darling. Tell me all about it.'

Helped by Qaris, Teti the Small made her way determinedly to the council chamber, where Moon, Heray, Neshi, Moustache and the Afghan were assembled. Like young King Ahmose, they looked grave.

Ahhotep helped her mother to sit down.

'The news from the Port of Kamose is bad,' revealed the queen. 'The soldiers are badly demoralized, and even Governor Emheb cannot give them back their courage. At the first Hyksos offensive, there will be a rout. I therefore think it vital to strengthen the front with almost all the weapons at our disposal.'

'The rebuilding of our fleet is far from completed,' warned Neshi. 'If we send all our boats and troops to the Port of Kamose, Thebes will be defenceless.'

'It will only seem to be,' Ahhotep corrected him, 'because if we can strengthen our lines enough the Hyksos will not get through. If they do succeed, it will be because we are all dead.

But you have become very cautious, Neshi. There was a time when you would have been the first to approve of this plan.'

'I do approve of it, Majesty, and unreservedly at that. Surrounding Thebes with a wall would achieve nothing. It is indeed vital to take a new initiative and to move the theatre of war as far north as possible, whatever the risks.'

Ill at ease in debate, the Afghan and Moustache were content to go along with this. At the thought of cutting down some Hyksos, they forgot the enemy's obvious superiority.

'Queen Ahhotep is right,' declared Teti. 'We must distance the danger from Thebes and protect the person of Pharaoh, who must grow in wisdom, strength and harmony.'

The queen saw from Ahmose's expression that he had nothing to add.

'Heray and Qaris,' she said, 'you are charged with the pharaoh's safety. You shall have the usual palace guard at your disposal and reinforcements whom I shall choose myself. If we are defeated at the Port of Kamose, a pigeon will bring you the order to leave with the king so that he may continue the struggle.'

The work was so terrifying that Minos dared not look at it. With a superhuman effort, he had succeeded in making the griffins' gaze unbearable. It seemed as if the two monsters flanking the emperor's throne were ready to leap forward and tear apart anyone who tried to approach.

'Just one more small thing,' rasped Apophis, 'and it will be perfect. The left eye lacks the last shade of cruelty that will make my two guardians utterly merciless.'

Swallowing hard, the painter asked the question that had been haunting him. 'What is to be my next task, Majesty?'

'You and your companions shall decorate the palaces in the Delta towns. Thanks to you, the gods of Egypt will disappear one after the other. Everywhere, people will undergo the ordeals of the bull and the labyrinth, and no one will dream of rebelling against me.'

So the emperor was allowing the painter to live in order to continue his propaganda work. Minos would never see Minoa again.

Leaving the artist, Apophis went to the small, secret room hollowed out in the centre of the fortress. No one could hear what was said in there.

The emperor sat down heavily on a sycamore-wood chair.

Soon, two guards announced the arrival of Commander Jannas.

'Come in and close the door, Jannas.'

Although accustomed to battles and death, the commander was impressed by the place and by this man who knew how to use his ugliness as a menacing weapon.

Apophis asked, 'Are you satisfied with our new security arrangements, Commander?'

'Yes, my lord. No Egyptian raid could possibly succeed, Avaris is impregnable.'

'But you don't think that is enough, do you?'

'Indeed, Majesty. I still believe it necessary to attack the enemy front, to break through it and destroy Thebes.'

'The time has come,' said Apophis. 'Launch the first wave of attack.'

14

Emheb was dazzled. Dazzled by the nobility of Queen Ahhotep, whose appearance at the prow of the flagship had transformed exhausted, despairing soldiers into tough fighters determined to die for her. Dazzled also by the measures that had turned the Port of Kamose into a true military base, capable of withstanding a Hyksos attack.

With his usual minute attention to detail, Moon had created an imposing barrage of war-boats. On the banks of the river skilled artificers had dug deep ditches which, when hidden by branches covered with grass and earth, would trap the Hyksos chariots. The archers would be drawn up in several lines, to cut down any enemy troops who got past the first obstacles. In addition, at Neshi's suggestion many large tents had been erected in the shade of the sycamores and palm-trees, for the troops to use while the stone-cutters were building the barracks. As for Moustache and the Afghan, they were submitting their troops to intensive training. And the queen had set another grand plan in motion: to dig subsidiary water-channels, which might prove decisive in the coming battle.

When the queen held aloft the Sword of Amon before the calm, confident army, each soldier felt invincible. The blade flamed in the dawn sun. Powerful rays of intense light flashed from it and touched their hearts. And Emheb felt ever more admiration for the queen, whom he had known since she was a passionate, stubborn girl, and whose faith in freedom never ceased to grow.

But one thing bothered him. 'How is Thebes being defended, Majesty?'

'There is not a single boat left there, not a single regiment, and the military base is almost empty. It is here that everything will be played out, Emheb. The Hyksos must not get past the Port of Kamose.'

The role of spy was definitely not an easy one to play, especially in the face of an adversary like Ahhotep. Getting a message to Avaris was extremely difficult anyway, and first a thorny question had to be asked: what information should be sent?

The queen had had the good sense to divide up the preparations for battle, assigning a specific task to each person, but she alone knew the entire plan. Was the abandonment of Thebes merely a bait? Would the Port of Kamose really be the main front, or would it serve as a rearward base for an offensive in the Delta? The spy could not answer these questions, or many others. And why had the emperor not attacked? Was it because he was having difficulties in Avaris which obliged him to remain there?

Watching and waiting patiently for the right moment: applying this strategy had already enabled the spy to kill two pharaohs, Seqen and Kamose. So common sense told him not to change it now.

The condemned man, a chariot officer who had dared criticize the emperor's waiting game, had just got past the third door of the labyrinth: a notable achievement. Evading the deadly traps, he was proving as cunning as he was quick. A gleam of interest flickered in Apophis's eyes.

In front of the fourth door, a privet arch, red earth was spread over the ground. The officer saw that it was studded with pieces of glass which, had he run across them, would have stabbed up into the soles of his feet. Having avoided this trap, he grew bolder and managed to get a grip on the arch. He found his balance, picked up speed and jumped over the danger zone.

That was his mistake.

In the greenery lurked a double-edged blade, which he seized with both hands. As the pain hit him, he let go and fell heavily on his back on the shards of glass. His neck pierced, he bled to death.

'Another useless idiot,' remarked Apophis. 'Did you enjoy it at all, Windswept?'

Sitting at the right hand of the emperor, his sister had watched the spectacle rather distractedly. The officer she had sent to his death had not been a good lover.

'I can't help thinking about my troubles.'

'What are they?'

'Minos has done everything you asked. Why won't you let him go back to Minoa?'

'Because I still need his talent.'

'The other Minoan painters are talented, too.'

'Minos is different – you know that very well.'

'What if I beg the emperor to grant me this favour?'

'The love of your heart will never leave Egypt.'

Moustache could not believe the gods had ever created a more beautiful work of art than She-Cat's body. He was not the only one to appreciate her beauty: she attracted many admiring looks from the soldiers, though they knew her husband's character well and so never overstepped the mark.

Whenever Moustache was with her, as now, he forgot the war, the war that had led him far into the south where he had met this Nubian with her long, golden-brown legs. When he joined the rebel movement, he had sworn that he would never become attached to a woman – given how slim a front-line soldier's chance of survival was, it was better to move from one mistress to another, as the Afghan did. But he hadn't counted on She-Cat's magic and her stubbornness. Once she had chosen Moustache, she had proved as tenacious as a jungle vine. And what a delicious prison that vine was!

Drawing away from him, She-Cat looked at him mockingly. 'What are you thinking about at the moment?'

'About you, of course.'

'But not only about me. Tell me the truth.'

Moustache gazed up at the ceiling. 'There's danger coming.'

She-Cat did not smile. 'You aren't afraid, are you?'

'Of course I am. It won't be easy, fighting one against ten. You could even say the battle is lost before it is begun.'

'Aren't you forgetting Queen Ahhotep?'

'How could I ever do that? Without her, Apophis would have conquered all of Egypt a long time ago. We shall die for the Queen of Freedom and not one of us will regret it.'

Someone knocked at the door. 'It's the Afghan.'

She-Cat wrapped herself in a linen shawl.

'Come in,' said Moustache.

'Sorry to bother you, but things are moving. Jannas and his troops have left Avaris and are heading south. The commander had a nasty surprise in the outskirts of Memphis: the people of the city had wiped out the Hyksos guard-posts.'

'The people will all be slaughtered.'

'Yes, probably, but they succeeded in slowing down Jannas's advance and warning us.'

'Is the queen going to send them reinforcements?'

'Only two regiments: yours and mine.'

'Then we'll be slaughtered as well.'

'That will depend on how quickly we move. The aim of the operation is to lure the Hyksos towards the Port of Kamose. It's tempting to pursue fugitives and kill them, isn't it? But, obviously, if we fail we die.'

Moustache began to dress. 'We must distribute strong beer to the men.'

'That's already been done,' replied the Afghan. 'Now we must explain the situation to them.'

'Explanations won't do any good. They'll have to be content to die as heroes, like their leaders.'

'Don't be so pessimistic.'

'Don't tell me we've known worse situations than this!'

'I won't.'

'I'm coming with you,' declared She-Cat.

'No you aren't,' retorted Moustache. 'And that is an order.'

The couple embraced for a long time, convinced that this would be their last kiss ever.

15

Windswept had been wrong to plead with the emperor and reveal her love for the painter. By trying to give Minos the happiness he dreamt of, she had placed him in danger. She decided to tell him she knew his true intentions, so that he would stop plotting against Apophis. Together, they would learn to endure reality.

Night had long since fallen, but the Minoan had still not come to her bedchamber. She lay there alone, lost in thought.

Eventually, unable to rest, she got up and went down the corridor that led to his workshop. It was empty.

Perhaps he was with his fellow painters. She found them in the dining-hall set aside for them, but Minos was not with them.

Anxiously, Windswept ran to his room. It, too, was empty.

In panic, she questioned several guards, but to no avail. Methodically, she searched the citadel. And at last she found him, in a shed where linen chests were stored.

Minos had been hanged from a hook strong enough to take the weight of his body.

Jannas went to see Khamudi. Each man was accompanied by his bodyguards. The commander would have dispensed with this measure, but it was Khamudi who paid the soldiers and, before beginning the conquest of Thebes, the situation must be clearly spelt out.

The two men dispensed with the usual polite formalities.

Jannas said bluntly, 'The Hyksos army consists of two hundred and forty thousand men. I am not planning to withdraw any men from Canaan or the Delta, nor, of course, from the capital. Therefore I shall leave with fifty thousand soldiers, to whom you must immediately pay a special bonus.'

'Has the emperor agreed to this?'

'He has.'

'I must check, Commander. Being responsible for public finances, I cannot make any mistakes.'

'Check, but do it quickly.'

'In your absence, I shall be in charge of the security of Avaris. Issue orders that all forces are to obey me without question.'

'It is the emperor's orders they must obey.'

'That is exactly what I meant.'

When Jannas inspected the army, he was disagreeably surprised to find that a lot of officers and men had become regular users of the drug sold by Khamudi. Some might fight even more fiercely in battle, but most of them had lost a great deal of their energy. Nevertheless, the Hyksos' weapons were so superior that the Egyptians could not possibly hold out for long.

Besides the destruction of the guard-posts, the outlying districts of Memphis held another unpleasant surprise for Jannas: a series of ambushes in which hundreds of Hyksos were killed. The slingshots and bows wielded by the rebels, who were as fast and deadly as hornets, proved formidably effective, and the chariots got stuck in the narrow alleyways so often that using them was pointless. So Jannas decided to take one house after another, then destroy all those harbouring rebels.

Cleansing the area around the great city took him several

weeks, so determined were his adversaries. Even when surrounded, they refused to surrender and preferred to die with
their weapons in their hands.

'These people are mad,' said his assistant.

'No, they merely hate us. The hope that the Queen of
Freedom keeps alive gives them almost supernatural courage.
When she dies, they will go back to being sheep.'

'Commander, would it not be a good idea to forget
Memphis and head south?'

'No, because the people of Memphis would rush out of the
city and attack us from the rear.'

The gates of the 'Balance of the Two Lands' refused to
open when Jannas reached them. That meant the rebels
believed they could withstand a siege.

Jannas was organizing it when his assistant reported an
attack by Egyptian regiments coming from the south.

'They have come to help the rebels, sir, and they are no
amateurs: our vanguard has been wiped out.'

Jannas realized that his task would be much less easy than
he had expected. Little by little the Egyptians had learnt the
art of war, and they were now a far from negligible power.
Moreover, they had the will to liberate their country.

'We must stop these regiments entering Memphis,' he
decreed. 'Part of our troops will encircle the city and the rest
will follow me.'

Moustache and the Afghan were not ordinary generals who
conformed to well-established custom, adopted a rigid battle-
plan and watched from afar as their men were killed. Their
early experience as rebels, used to surviving in even the worst
conditions, had taught them to act as promptly and destruc-
tively as possible. They therefore divided their troops, so that
in case of failure their losses would not be irreparable.

The Hyksos' over-strict discipline had been the rebels'
best ally. The Egyptians struck in successive waves, after

killing the officers and sinking the lead Hyksos war-boat. Some officers wanted to exploit their advantage by pushing the offensive further, but Moustache gave the order to beat a retreat aboard fast sailing-boats.

'We've only ten dead and twenty wounded,' reported the Afghan, 'and we did them plenty of damage. If all goes well, Jannas should give chase.'

'Our archers will kill the helmsmen,' said Moustache, 'and our strongest swimmers – led by myself – will pierce holes in the boats' hulls.'

'Don't overestimate your strength. And don't forget that you're here first and foremost to command.'

For a few hours, the two men wondered if Jannas would raze Memphis to the ground before pursuing them. But at high noon the first sails of the heavy Hyksos boats appeared.

Not a single word was spoken. Every man knew what he had to do.

The Hyksos scout's job was to detect any suspicious movement on the riverbank and to alert the lead boat immediately. He was getting more and more uneasy, even though there was no one and nothing suspicious to be seen.

Nothing, that is, except a thicket of tamarisks whose branches were moving in the wind; in fact, moving a little too much, as if enemies were trying to hide in them. But why would they conceal themselves so badly? The scout lay down on the path and watched. There was no further sign of life in the tamarisks. It must have been just the wind, after all.

He continued his exploration, turning to look behind him several times. The countryside seemed quiet, and there were no boats on the river. The Egyptians had fled south like rabbits, but they would not escape from Jannas's army. The scout climbed to the top of a palm-tree to signal to his colleague, who was inspecting the other bank, that all was well.

The same message reached the lead boat, which continued its slow progress up the river. Moustache waited until it was well within range before unleashing his archers, while the Afghan and his men killed the scouts.

But the Hyksos reacted so quickly that only by retreating hastily did the Egyptians manage to save themselves. Arrows whistled past the Afghan's ears, and he saw several young soldiers fall nearby.

'Our ambushes inflict nothing but scratches,' grumbled Moustache. 'Jannas doesn't care if he suffers a few losses. He has decided to advance, and we cannot stop him.'

16

Encircled and defenceless, Memphis was awaiting its total destruction, which the emperor was delaying so as to cause the citizens greater torture. Jannas's army was forging south, and the purge was proceeding apace . . . Apophis had plenty of reasons to be pleased. As for Minos's murder, that was a minor irritation. The other Minoan painters would do the work the emperor had planned.

Apophis knew the murder had been committed by Aberia on Tany's orders. But, as Minos had been plotting against him in a minor way and would have been sent to the labyrinth sooner or later, the emperor had decided not to punish his wife.

Windswept came in and bowed. 'I should like to ask a favour.'

'Forget that painter. He was unworthy of you.'

'I should like to take his body back to Minoa.'

Apophis was curious. 'What a strange idea. Why should you want to do that?'

'On one hand, to prevent King Minos's being angry, by telling him that his favourite artist died from natural causes. On the other, to seduce him and sleep with him in order to learn his thoughts and make him my slave.'

An evil smile lit up the emperor's face. 'You want to attack a king . . . Well, why not? You are as beautiful as ever, so you have every chance of succeeding. Ridding me of Minos's corpse and using it as a weapon against the Minoans is a fine idea. I shall place a ship at your disposal.'

Rascal landed on the deck of the flagship, just in front of Ahhotep. After congratulating and stroking him, the queen read the message he had brought. Then she convened her council of war.

'The good news,' she said, 'is that, although Memphis is surrounded, it is resisting and delaying part of Jannas's troops. The bad news is that the traps set by the Afghan and Moustache have not worked. A powerful, heavily armed force is heading towards us.'

'If I understand you correctly, Majesty,' ventured Emheb, 'you are not convinced that our front will hold.'

'It must hold.'

'Everything is ready to hold off an attack,' said Neshi. 'Jannas will certainly not expect strong opposition – he thinks we are fleeing towards Thebes.'

Another carrier-pigeon from the south alighted on the deck. It was one of Rascal's flock, and flew back and forth to the royal palace.

The short text made the queen turn pale. 'I must return to Thebes at once. My mother is dying.'

Taking advantage of Jannas's absence, Khamudi was arranging a dinner for the senior officers stationed in the capital, in order to offer them a fine quantity of drugs, houses in the Delta, horses and slaves, in exchange for their unhesitating cooperation.

Jannas would try to crush the enemy as the emperor had ordered – it was obviously necessary. However, the commander must not become enraged, empty the Delta garrisons and disorganize Avaris's defences. Khamudi had to ensure the safety of the emperor and the capital by avoiding any ill-advised ventures. From now on, no order issued by Jannas would be carried out without Khamudi's assent.

None of the senior officers Khamudi approached had rejected his invitation, so he was sure he was winning back all the ground he had lost. By ensuring that he had these men's friendship, Khamudi was sapping Jannas's authority and reducing his support. So the High Treasurer was in an excellent mood when he returned home, and eager to enjoy a lavish meal.

But the sight of Windswept waiting in the antechamber took away his appetite. There was such contempt in her beautiful eyes that it made him shiver.

'I wish to see your wife,' she said calmly.

'She . . . she is at the bedside of the lady Tany.'

'I shall wait for her as long as is necessary.'

'Would you like some refreshment?'

'That will not be necessary.'

'But please, will you not sit down and make yourself comfortable?'

'I prefer to remain standing.

Khamudi could not meet Windswept's gaze, which was no longer in any way that of a seductress. Luckily, just then his wife made a noisy entrance, calling loudly for her maid.

She, too, was astonished to see the visitor. 'Windswept! What a delightful surprise, but—'

'You ordered Minos's murder.'

'What? How dare you—'

'You wanted the head of the man I loved and you got it. That has made you think you're all-powerful, but you're wrong. You're nothing but a madwoman, and you will die as one.'

Yima ran to her husband. 'Listen to her, my darling. She's threatening me!'

Appalled, Khamudi tried to calm his wife down, while not angering the emperor's sister. 'It must all be a misunderstanding, and I am sure that—'

Windswept's eyes blazed. 'The murderers and their accomplices will be punished,' she promised. 'The fire of heaven will strike down upon them.'

Slowly, she stalked out of the villa, indifferent to the hysterical crying that shook Yima from head to foot.

With a kick, Jannas turned over the body of the Egyptian archer his men had at last managed to kill. Perched in a sycamore tree, the marksman had killed many Hyksos.

'Have the others been dealt with?'

'There is only one left, sir,' replied his assistant. 'And he soon will be.'

Jannas saw the sails of three warships burning; all three had been badly damaged and were in danger of sinking. 'Bring me the captains of those ships.'

The three captains hurried to him and saluted.

'You knew the risks,' snapped Jannas. 'Why did you not take the necessary precautions?'

'The enemy is very skilful, sir,' said the most experienced man. 'We did not make any mistakes.'

'Wrong. You were beaten by someone weaker than yourself, and that is unworthy of a Hyksos. It was your sailors who averted a disaster, so I shall choose the new captains from among them. As for you, your corpses will decorate the prows of your ships and show the enemy how we punish incompetence.'

Turning aside from the condemned men, Jannas proceeded to make the new appointments immediately.

'Both ashore and on the Nile, the way is clear now,' reported his assistant. 'We can move on without fear.'

'That is what the Egyptians want to make us to believe,' Jannas corrected him, 'and they have sacrificed a lot of brave men to do so. They are only pretending to give up, and are playing on our credulity. Those ambushes and skirmishes were only the prelude to their real trap, which has been in preparation for a long time. We shall therefore moor the fleet here and scour every inch of land until we have discovered the true positions of their forces.'

17

The queen's boat had beaten all records for speed. The moment it touched the quayside at Thebes, the gangplank was hastily put in place and Ahhotep disembarked. Bearers carried her quickly by travelling-chair to the palace, where she was greeted by Qaris, who was clearly overwrought.

'Is my mother still alive?'

'She is on her deathbed, Majesty.'

Ahmose came to meet Ahhotep. 'I have been constantly at my grandmother's bedside,' he assured her. 'She spoke to me about my duties and about the loneliness a king must experience, but she promised that she will always be beside me whenever fear enters my heart. Her only worry, Mother, was that she might not see you again.'

Ahhotep quietly opened the door to Teti the Small's bedchamber.

The old lady had had her servants lift her from her bed, and was sitting facing the setting sun. There was so little life left in her that she was scarcely breathing.

'I am here,' whispered Ahhotep, laying her hand on her mother's.

'That makes me very happy. I begged the goddess of the West to wait until your return. Have the Hyksos attacked?'

'Not yet.'

'They are making a big mistake in letting you organize our

defence. For you will succeed, Ahhotep. You were born to win Egypt's freedom, and you will win that victory for all of us, for those who are dead and for the generations to come.' Although extremely weak, Teti's voice was clear. 'Do you know what life is, my dear daughter? The sages wrote the answer in the hieroglyphs. Life is a knot on the belt that separates and links our thinking being and our animal being. It is also the thongs on our sandals that enable us to walk and make progress, the mirror in which we can see the sky, the flower that blossoms. Life is the ear that hears the voice of Ma'at and makes us alive, and the eye that gives us the ability to create.

'You possess all these qualities, Ahhotep, and you must use them so that a pharaoh may be truly reborn on the throne of the living. I have never doubted you, for there is nothing low or ignoble in your heart. You have survived adversity; the fire of hope has nourished your soul. I am going to rest in death, Mut, the divine mother. If the court of the afterlife grants me the gift of rebirth, my *ka* will strengthen yours.

'And now, will you put a little cream on my cheeks and red ochre on my lips? I don't want to take my leave looking unkempt.'

'Of course I will, Mother.'

In the few moments it took Ahhotep to fetch Teti's face-paints from the room where they were kept, her mother died. Concerned, as always, for elegance, she had not wished her daughter to hear her last sigh.

Keeping her promise, Ahhotep applied her mother's face-paint with great care.

Ahhotep perfumed the palace as never before. The gods were formed of subtle essences, and the sweet scents would enchant the nose of Teti the Small, whose body had been mummified according to the ancient rules. Djehuty, the High Priest of Amon, directed the funeral vigil during which the dead woman became at once a Hathor and an Osiris, thanks to the words of glorification.

Teti's heart of flesh was replaced by a stone scarab clad in gold, as it was for all great initiates. This would not bear witness against her in the hall of judgment and would guarantee her eternal youth.

As the Wife of God, Ahhotep presided over the funeral ceremonies for her mother, that remarkable woman who had prevented Thebes from dying and had taken part in every stage of the war of liberation. Teti and Ahhotep had very different characters, and had not been in the habit of exchanging fulsome confidences. But they had understood each other with a look, always steering the ship in the same direction.

When the entrance to the house of eternity was sealed, hundreds of swallows flew over the burial-ground on the west bank of Thebes, bearing away the righteous soul of Teti the Small. Tomorrow, at dawn, it would be reborn with the new sun.

Ahhotep suddenly felt so alone that she was tempted to give up an unequal struggle whose outcome was all too easy to predict. But that would be to betray her family and make her unworthy of an entire people whom she had persuaded to fight and never weaken.

Her son came and stood close to her. 'I shall never forget Grandmother,' he promised. 'When we have driven out the invaders, we shall pay her great homage. And, Mother, I haven't been idle while you were away. First, I have been reading a great deal; also, I watch people; lastly, I recruit.'

Ahhotep was astonished. 'Whom do you recruit?'

'New soldiers. I know all our forces must be concentrated on the Port of Kamose, but Thebes cannot do nothing. I carry out regular inspections of the naval boatyard, where our carpenters are building new war-boats, and I travel through the outlying districts and the countryside to recruit volunteers. The officers of the royal guard train them, and Heray sees that they are fed and housed. That's how you and my father created our first regiment, isn't it? Soon Thebes won't be defenceless any more.'

Despite his young age, thought Ahhotep, he was scarcely a boy any more. Within him, the office was already beginning to devour the individual.

'I am proud of you, Ahmose,' she said.

Suddenly, the young pharaoh frowned. 'I have been robbed: someone stole a pair of ceremonial sandals. It was Qaris who noticed, but we can't tell when they were stolen, because I hadn't worn them since the coronation.'

'Do you suspect anyone?'

'No. Dozens of people could have got into the room where they were kept.'

Was it really a simple theft, wondered Ahhotep, or was it something more sinister? Had the spy struck again? Harming the pharaoh, killing him like his predecessors: that must still be the spy's aim.

She asked, 'When you travel about, do you take all the necessary precautions?'

'As far as possible.'

'Is your bedchamber guarded at night?'

'Yes, by men I chose myself.'

'Apart from this theft, has anything else happened?'

'No, nothing.'

When they got back to the palace, Ahhotep and Ahmose had to console Qaris who, for the first time since Teti had appointed him head steward of the palace, felt unable to carry out his duties.

'I am too old, Your Majesties. Replace me with a younger, stronger man.'

'Teti the Small is irreplaceable,' declared the queen, 'and so are you, Qaris. How could I find a successor in the middle of a war? This palace must continue to live, and who but you would have the skill to see that all the daily rituals are properly carried out? You must pass on everything you know to King Ahmose.'

'You may rely upon me, Majesty.'

Mother and son spent the evening beside the sacred lake at the Temple of Karnak. Here, where the gods' spirit reigned, all conflict seemed utterly impossible.

'Come here often,' advised Ahhotep, 'so that you may detach yourself from immediate reality and soar above it, as if you were a bird. Spread out your thoughts as the bird spreads its wings and gaze upon the waters of the *Nun*, where life was born and to which it will return when time is at an end. The moment is your kingdom, Ahmose, eternity your wet-nurse; and yet it is here and now that you must combat the forces of darkness.'

'Are you leaving for the Port of Kamose tomorrow?'

Ahhotep tenderly embraced this young man who was threatened by a thousand deaths. 'First thing tomorrow, yes. Continue with your recruiting, and see there is no slackening of effort at the boatyard.'

'Without Grandmother, everything will be more difficult.'

'This is only the beginning of your trials.'

18

Windswept was the only passenger who was not paralysed with fear during the voyage from Egypt to Minoa. The first few days had passed without incident, but a storm transformed the next three into a living hell. Even the captain had been seasick, and three crew-members had been swept overboard.

Indifferent to the raging of the sea, Windswept thought only of Minos, of the intense happiness she had known with him, of the hours of pleasure that filled her thoughts constantly. Her lover seemed so close, yet she would never again hold him in her arms.

The Minoan officer who welcomed the emperor's sister when the ship reached the Great Island confined himself to brief courtesies, and escorted her to King Minos's palace at Knossos. Windswept did not even glance at the countryside as they travelled.

She had no greater interest in the palace – or, indeed, in the King of Minoa, a bearded old man with an imposing presence, who sat on a stone throne flanked by two painted griffins.

The sight of those two fantastical beasts jolted her from her apathy. They were at once splendid and disturbing, but did not bear the mark of her lover's genius. Windswept noticed that the reception hall was filled with dignitaries whose hair was meticulously dressed, either in long, wavy locks or in short curls. They were all fascinated by her beauty.

'Majesty,' she said, 'I have brought you the body of Minos the painter, to whom you granted the honour of bearing your name.'

'How did he die?'

'King of Minoa, I would speak with you alone.'

Murmurs of protest were raised against such insolence.

'Majesty,' said one of his advisers, 'do not take any risks, I beg you.'

Minos smiled. 'If you fear that such a beautiful woman may be driven by evil intentions, search her.'

'No one is to touch me,' ordered Windswept. 'You have my word that I carry no weapons.'

'That will suffice,' said Minos. 'Leave us, all of you.' He got up from his throne. 'Let us go and sit on that bench.'

Windswept gazed blankly into the distance.

'What use is so much beauty when the soul is filled with despair?' asked the king.

'I loved Minos the painter. I wanted to live with him, here in Minoa.'

'Am I to understand that his was not a natural death?'

'He was murdered,' admitted Windswept, her face contorted in pain.

The king let this sink in for a long time. 'Do you know who committed the crime?'

'A female assassin in the pay of the wives of the High Treasurer and Emperor Apophis. But the guiltiest person of all is Apophis himself. Nothing can be done without his agreement. He permitted Minos's murder because Minos was conspiring against him so that he could come back to Minoa. There was nothing I could do to save him.'

'I condemn this vile deed,' said the king, 'but what is the use of protesting?'

'The Hyksos must be destroyed,' declared Windswept solemnly.

'Has your grief robbed you of your reason?'

The Flaming Sword

'I have come to tell you two vital state secrets. The first is that there is bitter enmity between the emperor's right-hand man, High Treasurer Khamudi, and the commander-in-chief of the army and war-fleet, Jannas. Khamudi and Jannas hate each other and dream only of tearing each other apart. Jannas is a skilled and ferocious soldier, but Khamudi will defeat him, even it means doing harm to the empire.'

'But that would make no difference. The Hyksos forces are invincible.'

'Not any longer – and that is the second secret. Thebes has rebelled, and the troops commanded by Queen Ahhotep have proved extraordinarily courageous. Since her young son Ahmose was crowned Pharaoh, Egypt has regained its strength and resolution. Ahhotep has only one aim: to liberate her country.'

'She will never succeed!'

'The army of her elder son, Kamose, actually succeeded in breaking through all the Hyksos lines and seizing three hundred boats in the port of Avaris itself.'

The king was astounded. 'What? Surely you must be exaggerating!'

'Form an alliance with Ahhotep and stop relying on the Hyksos for help. If you do not, sooner or later Minoa will be destroyed.'

'But to cease being the emperor's vassal would be tantamount to signing my own death warrant.'

'Not if your alliance with Ahhotep brings about her victory.'

Minos got to his feet. 'I need to think. My steward will take you to your rooms.'

While a horde of servants attended to Windswept, the king assembled his close advisers and informed them of her revelations.

'She must be mad,' declared the envoy in charge of presenting tributes to Apophis. 'She sleeps with scores of

Hyksos dignitaries, encourages them to speak indiscreetly, and then denounces them to the emperor if she suspects them of the slightest reservation about him. How could she possibly be so much in love with Minos the painter that she hates her own people?'

'She appeared sincere to me.'

'It is a trap, Majesty. She is trying to seduce you, too, in order to know your intentions and draw down Appophis's thunderbolts on you. Neither Jannas nor Khamudi will disobey him. As for Queen Ahhotep, she's nothing more than a troublemaker whose rebellion will be punished with the greatest cruelty.'

The other advisers agreed.

The king seemed to hesitate. 'First of all,' he decided, 'we must get rid of her. I shall write to Apophis informing him that her ship was wrecked off our coast and that, in spite of our best efforts, we were unable to retrieve her body. As regards the rest, we shall think upon it.'

The commander of the chariot corps charged with encircling Memphis watched the progress of the tenth assault he had launched against the great white-walled city. True, he had seized most of the suburbs after fierce house-to-house fighting; true, the Egyptians were suffering heavy losses; but they were holding fast.

The entire city had risen up, convinced that the Queen of Freedom would fly to its aid. Memphis would eventually fall, but the siege would last a long time. So the commander had sent messages to Jannas and Khamudi, asking for reinforcements. With a few thousand more soldiers, he could force open the gates of the city.

Jannas's reply had been in the negative: busy with the reconquest of the South, he could not spare a single man. But, he said, there were such large reserves of infantry in the Delta that no doubt the High Treasurer would oblige.

Consequently the officer was astonished when he received the official message, written in the name of the emperor. Since the safety of Avaris was of prime importance, he must resolve the problem of Memphis on his own – the rebels' obstinacy would mean they would starve in the end.

Afraid of angering his superiors, the officer dared not press the point. He would carry out his orders to the letter, as a good Hyksos should, and would take whatever time he needed to knock down the white walls of Memphis and put its inhabitants to death.

19

When the flagship docked, all the soldiers in the Port of Kamose shouted for joy. The Queen of Freedom had returned to lead the Egyptian forces, increasing their potential tenfold; and she would first halt the Hyksos in their tracks, then retake the offensive.

Since the town had become a military base, it had changed greatly. Permanent buildings had replaced the tents, stone quays enabled supplies to be unloaded more easily, and a new boatyard ensured that the war-boats were properly maintained.

'What progress has been made?' Ahhotep asked Emheb.

'Everything is ready, Majesty.'

'Is Moon satisfied with his defences?'

'As satisfied as he will ever be.'

'We must deploy our men immediately. According to Rascal's last message, Jannas is not far away.'

The last clash with the regiments commanded by the Afghan and Moustache had been particularly violent. Jannas's army was winning victory after victory and continuing its slow southward progress, but it had lost two more warships and its losses were far from insignificant. Everyone praised his wariness. The Egyptians joined battle in the most unexpected places, using small units destined for certain death.

'The enemy does not lack courage,' Jannas admitted to his officers. 'We can be certain that they won't lay down their arms, but will fight to the last man.'

'The worrying thing, sir,' said his assistant, 'is that we still do not know exactly where Ahhotep has massed the main body of her troops. All our scouts have been killed – not one has survived to bring us that information. In my opinion, the queen has doubled back to Thebes, and that's where she will await us.'

'She would be taking an enormous risk,' objected Jannas, 'not only of military defeat but of the destruction of her capital. No, I believe she has established her main line of defence far from Thebes, certainly in Middle Egypt. I sense that we are close to our objective.'

Utterly exhausted, the Afghan and Moustache arrived back at the Port of Kamose with the tattered remnants of their regiments.

She-Cat and her assistants immediately began to tend the wounded, some of whose injuries were fatal. Fortunately, Moustache had suffered only a leg wound and multiple bruises, which would easily be healed by the Nubian's remedies.

Queen Ahhotep received the two men in her little palace, whose main room was a shrine in which she had laid the Sword of Amon.

'I am sorry, Majesty,' said the Afghan, 'but all we could do was to slow Jannas down, and we paid a high price for doing even that much.'

Moustache was as downcast as his companion.

'You carried out your mission perfectly,' said Ahhotep. 'You won us precious time, enough for us to dig channels and divert the water.'

A faint smile lit up the two warriors' tired faces.

'Then our men did not die for nothing,' said Moustache.

'Quite the opposite: they played a vital role. If you had not succeeded in slowing Jannas down, we would have had no chance of victory.'

'We killed many Hyksos and did some damage to their fleet,' said the Afghan, 'but they are still far superior in terms of numbers and weapons.'

'In your opinion, when will Jannas attack?'

'He has become so wary that he is advancing very cautiously,' replied Moustache. 'We must go on killing his scouts so that he does not find the Port of Kamose until the very last moment. I think it will take him three weeks to get here.'

'I agree,' nodded the Afghan.

Three weeks had passed since the last serious clash with the Egyptians. However, the Hyksos continued to advance extremely slowly. There was not a single boat on the Nile, and all the villages on the riverbanks had been abandoned.

'Obviously, the enemy must have retreated,' said Jannas's assistant. 'Should we not speed up our advance towards Thebes?'

Jannas shook his head firmly. 'We still do not know the enemy's exact position. But we can be sure the Egyptians are preparing more ambushes. For us to hurry would be suicide. It is better to gain territory cubit by cubit.'

'But we have not met any opposition for several days, sir.'

'That is precisely what worries me. The Egyptians must be regrouping in an attempt to bar our way.'

As the war-fleet rounded a bend in the Nile, the Hyksos saw the wall of boats created by Moon at the Port of Kamose. Their mouth watered with anticipation: a real battle at last!

Coldly Jannas analysed the situation. On the banks there were palm-trees and tamarisks, where Egyptian archers were no doubt hiding. In front of him was the major part of the enemy fleet, composed of boats which were swifter than his but also lighter.

'Commander, look! It's her!'

At the prow of one of the Egyptian vessels, whose standard was decorated with the sun-disc in its crescent-shaped ship, stood a woman wearing a gold diadem, dressed in a red gown and holding the Sword of Amon, which glittered in the sunlight.

Queen Ahhotep: it could indeed be no one else.

'She is taunting us and trying to lure us on,' said Jannas. 'The centre of the barrage will open, we will enter it and be caught in the trap. Clever – but not clever enough. Ahhotep has underestimated me, and that mistake will be her last.'

'What are your orders, sir?'

'We shall attack across the whole width of the river, and drive right through the barrage. The battle will be hard and there will be fierce hand-to-hand fighting, but the element of surprise will work in our favour.'

'What about our chariots?'

'We shall keep them in reserve to crush Thebes.'

The heavy Hyksos boats moved slowly into position. Surely the Egyptians would soon realize that their plan had not worked, and would disperse, becoming easy prey.

But nothing moved.

The queen is no coward, thought Jannas. She prefers to die rather than withdraw. A brave madness; but madness all the same.

Sheltered behind shields, the Hyksos archers made ready to return the enemy's fire. To their amazement, they did not have to fire a single arrow. The whole fleet, except for the ships transporting chariots, advanced peacefully towards the floating barrage, which it could destroy without difficulty.

Suddenly, the banks of the Nile seemed to be torn apart. Palm-trees sawn through at the base of their trunks were pushed down on to the attackers. Great thickets of tamarisks were dragged aside to unblock subsidiary channels, from which scores of war-boats emerged and rushed at the Hyksos.

It was a ferocious battle. There were archers with flaming arrows, grappling-irons for boarding vessels, furious skirmishing in which many men died. Then Ahhotep's fast, easily manoeuvrable war-boats joined the fighting, and several Hyksos ships were overrun, set alight and sunk.

White-lipped, Jannas ordered the retreat.

20

Ahmose was no longer a child. He had become a young man whose presence impressed everyone, and each day he gave yet more proof of his fitness for the office of pharaoh. Although less athletic than Kamose had been, he had the bearing of a resolute king, whose seriousness and ability to work hard astonished those close to him.

With the aid of Qaris, Neshy and Heray, his closest advisers, Ahmose had taken charge of the Theban province and the neighbouring regions, and agriculture there was flourishing. Thanks to the careful government for which he stood, the king could feed not only the civilian population but also the soldiers at the front, and could even build up reserves in case the Nile's annual flood was poor.

The damage caused by the wrath of Set was no more than a bad memory. At Ahmose's instigation, intensive rebuilding had been undertaken: those who had suffered most had been speedily rehoused and their living conditions improved markedly. Within a few months, all Thebans would have a suitable house or other living-quarters. A new city was being born, one which was even more pleasant to live in.

Almost every day the king went to the boatyard, where the carpenters were working hard, well aware that they probably held the key to victory. Egypt would need many war-ships, their main weapons against the Hyksos. Ahmose knew each craftsman, took an interest in his family and his health. Whenever he saw that one was exhausted, he ordered him to rest. But he dealt ruthlessly with idlers and malingerers, who were sentenced to forced labour. In the middle of war, the king would not tolerate cowardice in any form.

As he had promised his mother, Ahmose had also taken charge of the defence of Thebes. Travelling around the countryside and villages, he succeeded in creating a small army of volunteers willing to fight to the death to prevent the Hyksos from destroying Amon's city. He had no illusions about the effectiveness of this modest force, but its existence soothed the Thebans' fears and enabled them still to believe in a better future. Like his father before him, Ahmose trained true soldiers at the Theban military base, with a view to future battles.

The king was in a small town south of Thebes, enlisting new recruits, when he heard someone call for help. Accompanied by his hand-picked guards, Ahmose entered the farm building the shouts were coming from.

Two recruiting-officers were threatening to whip a dazzlingly beautiful young girl.

'What is going on here?' demanded the king.

'This traitor refuses to say where her brother is hiding. You ordered us to check the civilian status of every man in the province, Majesty, and that is what we are doing.'

'Well?' said Ahmose, looking straight into the girl's eyes. 'You had better explain yourself.'

She gave him a look as straight as his own. 'My parents are dead, and my brother and I take care of the farm they left to us. If he is forced to join the army, how am I supposed to manage on my own?'

'No one is forced to join my army. But your brother may be no more than a fugitive. How can I tell if what you say is the truth?'

'In the name of Pharaoh, I swear it is.'

'Leave us,' Ahmose ordered his men. He could not stop gazing at the young woman, who was tall, naturally elegant, and proud, with the bearing of a queen. 'You are in fact standing before Pharaoh. What is your name?'

'Nefertari.'

'Nefertari, "the Beauty of Beauties". The name was well chosen.'

The compliment did not make the young woman blush. She merely said, 'About my brother, Majesty, what is your decision?'

'Since you have given me your word, he shall continue to tend his farm. It is too much work for one man, so I have decided to grant him the assistance of two peasants, who will be paid by my government.'

At last she showed emotion. 'Majesty, how can I ever thank you?'

'By leaving this place and accompanying me to the palace.'

'To the palace? But . . .'

'Your brother no longer needs you, Nefertari, and your place is no longer here.'

'Are you forbidding me to see him again?'

'Of course not. But we are at war, and we must all play our parts to the best of our abilities.'

'And mine is not to help my brother?'

'It is now to help your king.'

'But how?'

'A woman who knows how to manage an estate is undoubtedly good at organizing. I need someone to supervise the weaving workshops that make sails for our warships, and to help Steward Qaris, whose strength is beginning to fail. It is a heavy responsibility, but I believe you are capable of taking it on.'

An infinitely sweet smile lit up Nefertari's face.

'Then you accept?'

'I know nothing of the court's customs, Majesty, and I—'
'You will learn quickly, I am sure.'

The royal procession was approaching Thebes when the commander of the guard halted. Immediately several soldiers surrounded the pharaoh and Nefertari.

'What is it?' asked Ahmose.

'A sentry was supposed to meet us at this guard-post, Majesty. He is not here, so I would advise you to send out scouts.'

'We ought not to separate,' objected the king.

'Majesty, going any further might be dangerous.'

'I must know what is happening.'

Everyone was thinking about the Hyksos attack, which must have begun, and the sack of Thebes, whose streets would be littered with corpses. Not a single building would escape the flames.

'There's no sign of smoke, Majesty.'

The first guard-post they encountered had also been deserted. Had its soldiers fled, or hurried to the city to help their comrades?

Nefertari listened intently. 'I can hear singing coming from the city.'

They went a little closer. It was indeed singing: joyful singing!

An officer came running towards them, gasping for breath. Ahmose's guards brandished their spears.

'Majesty,' cried the officer, 'we have just had a message from the Port of Kamose: Queen Ahhotep has beaten the Hyksos – they're in full retreat!'

21

Wearing his usual striped headdress, Jannas appeared before the emperor, whose face was alarmingly pale.

'I require the truth, Commander.'

'Half my fleet was destroyed at the Port of Kamose, but our chariot corps is intact, and I inflicted severe losses on the enemy. Nevertheless, there may be a counter-attack, so I recommend destroying Memphis.'

'There is a more urgent matter,' said Apophis. 'That damned city's rebellion has led others to follow suit. Several towns in the Delta are rising up against us. You are to take action immediately.'

As he was leaving the fortress, Jannas encountered Khamudi, who looked angry. Surrounded by their bodyguards, the two men glared at each other defiantly.

'Your campaign was hardly brilliant, Commander,' sneered Khamudi. 'You were supposed to destroy all the Egyptians, but Queen Ahhotep is still alive.'

'Why did you not send reinforcements to my troops besieging Memphis?'

'Because the emperor did not wish it.'

'Did you actually speak to him about it?'

'I will not allow you to question my word, Commander.'

'Your word? There is no such thing, Khamudi. Today, the

very safety of the empire hangs in the balance, and it is my task to ensure it. Do not obstruct me, or else . . .'

'Or else what?'

Turning aside contemptuously, Jannas continued on his way.

The members of Ahhotep's council of war were all jubilant.

'You have won a magnificent victory, Majesty,' said Moon. 'It is only a pity that Jannas did not order his chariots to disembark, because they would have fallen into our ditch-traps.'

'Victory is an exaggeration,' replied the queen. 'We lost a great many sailors and war-boats, and Jannas himself is unharmed.'

'That is true, Majesty,' observed Emheb, 'but this time the enemy suffered more than just scratches. It was Jannas in person whom you forced to withdraw. Who could have dreamt of a result like that when we began our fight?'

'The latest news from the Delta is quite good,' added Moon. 'Part of Memphis is resisting the Hyksos siege, and several other cities are ready to rise up.'

'It's too soon – much too soon,' said Moustache. 'The rebels will all be slaughtered.'

'Can we not at least help Memphis?' suggested the Afghan.

'It is essential that we do,' said the queen. 'We must send them food and weapons, so that they can find new ways of pinning down the Hyksos.'

'That is our speciality,' nodded the Afghan. 'Moustache and I will mobilize all the rebel networks and poison the attackers' lives. From now on, they will not spend a single peaceful night. Their food and their water will be poisoned, their patrols attacked, their sentries executed.'

It began in the city of Bubastis, on the vast plains of the Delta.

First of all, a few bold young men killed two Hyksos

security guards who tried to throw them in prison. Then some women joined in, to fight the soldiers charged with deporting them to Tjaru. Finally, the people of the city, armed with hatchets and sickles, attacked the barracks and trampled its occupants underfoot. Exulting in this unhoped-for triumph, the rebels celebrated by burning the clothing of the torturers they had killed. Tomorrow, the whole city would rise up!

But then, as dawn broke, they heard the neighing of horses, growing louder and louder. Orders rang out like whip-cracks, clear and precise.

'It's Jannas's chariots!' cried a young man fearfully.

On the plains, no one could withstand the Hyksos' deadly weapon. After a brief parley, the Egyptians walked out in front of the hundreds of chariots, which were drawn up in perfectly straight lines, and threw down their weapons.

'We committed an act of madness,' shouted one of them, 'and we beg for pardon!'

They knelt in submission.

'A bloodless victory,' commented Jannas's assistant.

'With or without weapons, rebels are rebels,' replied the commander. 'Sparing their lives would be a sign of weakness and would rebound against us.' He raised his arm and brought it down sharply, ordering the attack.

Indifferent to their victims' screams, the Hyksos charioteers crushed every last one of the rebels beneath their wheels. Jannas used the same methods at Hwt-Heryib, Taremu and all the other towns where madmen had dared to rebel against the emperor.

Surrounded by his bodyguard of Libyan and Cypriot pirates, High Treasurer Khamudi paraded in his new fringed cloak. His profits from the drugs trade were still growing, and so was his immense fortune, but he was concerned that his success might be threatened by Jannas.

The commander's failure at the Port of Kamose had not

damaged his popularity at all. It was incomprehensible, as if most of the army's senior officers simply could not admit that this blinkered soldier was leading them to their doom. Moreover, Khamudi had not yet managed to subvert even one of Jannas's general staff or bodyguards. They were all soldiers who had fought under Jannas for many years and believed in him implicitly. But Khamudi would find a weak link eventually.

In accordance with the emperor's orders, Jannas had killed all the rebels in the Delta cities. The whole army spoke glowingly of him, and this very morning he was to be publicly congratulated by Apophis for his services to the empire. There would be no mention of the humiliating defeat at the Port of Kamose – still less of Queen Ahhotep, who was still defying the Hyksos. If everyone else was becoming blind and deaf, who but Khamudi could save the empire? Yet he, the only one aware of the true dangers, was going to be forced to bow the knee to Jannas.

His secretary brought him a confidential and urgent message from the Hyksos fortress which kept watch on the roads leading to the mountains of Anatolia.

When he had read it, Khamudi at once requested an audience with the emperor, whom he found conversing with Jannas.

'Alas, Majesty,' he said, 'there's bad news, very bad.'

'You may speak freely in front of Jannas,' said Apophis.

'The Anatolian mountain peoples have rebelled again and have attacked our principal fortress. Its commander is asking urgently for help.'

'I predicted this, Majesty,' said Jannas. 'Those people will never submit. If we want to be rid of them, we shall have to kill every last one of them.'

'You are to leave immediately for Anatolia, and put down this rebellion,' ordered the emperor.

'But what about Queen Ahhotep?'

'The Delta has been pacified, and Avaris is impregnable. Thanks to my spy, I now know how to barricade the queen and her son in their lair. Today, nothing is more important than re-establishing total control of Anatolia.'

22

Contrary to what many soldiers had hoped, Queen Ahhotep did not march on Avaris but confined herself to providing essential help to Memphis, so that the rebels there could continue to hold off the Hyksos.

For several nights now the sky had been turbulent, and energy was no longer circulating normally. The message from the moon-god, Ah, was unambiguous: King Ahmose was under threat. Without the slightest doubt, Apophis had put a curse on him.

'Will you at last permit me to return to Edfu, Majesty?' asked Emheb. Despite his great strength, he was clearly very tired.

'You know I cannot do that,' replied Ahhotep gently. 'Whom else could I rely on to ensure that there is no slackening of effort at the Port of Kamose? But I am convinced that Jannas will not counter-attack immediately, so, although you must stay on the alert, you may be able to rest a little before the next battle.'

The queen's smile was so enchanting that Emheb did not press the point.

'I must return to Thebes,' she said. 'As soon as we are ready, we shall go on to the offensive.'

'I shall be at your side, Majesty.'

*

Thebes would gladly have marked the victory at the Port of Kamose with a great feast, but how could they celebrate when the king was ill? The doctors could not understand why he could no longer set foot on the ground without unbearable pain. No remedy relieved it, and the doctors' conclusion was deeply worrying: it was an unknown sickness which they could not cure.

Despite this severe handicap, Ahmose kept up his pace of work. Whenever he could not walk his guards supported him, and he continued to travel all over the countryside to recruit new soldiers. Qaris and Heray advised him to take things more slowly, but he paid them no heed although he was growing weaker by the day.

The only thing that comforted him was the presence of Nefertari, who was so tactful yet efficient that she had won the heart of everyone who worked at the palace. Helping this marvellous young woman learn the customs and rituals of the court had made Qaris feel young again.

The steward was smiling as he informed the king, 'Your mother is coming, Majesty.'

'We shall receive her in the great audience chamber,' decided Ahmose.

There was rejoicing on the quayside. As soon as Queen Ahhotep set foot once again on Theban soil, her way was strewn with flowers by the citizens of the capital, eager to acclaim the heroine who had won such an incredible victory over the Hyksos.

At the entrance to the palace, the dignitaries formed a guard of honour. When Ahhotep entered the audience chamber, Pharaoh Ahmose bowed his head as a sign of veneration.

'Homage shall be paid unto you, my mother, for you have come once more to save Egypt. The spirit of Amon is within you and guides you. Through me, the love, respect and trust of the people of the Two Lands are offered to you.'

Moved to tears, Ahhotep prostrated herself before the pharaoh.

'Please stand up. It is we who should bow the knee before the Queen of Freedom.'

After conducting a long and intense ritual at Karnak, during which the Wife of God called upon Amon to become incarnate in the stones of the temple and in the hearts of men, mother and son found themselves alone once more.

Ahmose did not attempt to hide his pain, or the extent to which his health had declined.

'It was Apophis's spy who stole your sandals,' said Ahhotep. 'He sent them to the emperor so that he could curse them and prevent life from flowing through your feet.'

'What can we do?'

'High Priest Djehuty knows the incantations of Thoth that will destroy the curse. So that each part of your body may be protected from now on, I shall lay the amulets of resurrection upon you.'

These incantations dated from the time of the great pyramids, and opened up the paths of the afterlife to the reborn soul, whether those paths were of fire, water, air or earth. On the soles of the king's feet, the High Priest drew the outline of sandals which would permit the wearer to travel across any space. And when Ahhotep laid the amulets on the nape of the king's neck, she ensured that all his vital energy centres were protected.

Being able to walk without pain was like a rebirth to Ahmose. The blood flowed round his body normally, and all his former energy returned.

'I owe you my life for a third time,' he told his mother. 'After giving me birth and crowning me pharaoh, you have now given me back my life-force.'

'The emperor was right, Ahmose. You are indeed the

future of Egypt. But now tell me, who is that beautiful young woman who cannot take her eyes off you?'

'So you have noticed her.'

'One would have to be more sightless than a blind man not to.'

'If you consent, Mother, I should like her to become my Great Royal Wife.'

'Did you think long and hard before taking this decision?'

Ahmose hesitated. 'No, I took it in a moment.'

'What is her name?'

'Nefertari. She is the daughter of peasants, but she was born to be a queen.'

Ahhotep saw her son in a new light. So this patient, serious young man with the iron self-control was capable of deep passion.

The queen's long silence worried Ahmose. Of course, she had already judged Nefertari. And if she was opposed to the marriage, what could he do? The thought of life without the woman he loved was impossible, but so was the prospect of losing Queen Ahhotep's support.

'Will you not speak with her, Mother?'

'That will not be necessary.'

'Is it her lowly birth?'

'Your father was a gardener.'

'You think she and I have not taken enough time to think, but—'

'Nefertari has the eyes of a Great Royal Wife, my son. And it is vital that the pharaoh should be personified by a couple.'

Apophis congratulated himself. In sending him Ahmose's sandals, his spy had provided him with an effective way of neutralizing a young warrior who might one day have become a threat. By harming Ahmose, the emperor would break Ahhotep's heart and mother and son would both be made powerless.

Christian Jacq

Apophis had placed the sandals in a large glass vase filled with scorpions' venom, and was on his way up to the ramparts of the citadel, to expose it to the midday sun. Once heated, the poison would become corrosive, and as the days passed it would eat into the lower limbs of the madman who dared claim to be pharaoh. Little by little, the pain would become unbearable, and Ahmose would eventually kill himself rather than suffer any longer.

As the emperor climbed the steps, his ears were assailed by his wife's screams. Day and night, Tany was tormented by hideous nightmares, and Yima had to give her larger and larger doses of drugs. It was a long time since Apophis had visited his half-crazed wife. He had to admit, though, that her idea of getting rid of Minos had been a good one. The painter's death had led to that of Windswept, who had become far too much of a nuisance – sooner or later, he would have given her to the bull.

Although the rays of sunlight had not yet struck the glass vase, it became burning hot. Apophis set it down on the ramparts. Scarcely had he done so when the vase exploded, and the venom poured all over his feet, burning them as though it were acid.

23

In Anatolia the fighting was ferocious, and frequent rebel attacks were preventing Jannas from achieving a final victory. But in Egypt time had stopped in its tracks, and so had the war. Memphis remained divided in two: one part under Hyksos control, the other in the hands of the Thebans, who were supplied with food and equipment by the troops at the Port of Kamose.

Month after month, Queen Ahhotep, who was still dazzlingly beautiful though she was almost fifty, consulted the moon-god, who told her to be patient. With joy, she witnessed the birth of a new royal couple, Ahmose and Nefertari. The profound love that united them was complemented by an increasingly strong sense of their office and their duties.

Each evening, Ahhotep meditated beside the sacred lake while the swallows soared overhead, souls from the afterlife who were regenerated in the sunshine.

Her son, now an austere young man of twenty, came to join her. 'We shall soon celebrate the eleventh year of my reign, Mother, and Egypt is still occupied. In the past, I did not feel I could fight like my father and brother. Now I know I can.'

'That is true, Ahmose, but the omens are still unfavourable.'

'Must we heed them?'

'Haste might be dangerous – even fatal.'

'The Hyksos have not retaken any of the positions they lost, many warships have been launched from our boatyard, and we have mobilized thousands of men. Why put off the battle?'

'It pleases me to hear you talk like that,' said Ahhotep. 'Liberating our country must always be our foremost concern. But only the gods' assent and the breath of Amon will give us the strength we need.'

'Then we must enlarge Karnak and the god's shrine at the military base. I shall attend to the matter first thing tomorrow.'

Apophis's feet and ankles were so painful that he had to be carried everywhere on a pine-wood throne by two Cypriot guards, whose tongues he had had cut out. Although he seemed more and more passive and less and less talkative, the emperor continued to govern without delegating even a scrap of his power.

Jannas was reimposing Hyksos control in Anatolia at the cost of thousands of deaths, while Khamudi did the same in the Delta by means of deportations. And the ruin of Memphis, which was still under siege, favoured the expansion of Avaris as a trading centre.

But there remained Queen Ahhotep and her puny little king. True, they had given up fighting and were pinned down in their positions, but their very lives were an insult to Hyksos greatness. As soon as Jannas returned, he must think up a new way of destroying them.

When the curse of the sandals had turned against him, the emperor had felt an even greater desire to destroy the queen, whose magic rivalled his own. It would be the most satisfying victory of his entire reign.

Beneath a threatening sky, Apophis was carried to the Temple of Set, where he was currently the sole High Priest. Who but himself could really communicate with the thunder?

As he entered the shrine, where animals were being sacrificed to Set, the emperor felt a fierce pain in his feet and he realized at once that something important was about to happen.

Seizing the blood-soaked head of a sacrificed donkey, Apophis gazed deep into the animal's eyes.

And he saw. He saw Thebes, a queen and her son. He saw a pact sealed between them, and knew that this alliance would have all the power of an army.

He called once again upon Set, bidding him to unleash his power against these enemies and separate them for ever.

On the morning of the third day of the first month of the first season of the eleventh year of the reign of Ahmose, the pharaoh left by boat to set in train the building of Amon's shrine at the military base.

On the same morning, Djehuty, High Priest of Karnak, at last managed to reassemble the ancient calendar of favourable and unfavourable times, which had come to him in disjointed fragments. As he put the final touches to this vast puzzle, the learned scribe had a terrible shock. Ordinarily the very model of self-control, he could not prevent himself running full tilt to the palace, where Ahhotep received him immediately.

'Majesty, all royal activities must be halted and the king given extra protection. Today is the day of Set's birth, and if the emperor knows it he will unleash his thunder against us.'

'Pharaoh Ahmose is on his way to the military base. I shall try to join him there.'

'Do not take any risks, I beg of you! You may fall victim to the heavens' fire, too.'

But the queen paid no heed to the High Priest's warning.

Before she embarked, he handed her a strip of linen on which an ancient incantation was written. 'Place this round the pharaoh's neck,' he advised. 'It may perhaps save his life.'

When he had unleashed the terrible storm that had destroyed much of Thebes, Apophis had allied himself with the clouds and the winds. This time, in addition to a storm which raged over the city and the burial-ground on the west bank of the Nile, he let loose the river's fury.

In a few minutes, the water began to boil, and enormous waves attacked both the riverbanks and the hull of Ahmose's boat, which was nearing the military base.

At Karnak, in the palace, at the entrance to the burial-ground and inside each house, the Thebans obeyed Ahhotep's instructions by making offerings to the dead and burning clay figurines on which the name of Apophis had been written. Djehuty took the additional precaution of placing a cornelian eye on the wax effigy of the emperor, so as to destroy the evil eye with which he was seeking to lay waste Thebes.

Aboard a boat sailing north, Ahhotep firmly gripped the gold sceptre with the head of Set. The god of storms was now not her enemy but her ally. Having captured his thunder, the queen no longer feared his violence. Within the sceptre the energies of heaven and earth were united.

Ahhotep thought only of the pharaoh. Even if she died in the attempt, she must save him.

Ahmose helped the crew lower the sails so that the smallest possible surface faced the raging wind, which was spinning the boat spin round and round. Without its rudder, which had snapped off, the captain could not steer towards the bank.

Only the pharaoh's calmness stopped the sailors panicking. When all seemed lost, Ahmose issued an order which the crew obeyed to the best of their ability, and in so doing prevented the vessel from sinking.

Emerging through the torrential rain, the queen's boat

116

reached the pharaoh's. She raised the sceptre towards the mass of clouds, and the rain began to slacken.

The timbers of the royal vessel made a sinister cracking noise. Several holes opened up, letting in water.

Ahhotep intoned the words written on the linen strip: 'The universe of the stars obeys you; the light rests upon you.'

The boat stopped spinning. Just before it sank, its occupants jumped on to Ahhotep's boat and she immediately tied the linen band round her son's neck.

The storm died down, and Thebes emerged from it almost unscathed.

24

Never had the security measures around the fortress at Avaris been so spectacular. It was the time of the tribute ceremonies, and in Jannas's absence High Treasurer Khamudi was determined to prevent any untoward incidents. The towers and ramparts bristled with watchful archers, and the pirates who formed the emperor's personal bodyguard had orders to arrest and kill any suspicious persons.

In this oppressive atmosphere, the envoys from the countries that had submitted to the Hyksos, and their gift-bearers, were given permission to enter the fortress through the main gate. Then, under heavy escort, they were ushered into the audience chamber of Apophis's palace.

Seated on his pine-wood throne, flanked by the two griffins, the emperor enjoyed the fear of his guests, who dared not raise their eyes to look at the tyrant, sitting above them swathed in a voluminous dark-brown cloak. Even the beauty of the Minoan-style frescoes had a disturbing aspect, as if the bulls were about to come charging out at the visitors.

In both summer and winter, the place was icy cold. The emperor exuded a chill which prevented the slightest breath of warmth from entering.

The envoys and their entourages lay prostrate before Apophis for a long time. He savoured this moment, which confirmed his omnipotence over the most extensive empire the world had ever known. His right hand caressed the gold pommel of his dagger, with which he could inflict death on anyone he chose, whenever he wished. It was because they had forgotten this aspect of true power that the pharaohs had been defeated.

With a disdainful gesture, Apophis ordered his vassals' representatives to stand up.

'A few Anatolian barbarians have tried to rebel,' he declared in his rasping voice, which made everyone present shiver. 'I have sent Commander Jannas to exterminate them. Anyone who gives them aid, in any way whatsoever, will suffer the same fate. Now I consent to receive your homage.'

Gold and silver ingots, fabrics, costly and elegant vases and pots of priceless ointments were laid before the throne. But Apophis's ugly face did not brighten and the atmosphere remained tense. The Minoan envoy was the last to offer his gifts: gold rings, silver cups and lion-headed vases.

'That is enough!' bellowed the emperor. 'Your tributes are even more ridiculous than your predecessors'. Do you not realize who it is that you dare to mock?'

'My lord,' said the Phoenician envoy nervously, 'we have done everything possible. I beg you to understand that the rumours of war are very harmful to trade. And also long periods of bad weather have prevented our ships from putting out to sea. So the trade in goods has been less good than normal, and we have grown poorer.'

'I understand, I understand. Come here.'

The Phoenician recoiled. 'I, my lord?'

'Since you have given me an explanation, you deserve a reward. Approach my throne.'

Trembling, the envoy obeyed.

Flames darted from the griffins' eyes; flames as intense as they were short-lived. His face ablaze the Phoenician howled with pain and rolled about in the heap of gifts to try and put out the fire consuming him. Dumb with terror, those present witnessed his death-throes.

'That is the punishment reserved for anyone who dares treat me with insufficient respect,' stated the emperor. 'You, the Minoan envoy, what have you to say for yourself?'

Although old and sick, the diplomat managed to contain his fear. 'We could not give any more, my lord. Our island has suffered greatly from rain and gales, which destroyed most of our crops. In addition, the accidental death of some of our best craftsmen in a fire has caused chaos in our workshops. As soon as the situation has returned to normal, King Minos the Great will send you more tributes.'

For a few moments, everyone thought these explanations had calmed the emperor's cold fury. They were wrong.

'You have all insulted me,' he continued. 'These miserable offerings show that you are refusing to pay your taxes and that you are all rebels. First thing tomorrow, regiments will leave for the provinces of my empire, and those responsible for this insurrection will be put to death. As for you, you ridiculous envoys, I shall grant you a fitting end.'

Using the great axe, which she wielded as well as any headsman, Aberia had beheaded all the gift-bearers. As for the two Nubians and the three Syrians who had tried to rush the guards and escape, she had enjoyed cutting off their feet before strangling them.

The rejoicing was not yet at an end: like the other Hyksos dignitaries, she was about to watch the great game Apophis had devised.

Before the citadel a rectangle had been drawn. Inside it were twelve white and twelve black squares, arranged alternately.

Their hands tied behind their backs, the twenty-four envoys from the provinces of the empire were brought forward by guards.

'You will be untied,' announced Apophis, who was seated in a travelling-chair overlooking the gaming-board, 'and you will be given weapons. Twelve of you will form one army, the other twelve the opposing one.'

Speechless, the envoys bowed to Apophis's instructions.

'Whom shall I play against? Ah yes, against you, my faithful Khamudi.'

The High Treasurer would happily have dispensed with this favour. There was only one possible thing to do: let the emperor win.

Appophis turned back to the prisoners. 'Do exactly what I order you to do and respect the rules of the game,' he warned them, 'or the archers will kill you. You are now nothing but pawns, to be moved around by myself and Khamudi.'

From the oldest to the youngest, the envoys trembled.

'Persian, advance one square straight ahead,' ordered Apophis.

Khamudi moved forward the Nubian, who was armed with a spear, to confront him.

'The Persian must try to kill the Nubian,' decided the emperor.

In terror, the two envoys stared at each other.

'Fight,' snapped Apophis. 'The victor will drag the loser's corpse out of the game and take his place.'

The Persian wounded the Nubian on the arm, and the Nubian dropped his spear.

'I have defeated him, my lord!' quavered the Persian.

'Kill him or you are dead.'

The spear came down once, twice, three times. Then the Persian dragged the bloody body out of the rectangle and stood at the head of Apophis's pawns.

'Your turn, Khamudi.'

If he allowed himself to be defeated too easily, the High Treasurer risked displeasing the emperor.

'The Syrian is to attack the Persian,' he announced.

121

The Persian tried to run, but the archers stopped him by firing arrows into his legs. And the Syrian smashed his skull with his club.

'Do not forget that the victors' lives will be spared,' added Apophis.

From that moment, the 'pawns' killed each other in quick, vicious duels. Khamudi played well, making the game interesting but enabling Apophis to win decisively. At the end, the emperor had only one pawn left, the Minoan envoy.

Numb, not knowing where he had derived such energy, the old man gripped the bloody dagger with which he had killed three of his colleagues.

'As you are a victorious soldier, your life shall be spared,' decreed the emperor.

The Minoan let go of his weapon and staggered out of the gaming-board.

'But as a traitor,' Apophis added, 'you must be punished. Lady Aberia, deal with him.'

25

The five men disembarked at a deserted spot on the Egyptian coast, after which their boat immediately put out to sea again. Then, instead of taking the route to Sais, they moved away from the green fringe of the Delta and headed into the desert. Armed with rough maps showing a number of water-holes, they hoped to avoid any confrontations on the long journey that would lead them to the province of Thebes.

Several times they were almost intercepted by Hyksos patrols, by nomads, or by caravans. Halfway to their destination, they began to fear they would die of thirst, for one of the wells on their map had dried out. They had to detour to the edge of the desert, to the cultivated area, to steal fruit and water-skins from a farm.

Two of them did die. The first collapsed, exhausted; the second was bitten by a cobra. If the other three had not been well-trained footsoldiers, used to moving about in hostile terrain, they would not have survived their ordeal – they had never imagined it would be so harsh.

Less than an hour's march from the military base at Thebes, they ran into an Egyptian patrol. At the end of their strength, thin as skeletons, they fell to their knees in the sand.

'We have come from the island of Minoa,' croaked one of them, 'and we have a message for Queen Ahhotep.'

*

Christian Jacq

Neshi had interrogated the three men separately; each claimed they had been sent by Minos the Great. As their accounts tallied, he agreed to their request.

Washed, shaved, fed and dressed in new kilts, they were taken under guard to a small room in the Theban palace, where the queen and Pharaoh Ahmose were studying a report by Heray on the army's supply system.

'I am Commander Linas,' declared a bearded, square-faced man, 'and I shall speak to no one but the Queen of Egypt.'

'You and your two companions must bow before Pharaoh,' ordered Ahhotep.

She had such authority that the three Minoans obeyed.

'Why did you undertake this arduous journey?' she asked.

'Majesty, the King of Minoa's message is strictly confidential, and . . .'

'The guards will take your friends back to their rooms. You shall remain here. The pharaoh and I will hear you.'

Linas, who was accustomed to giving orders, not taking them, sensed that it would be as well not to displease this woman.

'Minos the Great has ordered me to invite you to Minoa, Majesty. He wishes to converse with you about plans which are as important for your country as for our own.'

'What plans?'

'I do not know.'

'Have you brought no written message?'

'No, Majesty.'

'Why should I deliver myself into the hands of one of the Hyksos' principal allies?'

'Because of the laws of hospitality that obtain in Minoa, you will be in no danger: in our land, a guest is sacred. King Minos will welcome you in a manner worthy of your rank, and, whatever the outcome of your discussions you shall leave free and unharmed.'

'How can you guarantee that?'

'I am not only a commander in the Minoan war-fleet, but also King Minos's youngest son. Naturally, I shall remain here in Thebes until your return.'

Neshi, Heray and Qaris all agreed that the invitation was a crude trap laid by Apophis to lure Queen Ahhotep into enemy territory and capture her. The only possible response was to send Linas and his companions back to Minoa.

'But supposing the king is sincere?' suggested the queen. 'Minoa finds Hyksos domination hard to bear. Her people are proud, her culture rich and ancient. Her relations with Egypt have always been excellent, because the pharaohs, unlike Apophis, did not try to subjugate her.'

'That is true, Majesty,' said Neshi, 'but in the current situation—'

'Precisely. The current situation is not at all favourable to Minoa. Let us suppose King Minos is afraid that he will be attacked and deposed, that he suspects Apophis of wishing to lay Minoa waste. What can he do, except form an alliance against the Hyksos? Despite all his efforts, Apophis has not succeeded in keeping our victory secret. The news of that victory, however minor it may have been, must have reached Knossos. Minos now knows that the Hyksos are no longer invincible. If Minoa rebels, other conquered lands will follow suit, and the empire will begin to disintegrate. Destiny is offering us an unexpected opportunity, and we must seize it.'

Ahhotep's reasoning was tempting, but old Qaris refused to be swayed. 'If the king is intelligent and shrewd, he probably hopes we take that view – and the trap is all the cleverer. I detect here a new sign of Apophis's cunning. As he has failed to kill you himself, he is using the services of a faithful vassal who offers you a tempting glimmer of mad hope.'

'Qaris's voice is the voice of reason,' agreed Heray.

'To which I have never listened,' said the queen, 'since the moment when I decided to fight the Hyksos. You all know that we cannot win this war without taking risks. This invitation is the sign I was hoping for.'

Qaris turned to Ahmose. 'May I beg Pharaoh to persuade the queen not to do this?'

'If you die, Mother,' said the king sombrely, 'what will become of us?'

'You have been crowned and you rule Egypt, Ahmose. First of all, you should go to the Port of Kamose, and you should continue to support the rebellion in Memphis so that only the Delta remains safe territory for the Hyksos. While you await the results of my discussions with King Minos, you should build more and more war-boats. If the invitation really is a trap, Apophis will be sure to gloat publicly over it, and you must then attack him. If, on the other hand, King Minos agrees to become our ally, we shall be in a much stronger position.'

'Am I to understand, Mother, that you have already made your decision?'

Ahhotep's smile would have charmed the sternest of opponents. 'Yes, because I know you are capable of ruling.'

Ahmose knew that the death of the Queen of Freedom would be far worse than any military reverse. But no one could persuade Ahhotep to change her mind.

'I have always agreed with your plans, Majesty,' said Neshi, 'but I cannot support you in this, for one simple reason: it would be impossible for you to reach Minoa. You would first have to cross Middle Egypt, then get through the Delta – which is entirely in the hands of the Hyksos – and finally find a ship with an experienced crew.'

'There is another way, the one by which Linas and his men reached us.'

'Through the desert? But, Majesty, that is an exhausting, highly dangerous journey.'

'The expedition will include Egyptian sailors and Linas's companions, who can give us detailed information about which tracks are safe. As for the ship, we shall transport a boat in sections and assemble it on the coast at the point of departure.'

'Majesty,' said Neshi, 'this plan . . . this plan is . . .'

'I know, it makes no sense. But just imagine if I succeed!'

Only one thing worried Ahhotep: that the emperor's spy would discover her plan and bring her journey to an abrupt end by prompting Hyksos intervention.

26

The sadness in Way-Finder's eyes was matched by the despair on Young Laughter's face. But Ahhotep could not yield to their entreaties. She explained to them that crossing the desert, and then the sea, was much too dangerous for them and that, in any case, they had important work to do. Way-Finder must continue to guide the other donkeys as they delivered equipment to the army, and Laughter must watch over Ahmose. Like his father, Old Laughter, the huge hound had become a formidable guard-dog, ready to fight to the death to save the king. The two faithful servants pretended to be content.

'But I wish I could take you with me to protect me,' she whispered.

As the sun set, the heat of the day began to wane. A gentle breeze wind began to blow from the north, strenuous work in the fields stopped, and all over the countryside the sounds of flutes could be heard. Ahhotep thought of her dead husband and son, and knew that they were sharing the banquet of the gods.

Nefertari came in and bowed. 'Your evening meal is ready, Majesty,' she said. 'Oh, forgive me. I have interrupted your reflections.'

'This is not the time for reflecting on the past. There is too much to do building the future.'

As she looked at the Great Royal Wife, Ahhotep mused that Ahmose, ordinarily so cautious, had been right not to hesitate over his marriage. Although blessed with gifts which could have earned her a life of easy contentment as a prosperous lady, Nefertari had the soul of a queen: conscientious, radiant, caring more about the destiny of her country and her people than she did about her own.

'If I do not return, Nefertari, you must fight at the pharaoh's side. Without your radiance and your magical power, he will lack the energy necessary for victory. It was Isis who brought Osiris back to life, and it is the Great Royal Wife who fills the king's soul with the flame of just deeds. Above all, do not waste your time on unworthy tasks or your words on banalities.'

Nefertari's unflinching gaze belied her delicate appearance. 'I promise, Majesty.'

'Now we can have our meal.'

Ahhotep was extremely pleased to have retaken control of the road to the oases: the Nubians and Hyksos could no longer use it to send each other official messages. In the Great South, which was now under Egyptian control, the King of Kerma seemed content with his wealth and his pampered life, far removed from the war. Ahhotep was still wary, and feared that his warlike nature might be reawakened. But, hoping that she was mistaken, she put such thoughts aside and enjoyed the harsh beauty of the desert, even though it was hostile to humans.

The men were suffering, but they were so proud to have been chosen to accompany Ahhotep that they made light of their difficulties. Only the two Minoans, who had been firmly invited to carry their share of the load, looked unhappy. Eventually the good food and wines cheered them up, and rest periods at the oases put them in a better temper. They consented to answer the queen's questions as she asked them about life in Minoa, where, according to them, there was a pronounced taste for games, celebrations and fashion.

They all had to be constantly on the alert, and Ahhotep slept with one eye open. If the spy had been able to warn the emperor, the Hyksos would travel to the ends of the earth to capture the queen.

The last week of the journey, when they had to cross the coastal marshlands, was particularly arduous; the travellers almost wished they were back in the desert. They had to wade for hours through stagnant standing water, with snakes brushing against their legs and under constant attack from mosquitoes. Much use was made of She-Cat's remedies and ointments, but the Egyptians were convinced that they really owed their lives to the protective magic of the Wife of God, who shared their trials without a word of complaint.

Fortunately, the expedition encountered not a single enemy patrol, and eventually reached the coast safely. To the Egyptians it was a new world: a sandy beach, waves, salt water constantly in motion. At the Minoans' suggestion, they dared to bathe in it. The water felt heavy and sticky, although it made them feel much better after the water of the marshes.

Ahhotep allowed the men to relax, only too happy that they were all alive. Surely, she thought, that must be a sign that she had made the right decision? All the same, she did not lower her guard.

'The demons of the sea are even more formidable than those of the desert,' she warned them as they ate beneath the stars. 'We know the Nile's whims well, but the caprices of this immense ocean may take us by surprise. Nevertheless, we must cross it.'

Watched sceptically by the two Minoans, the Egyptians assembled a boat designed for long journeys. With its double mast, constructed from two oblique shafts joined at the top, its flat-roofed cabin, new sails, oars and sturdy rudder, it looked very fine.

'Are you planning to sail all the way to the Great Island in . . . that?' asked one of the Minoans.

'Our ancestors did,' replied Ahhotep.

'But, Majesty, you do not know all the dangers that lie in wait for us. With a good following wind, it takes only three days to cover the distance between Minoa and Egypt,* but going from Egypt to Minoa will take almost twice as long because we shall be sailing into the wind. Besides, the winds are gusty and unpredictable, and the swell is dangerous – and then there are the storms. In short, the boat's hull must be able to withstand tremendous pressure from the wind and waves.'

'It will.'

'Also, if the weather is bad and the clouds hide the stars from us, we shall lose our way.'

'Not with the map I have. Our ancestors, who often sailed to and from Minoa, left us invaluable documents, and you would be wrong to scorn their knowledge. Do you know, for example, why it is stated that the length of the *duat*, the intermediary world between the sky and the underground ocean, is 3,814 *iterus*, to use a map-maker's term? Because it corresponds to the perimeter of the Earth.† The sea may frighten many Egyptians, but our people have included great navigators and we know how to tame it.'

'But, Majesty, this crew certainly does not!'

'Then this will be an opportunity for them to acquire that knowledge.'

When they saw how well the queen's sailors handled their vessel, the Minoans were slightly reassured. But they knew how suddenly the ocean's fierce storms could strike, and

---

*About 500 kilometres.

†3,818 *iterus* = 39,894.48 kilometres. This information, provided by the tombs in the Valley of the Kings, was probably known before (see J Zeidler, 'Die Länge der Unterwelt nach ägyptischer Vorstellung', *G*ttinger Miszellen 156, 1997, pp 101–12).

were afraid the crew would panic if anything went wrong. The wind veered several times, and at dawn on the third day the sea became very rough. The captain reacted by adjusting the sails and the course of the boat, whose manoeuvrability was a great asset. The crew adapted surprisingly quickly, not once losing their confidence.

And each night Queen Ahhotep conversed with the moon-god, asking him for a peaceful crossing.

On the evening of the fourth day, the two Minoans suddenly thought they were seeing things. 'Look over there! It's our island, the Great Island!'

'Let us pay homage to Amon, master of the wind, and to Hathor, queen of the stars and of sailing,' said Ahhotep. 'Without their aid, we would not have reached our destination safely.'

The queen laid bread, wine and a phial of perfume on a small altar, and everyone bowed their heads in meditation.

'Ships in sight,' announced the captain.

Four warships were closing swiftly on the Egyptian boat.

'They think we're an enemy boat, and they're going to ram us,' cried one of the Minoans.

Indeed, the warships' course left no doubt as to their intention. Ahhotep gave the order to lower the sails and went to stand at the prow, presenting an ideal target for Minos the Great's archers.

27

Khamudi paced back and forth in his villa like a caged bear. Although he had doubled the number of guards who protected him day and night, he no longer dared go out.

'Why are you so afraid?' asked his wife. 'Surely Jannas isn't going to attack our house?'

'He's quite capable of doing so. There is now only one obstacle between him and imperial power: myself. He and I both know it, believe me.'

'But you're still the emperor's right-hand man, aren't you?'

Khamudi sat down heavily in an armchair and drained a cup of white wine. 'Apophis is getting old. Every day he's a little less lucid.'

Yima was shocked. 'That's the first time I've ever heard you criticize the emperor.'

'It isn't a criticism, it's an observation. If we want to preserve the empire's power, Apophis needs more and better help.'

Yima understood nothing of politics, but her husband's worry made her afraid she might actually lose all her money and possessions. 'Are we in danger?'

'No, because the emperor still trusts me.'

'Would he dare put his trust in anyone else?'

'Jannas is trying to persuade him to, because Jannas and I

are enemies and he is determined to reduce my influence on all the leading government officials. In other words, he wants to get rid of me.'

Yima turned pale. 'Is that just rumour, or do you know it for a fact?'

'I have carried out a detailed investigation, and all the evidence points one way. As soon as he returns from Anatolia, Jannas will try to remove me from power.'

Yima sat on Khamudi's knee and covered him with nervous kisses. 'You won't let that happen, will you, my darling? You won't let him steal our fortune?'

'Not if you help me.'

'How?'

'You still have the empress's ear, haven't you?'

'Yes, but she is a crazed old woman, ill and powerless.'

'All the same, she gave the order to kill Minos.'

'Jannas is a much bigger and more dangerous target.'

'Indeed he is. So you must convince Tany that he's leading the empire to ruin. After all, Jannas's incompetence led to the attack on Avaris and to her illness, didn't it? That man is the cause of all our troubles. If we don't kill him, he'll certainly kill us.'

Yima seemed to understand. 'Supposing he has been killed in Anatolia?'

'According to his latest message, he'll be back here in less than a week – no doubt he'll be greeted as a conquering hero.'

His old striped headdress and his clothes, which were scarcely better than those of a simple soldier, reflected Jannas's indifference to the cheering that punctuated his march to the citadel. Soldiers, guards citizens were celebrating a great triumph. Only the emperor must know the truth: that the celebrations were utterly unjustified.

In accordance with custom, it was Khamudi, as head of

security, who greeted the commander. 'Did you have a good journey?'

'Can the emperor receive me immediately?'

'He is taking his afternoon rest. I am ordered to hear your report and pass it on to him.'

'That is out of the question.'

'Commander! That is the usual procedure, and—'

'I don't care about procedure. Now that I am back, I shall again take charge of the safety of the capital and of the emperor. Go back to your finances and your drugs-trafficking, and above all do not try to stop me entering the citadel. I shall wait there until Apophis awakes.'

Furious, Khamudi stood aside.

Despite all the cares that weighed him down, Jannas had dozed off. An icy breath jolted him abruptly awake. The emperor was standing right in front of him.

'You have been away a very long time, my friend. Have our troops grown soft?'

'The situation is grave, my lord.'

'Follow me.'

The two men shut themselves away in the little room at the centre of the palace, where no one could hear them.

'Has Asia been pacified, Jannas?'

'I have killed thousands of rebels and their families, burnt hundreds of villages, slaughtered entire herds, and brought terror wherever I went. Everyone knows that to offend the emperor of the Hyksos leads to implacable punishment.'

'You have not answered my question.'

'No one dares face us in pitched battle, because nothing and no one can withstand our chariots, but there are interminable ambushes, minor clashes and skirmishes. Normally, I would simply have wiped the rebels out, but a new class of real warriors has succeeded in uniting the tribes and sweeping away the local rulers to form a new power. They call themselves Hittites.'

'Why did you not simply wipe out the Hittites?' demanded Apophis.

'Because they know every inch of their mountains and can survive in even the most difficult conditions. Even when they are starving and dying of cold, they still fight like wild beasts and lay murderous ambushes for us. I hanged their wives, disembowelled their children, razed their houses to the ground, and still they did not surrender. If I had sent my men into the gorges and the ravines, they would have been slaughtered.'

The emperor's harsh voice grew menacing. 'Then what do you suggest?'

'I have left in position enough men forces to keep the Hittites pinned down in their enclave. In the short term, they are not a serious threat. However, on our homeward march I reflected at length. In Anatolia there are the Hittites, in Egypt there is Queen Ahhotep. The two cases are comparable: pockets of rebellion which must be annihilated if we are not to see them grow stronger or, worse, infect other regions.'

'That is precisely the sort of catastrophe I ordered you to prevent.'

'Majesty, I have done all that was possible with the means at my disposal.'

'That is for me to judge, Commander.'

'Majesty, you can of course send me to the labyrinth or consign me to the bull, but my death would not solve any of the problems facing the empire.'

The emperor did not like Jannas's tone, but he recognized the validity of his arguments. 'What exactly do you want?'

'Full powers.'

Apophis remained rigidly motionless for endless seconds. Then he said, 'And what does that mean?'

'I regret to have to say that the High Treasurer has more

than once interfered in military matters and has acted in a way which undermines my authority. By doing so he has weakened us. Let him confine himself to his role as an administrator – and stop trying to suborn my senior officers.

'As for my plan, it is this is: to use almost all our forces, except for a single regiment which will protect Avaris, in order to achieve three things as quickly as possible. The first is to raze the city of Memphis to the ground. The next is to break through the Egyptian front, destroy Thebes and bring you back Queen Ahhotep and her son, dead or alive. The last is to crush the Hittites, by obliterating the whole of Anatolia if necessary. My inability to achieve complete success was due solely to the dispersal of our men to several fronts, which was Khamudi's doing. We must therefore put an end to the dissension between him and myself, and destroy our enemies. There is only one way to do so: at each stage, we must use our full military power. That is how the Hyksos conquered their empire, and that is how you will enlarge it.' Jannas was well aware of the risk he was taking but, as commander-in-chief of the army, he could not bear not to succeed.

'Have you finished?' asked Apophis.

'I have nothing to add, my lord, except that my only concern is for the greatness of the Hyksos Empire.'

28

The captains of the Minoan war-boats were preparing to ram the enemy ship and to order their archers to fire, but Ahhotep's appearance halted them where they stood. With her gold diadem and her long red gown, she truly possessed the bearing of a queen. Could this possibly be that Egyptian woman who the storytellers said had driven back the Hyksos? None of the sailors in her crew looked warlike . . .

Then one of the captains recognized the two Minoans, who were waving frantically. Immediately the attack was halted, and the Egyptian ship was guided into port.

The two Minoans were the first to step on to their native soil. They explained to an officer that they were royal envoys returning from a secret and dangerous mission, and that Queen Ahhotep requested an audience with King Minos.

Following a stormy discussion, the situation calmed down. None of the crew was permitted to disembark, and the boat would remain tied up and under permanent guard in the port, where cargo-vessels were unloading jars of oil.

The queen was invited to climb into a large, comfortable chariot drawn by oxen.

'One moment,' she said. She told her ship's captain not to attempt anything, but to await her return calmly. Then she turned to the two Minoan envoys and said, 'I ask you to guarantee the safety of my sailors, and to give me your assurance that they will be well treated and properly fed during my absence. If you do not, I shall leave Minoa this instant.'

While the Minoans discussed what she had said, Ahhotep examined the chariot's massive wheels with great interest. Egypt had made wheels as long ago as the time of Djer, notably to move military towers designed to attack Libyan strongholds across hard terrain. But wheels were useless in soft sand and, in any case, for transporting materials, men or animals, the Nile had no equal. The Hyksos invasion, however, proved that the Egyptians had been wrong to forget the wheel. The queen began to form a plan to be put into action on her return – assuming, of course, that King Minos did not take her prisoner.

The Minoans ended their discussion, and helped Ahhotep mount into the chariot.

As they travelled along, Ahhotep had the chance to see Minoa for the first time. Forests of pine and oak crowned a succession of hills. The road leading to the capital, Knossos, was lined with guard-posts and small inns, and she could see the hills that rose above the valley of Kairatos, where cypress trees grew. In the distance was Mount Iuktas. How different this land was from her own, and how much she already missed Egypt!

The city of Knossos was open: there were no fortifications, no ramparts, but instead busy, narrow streets filled with workshops and shops. Many people were curious and came out of their homes to marvel at the beautiful stranger, who smiled at them and gave signs of friendship. Very quickly, the atmosphere relaxed; women and children wanted to touch the queen, who, to them, had come from another world, and whose legend held that she was the bearer of good fortune.

Overwhelmed, the guards tried to push the onlookers back, but Ahhotep stepped down from the chariot and went to greet them. Immediately calm returned, soon to be replaced by the cheers of a happy crowd who had taken this beautiful, warm-hearted woman to their own hearts.

On foot, crowned with lilies and accompanied by laughing children, the Queen of Freedom made her entrance into the royal palace of Knossos, whose guards dared not bar her way.

The imposing palace was sheltered behind thick walls. From the river, stepped terraces could be seen, hiding a vast courtyard a hundred and twenty cubits long and sixty wide. Each side of this rectangle faced one of the cardinal points. Oblong windows with crosspieces, painted red, opened on to the courtyard, which was a most agreeable place to be when the weather was at its hottest.

An officer led the queen along a corridor whose walls were decorated with axes and bulls' heads. The throne room was less austere. In remarkably delicate and lifelike colours, the painters had created enchanting scenes of crocus-gatherers, young girls with delectable bodies, women carrying precious vases, cats, hoopoes, partridges, dolphins and flying-fish. Spirals and palm-leaves decorated the ceilings.

Every single noble of the Knossos court was present, and their eyes all turned towards Ahhotep.

Clean-shaven, and dressed in short, multicoloured, wrap-around kilts, the men clearly took great care in dressing their hair: some wore it in long, wavy locks alternating with shorter, curled sections, while others had spirals which hung over their foreheads. Some wore leather boots, others long socks.

The women vied with each other in elegance and were evidently eager to seek out the latest fashion. There were long skirts, short skirts and ones with many-coloured panels, transparent bodices, gold jewellery, and agate and cornelian necklaces, showing the Minoan women's taste for luxury.

But Ahhotep outshone them all, although she had opted for simplicity, with her traditional gold diadem and an immaculately white linen dress. Subtle face-paint emphasized her perfect features.

She turned her gaze upon the high-backed gypsum throne, flanked by two griffins. It was occupied by a bearded old man with great presence. In his right hand he held a sceptre, in his left a two-headed axe, the symbol of the thunderbolt he used against his enemies.

Ahhotep bowed. 'Majesty, Pharaoh Ahmose offers you his good wishes for the health of yourself and of Minoa.'

King Minos contemplated her. So she really did exist, and she was here in his palace, alone and without an army, utterly at his mercy. He could have her arrested and sent to the emperor, or execute her himself and send her head to Apophis.

His decision astounded the court. 'Come and sit at my right hand, Queen of Egypt.'

Since the death of his wife, Minos had lost all interest in women. To pay such homage to a foreign queen was certainly not in accordance with custom, and specialists in court ritual were shocked. But when Ahhotep took her place on a gilded wooden throne decorated with geometrical figures, they forgot their criticisms.

'Is this palace worthy of comparison with the one at Thebes?' asked the king.

'It is much larger, better built and more beautifully decorated.'

'And yet the Egyptians are said to be unrivalled builders,' said Minos in surprise.

'Our ancestors were, but compared to them we are mere dwarves. But we are waging a war, and the only thing that matters is the liberation of my country. If destiny favours us, everything will have to be rebuilt and we shall then follow the example of our predecessors. Majesty, I pray that the Great Island may be spared the misfortune that has stricken Egypt.'

For that simple but provocative declaration alone, King Minos, as a vassal of the Hyksos emperor, ought to have thrown the woman in prison.

'What do you think of my court?' he asked.

'It is as beautiful is it is refined. And I see no Hyksos here.'

Most of the Minoan nobles were of the opinion that Ahhotep had far overstepped the mark, but the king seem unconcerned.

'I trust your journey was not too wearisome?'

'Fortunately, the sea was calm.'

'My people love music, dancing and games. So, without further delay, I invite you to a celebratory meal in your honour.'

The king rose, and Ahhotep followed suit. Side by side, the two rulers left the throne room and went out into the garden, where tables had been set out, decked with flowers and groaning with food.

29

At the end of the banquet the court headed for the square. Acrobats and dancers performed, before giving way to the most exciting spectacle of all: the trial of the bull. The one that entered the arena was enormous, fully the match of Egyptian wild bulls, which experienced hunters considered the most fearsome animals in all creation.

For the agile, swift-footed performers, the 'trial' consisted of angering the beast so that it charged headlong at them. At the last moment, they seized its horns and, in a perilous leap which made the audience shiver, sprang over its back and landed behind it. The young men were so skilled that not a single mishap marred the game.

'Majesty,' asked Ahhotep, 'what will happen to the bull?'

'We shall set it free. To kill such a noble animal, the embodiment of royal power, would be barbarous.'

'What does that strange design represent, there on the wall of the arena?'

'The labyrinth, a symbol linked to the bull. It was built near Knossos and housed a spirit with terrifying power, the Minotaur. Guided by a thread Ariadne gave him, the hero Theseus entered the labyrinth, killed the monster and escaped with his life.'

'Majesty, do you think Ariadne's thread might link our two countries together?'

Minos rubbed his beard. 'If I understand you correctly, you have tired of the entertainment and would like to discuss more important matters.'

'Egypt is at war, my lord. However impressive your welcome, I cannot tarry here long.'

The king paused; the air was heavy with menace. 'As you wish. Let us leave the court to enjoy themselves and withdraw to my private quarters.'

The old man walked with difficulty, but it was clear that his vital energy was undimmed. Ahhotep was glad to be negotiating with a true king.

He showed the queen into an office decorated with rural scenes. On shelves lay wooden tablets covered with writing.

'How difficult it is to govern a country,' he grumbled. 'One moment's inattention and chaos beckons.'

'But is it not even more exhausting to have to account for everything you to do a tyrant like Apophis?'

The king poured red wine into two silver cups, handed one to Ahhotep and sat down in a sturdy armchair, while the queen sat on a bench covered with multicoloured fabric.

'How is my son, Linas?'

'When I left Thebes, he was extremely well and seemed to like our modest capital very much. I must stress that it was he who decided to stay in Egypt until my return.'

'Those were my orders. If I had not given you a guarantee of that magnitude, would you have come to Minoa?'

'In fact, he is not your son, is he?'

The king avoided her eyes. 'No, he is not.'

'Now may I know the reasons for your invitation?'

'I, a faithful vassal of the Hyksos, receiving their greatest enemy on my island . . . Why did you not refuse when you were invited into such a clumsy trap?'

'Because it is not a trap. You know that the Hyksos want to destroy you, and you cannot fight them alone. That is why you are planning an alliance with Egypt.'

Minos gazed at Ahhotep for a long time. 'What supernatural force enables you to confront the emperor?'

'The desire for freedom.'

'And you will never give up?'

'My husband and my elder son died in battle, and my younger son is now Pharaoh, firmly determined to carry on the fight, even if we are outnumbered ten against one. Thanks to our carpenters' hard work, our war-fleet now rivals that of the Hyksos.'

'But on land their chariots will crush you.'

'We have not yet found a way to defeat them, that is true, but I am convinced that one exists.'

The king sat back in his chair. 'Windswept, the emperor's sister, came to the Great Island to tell me that her lover, a Minoan painter I thought highly of, had been murdered on Apophis's orders. As an act of vengeance, she told me two vital secrets. First, she confirmed your existence and your military successes.'

'My son Kamose led an attack against Avaris, and our men repelled a counter-attack led by Commander Jannas himself. At the moment, we control Upper Egypt, a fact which the emperor is trying desperately to keep hidden.'

'By using our trading-fleet, I can spread the truth across many lands.'

'Then Apophis's vassals will know that he is not invincible, and the rebellion will grow.'

'Do not hope for too much, my lady: not everyone has your courage. Nevertheless, it is possible that such news would shake the empire to its foundations.'

'Have you made up your mind to act?'

'First, I must tell you the other secret Windswept shared with me. There is bitter rivalry between the two men charged with carrying out Apophis's wishes: Commander Jannas and High Treasurer Khamudi. They hate each other, and, although for the moment their enmity is concealed, eventually it will explode into the light of day, weakening the Hyksos regime in the process. Apophis is growing old, and the war of succession is being prepared. Who will win it?'

'That matters little,' said the queen. 'The important thing is to take full advantage of this opportunity. Whichever of them emerges the victor will be no less a tyrant than Apophis at his worst, so we must act before he takes power.'

'Minoa is a very long way from Egypt, and I must think first and foremost of my own country.'

'If you will not fight at my side, may I at least be assured that you will not fight for the Hyksos?'

'Such a promise cannot be given without mature reflection, for the consequences might be fearsome.'

'I believe you have only one course of action, my lord: to recognize my sovereignty over the Mycenean islands, most notably over yours. As Queen of the Distant Shores, I shall offer you protection, and Apophis's anger will be unleashed against me and me alone.'

Minos gave a half-smile. 'Are you sure you will not be more demanding than the emperor?'

'All I ask is your word that you will not betray me. You will remain King of Minoa, your country will remain independent, and we shall exchange envoys and tribute-gifts.'

'There is another course of action. I am a widower, and my country has no queen. You would be safe here, and my people would readily accept you.'

'My lord, I am faithful to one man, Pharaoh Seqen. As the Wife of God, I try constantly to strengthen the King of Egypt's power and to draw Amon's goodwill to him. My place is at the heart of my army – to take refuge with you would be cowardice of the most disgraceful kind. I therefore ask you again to recognize my sovereignty, to spread the truth by means of your trading-fleet, to give the Hyksos no further assistance, and to prepare the Great Island to withstand an attack by Jannas's war-fleet.'

146

'You ask a very great deal of me, Queen Ahhotep!'

'But I have told you what you wanted to know, have I not?'

Minos did not reply.

Eventually the queen broke the silence. 'What happened to Windswept?' she asked.

'She drowned – a most unfortunate accident. But now, my lady, it is time to go and rest.'

'When shall I have your answer?'

'When the right moment comes.'

The apartments set aside for the Queen of Egypt were luxurious, and included a bathing-room and a lavatory whose wooden seat was right above a water-channel, part of the drainage system underneath the palace. Rainwater flowed down terraces through mortared pipes, and all the various branches ended up at one large collecting pool.

Her bedchamber was provided with beautifully carved and painted wooden furniture. On a porphyry table stood cups decorated with spirals, and conical and lion-headed vases containing water, wine and beer. As for the bed itself, it was most comfortable.

As she lay down, Ahhotep wondered if she would ever emerge from this gilded prison.

30

'I am sorry, my lord,' said the guard. 'The emperor is ill and will not receive anyone today.'

'Not even me?' demanded Khamudi in astonishment.

'My orders are strict, High Treasurer: no one.'

It was the first time Khamudi had ever been refused admittance to see Apophis. True, Jannas had also been turned away, but the High Treasurer's privileged position had just been wiped out.

Anxiously, Khamudi questioned those faithful to him to find out how long the conversation between Jannas and the emperor had lasted. More than an hour! Usually, all that happened was that the emperor issued brief orders. This time there must have been long, important discussions.

Jannas himself, Khamudi learnt, was at the main barracks in Avaris, surrounded by his most senior officers. In other words, he was holding a meeting of his general staff – and the High Treasurer had not been invited to attend.

On the verge of nervous exhaustion, Khamudi went home.

'Back already?' simpered Yima. 'You've come because of me, of course! Come, my dear one, I shall—'

'We are in danger.'

Yima's simper vanished. 'Why? What has happened?'

'I am convinced that Jannas has asked the emperor to grant him full powers.'

'But surely Apophis will have refused?'

'I'm afraid he may not have. He refused to receive me, and Jannas is at this moment telling his generals about his plans.'

'Can't you find out what they are?'

'Yes, but by then it will be too late. Anyway, I think I know what he wants: total war, in Egypt as well as in Anatolia, using all our forces. If he gets his way, either my status and authority will be reduced to almost nothing, or else I shall be executed for trying to thwart Jannas's plans. Soon his henchmen will come to arrest us.'

'We must escape at once!'

'It would be useless to try. Jannas will have stationed men on all the routes out of Avaris. And where would we go?'

'You must force your way in to see the emperor!'

'That's impossible.'

'But then . . . what are we going to do?'

'Fight with every weapon we have. Have you convinced Tany that Jannas, the man who failed to defend Avaris, is also responsible for her illness?'

'Yes, oh yes!'

'Go and see her and explain that he has an insane plan to wage war on all fronts at the same time, and that he will leave only the imperial guard in the capital. If the Egyptians attack again, they will have no difficulty in taking the citadel, and Tany will be captured and tortured.'

Without bothering to paint her face or change her dress, Yima ran to the empress's apartments.

Jannas was pleased with the way things had gone. The generals had unreservedly approved of his plans. Neither Anatolian nor Egyptian rebels could continue to defy the Hyksos Empire. They must be attacked and mercilessly destroyed, to show that the emperor's army had lost none of its efficiency. Even the officers bought by Khamudi had rallied to the commander's cause. As for Khamudi himself, he would be arrested within the next few days, then sent to one of the two death-camps he was so proud of.

However, even while contemplating the inevitable sequence of events, Jannas was not fully satisfied. Although in practice he would have sole and absolute command of the Hyksos forces, he had not obtained Apophis's explicit agreement. To a soldier who had always obeyed the emperor's orders, this vagueness was annoying. He still hoped to acquire full powers unequivocally, and decided that he would lay siege to Apophis's apartments until he obtained the necessary official declaration. The emperor knew that he could not refuse.

If the old man refused to face reality and by doing so condemned the Hyksos Empire to death, Jannas owed it to himself to save it. If Apophis persisted, the commander would have to get rid of him.

His assistant interrupted his troubled thoughts. 'Sir, there's a terrible scandal. People are saying you have had your servants beheaded so as to present their corpses to the Temple of Set before setting off on campaign.'

'That is nonsense!'

'An accusation of murder has been lodged against you by High Treasurer Khamudi.'

'We shall go to my house at once and prove the absolute falsity of these allegations.'

When Jannas, accompanied by his bodyguards, arrived at his house, there was no sign of the sentry who should have been guarding the gate. Fully alert, they went into the grounds.

'Split up and surround the house,' Jannas ordered his men; his assistant remained at his side.

The front door was wide open. The admiral called his steward. No reply. Cautiously, he went inside.

The steward lay in the entrance hall, his throat slit. The pool of blood was still warm and wet.

'The murderers must have only just left,' said his assistant.

Although he had both ordered and participated in many massacres, Jannas seemed lost. He had never dreamt that anyone could confront him in his own home and attack his household.

With wary steps, he crossed the hall and entered the reception chamber. On a chair, in a grotesque posture, sat the body of his chambermaid. At her feet lay her severed head. Not far from her were the bodies of the cook and the gardener, their bloody heads laid on their bellies. His assistant vomited.

Stunned, Jannas slowly walked into his office. His secretary had been hacked to death with an axe, and his head lay on a shelf.

'I shall continue to explore this charnel-house,' Jannas told his assistant. 'You must go and see if my men have spotted anyone. If not, tell them to join me here.'

In the commander's bedchamber were the last three serving-women, also decapitated. The bed, chairs and walls were covered in blood. Not a single member of his household had been spared.

Jannas snatched up a jar of fresh water and poured it over his face. Then he left the house and called for his assistant. To his surprise there was no answer.

He went round the corner of the house and almost tripped over the body of one of his guards, an arrow sticking out of the back of his neck. Ten paces away lay his assistant, who had been killed in the same manner. A little further off lay other guards.

Petrified for a moment, Jannas realized that he must flee.

Two enormous hands closed about his throat. He jabbed his elbow into his attacker's stomach to try get free, but the lady Aberia took the blow without batting an eyelid.

'No one is stronger than the emperor,' she told him as she strangled him savagely. 'You dared to defy him, Jannas, and that insolence merits death.'

The commander fought with every last bit of his strength, still clutching at his killer. As he died, his larynx crushed, with his last breath he cursed Apophis.

Khamudi had been watching from a safe distance, surrounded by the Cypriot pirates who had cut down Jannas's staff and guards. Now he came nearer.

'It is done, High Treasurer,' said Aberia.

'Disembowel him with a sickle. Officially, his gardener murdered him in order to steal from him.'

31

Ahhotep had just dozed off when her bed shook so violently that she almost fell out of it. The furniture creaked, and a vase fell off a shelf and broke. Calm returned for a few moments, then another tremor, even stronger than the first, made the queen get up. The ceiling of her bedchamber had cracked. Up above, she could hear shouting.

Ahhotep tried to leave the room, but the door was locked from the outside.

'Open this door immediately,' she ordered.

An embarrassed voice replied, 'Majesty, my orders—'

'Open it or I shall break it down.'

The man who let her out was no ordinary guard. He was Minos's private secretary, and – like the king – spoke passable Egyptian.

'Am I a prisoner, then?' asked Ahhotep.

'No, not at all, but your safety—'

'Do not trifle with me: I want the truth.'

The secretary gave in. 'King Minos has gone to the sacred mountain, Majesty, to hear the oracle of the bull in the cave of mysteries. Ordinarily, he goes there only every nine years. Because of the exceptional nature of the question he must ask, he has broken with tradition, which may be very dangerous. Sometimes the reigning king does not emerge from the cave, and has to be replaced. At the court, many believe that King Minos has made a double mistake: inviting you to Knossos, and submitting to this ordeal.'

'Most of the court favour the Hyksos, do they not?'

'Let us say they fear the emperor's anger, Majesty – and with good reason. Your presence has persuaded more than one to change his mind, but there are still some who refuse to do so and who might prove dangerous. In his absence, the king asked me to watch over you, and I believe the best way to do that is to lock you in your room, which will be guarded day and night.'

'How long will it be before King Minos returns to Knossos?'

'His consultation with the oracle will take nine days.'

'And . . . what if he does not return?'

The secretary looked perturbed. 'That would be a tragedy for Minoa. I fear there would be a fierce struggle for the throne and the victor would be a supporter of the Hyksos.'

'Then do not lock me up any longer. I must be free to move about.'

'As you wish, Majesty. But I beg you not to leave this wing of the palace, where every guard can be trusted.'

'I understand.'

'Your food and drinks are tasted by my cook, so you can eat and drink absolutely safely. And may I say, Majesty, that I hope fervently for the king's return and for your plans to come to fruition.'

'Are these earth tremors common?'

'They have happened more and more often in the last two years. Some people claim they express the anger of a volcano whose peace was broken by the Hyksos when they murdered some Cypriot pirates on its slopes. The tremors are impressive but do not cause serious damage. The palace at Knossos is so strongly built that you have nothing to fear.'

'I should like to speak with you each day about how the situation is developing.'

'It shall be as you wish, Majesty.'

Aboard the Egyptian ship, at anchor in the little Minoan port where jars of oil were stored, the mood was not optimistic. There was no contact between them and the natives. Soldiers brought them two meals per day and jars of water. No wine or beer.

They were forbidden to disembark, and the captain's only attempt had ended at the bottom of the gangplank. Threatened by spears, he had had to retrace his steps.

'We'll never come to an understanding with these people,' said the helmsman.

'In the past, before the Hyksos invasion, we used to trade with them,' the captain reminded him.

'That may be so, but they're our enemies now.'

'Perhaps Queen Ahhotep will succeed in making them our allies. It wouldn't be her first miracle.'

'You're dreaming, Captain. Minoa is a vassal of the emperor and will remain so. Otherwise Jannas will turn it into a desert.'

'Let me dream anyway.'

'It would be better to face reality. We have been stuck here for ten days and have had no news of the queen. Wake up, Captain.'

'What do you mean?'

'Ahhotep must be either dead or a prisoner. Soon the Minoans will come aboard and kill us. We must get away as soon as possible.'

'What about the mooring-ropes?'

'We have two good divers, who can cut them during the night. At dawn we can weigh anchor and row out of port.'

'The archers will fire on us,' objected the captain.

'They won't be able to see clearly in the dawn light. And we shall fire back.'

'Minoan ships are bound to give chase.'

'I am not so sure about that. They know we're inexperienced at sea and will expect us to be wrecked – besides, we're faster than they are. With the maps and a little luck, we'll get back to Egypt.'

'I cannot abandon Queen Ahhotep.'

'Her fate is sealed, Captain. At least save your crew.'

It was a bitter thought, but he could not help acknowledging its truth. 'Very well, helmsman. Warn the men. We leave at dawn.'

Ten days had passed, and still King Minos had not returned from the cave of the oracle. He must be dead, thought Ahhotep, which meant a war of succession was about to start. She would be merely a pawn in that vicious fight. Either the new ruler would execute her and dispose of her body, or he would hand her over to Apophis. According to what Minos's secretary had told her, all the claimants believed she was a danger which must be got rid of.

If she did not manage to leave the palace in the next few hours, Ahhotep would never see her country again. But the wing in which she was staying was now guarded by new soldiers, who would never let her pass.

How could she get away? All she could think of was to disguise herself as a maidservant and try to escape with other members of the household. Then she would have to get out of Knossos and make her way to the port – but would her ship still be there? Ahhotep refused to think of the obstacles that would lie in her way. As soon as the maidservant entered the room to change the bedlinen, she would knock her unconscious.

There was a soft knock on the door, and a whisper: 'It is King Minos's secretary, Majesty. Open the door quickly.'

Was he accompanied by a host of soldiers? This time there was no way out.

Ahhotep opened the door. The secretary was alone.

'There can no longer be any doubt: the king has died in the cave of mysteries,' he said. 'The priests are demanding a delay before announcing the succession. This is your only chance of escape, Majesty. Get into my chariot; I will take you to the port.'

'Why should you take such a risk?'

'Because I believe in an alliance between Egypt and Minoa. For my country, as well as yours, there is no other way of escaping from Hyksos tyranny. That is the position I shall defend at court and before the new ruler – even though I have no hope of being listened to.'

Stealthily, they made their way out of the palace and round to the stables. The chariot was waiting, ready, and they set off at once along the road to the port. At every moment, the queen expected to be stopped, but Minos's secretary was known and recognized, and they passed all the guard-posts unhindered.

The Egyptian ship was still at the quayside, guarded by some twenty footsoldiers, who refused to let them pass.

'You were ordered not to let anyone disembark,' said the secretary to an officer. 'Queen Ahhotep is going aboard, not disembarking.'

The officer considered for a moment, then stepped aside.

Though his nerves, like the rest of the crew's, were stretched to breaking-point, the captain dared not show his joy. 'We were sure we would never see you again, Majesty, and we were ready to leave.'

'You would have been right so to do. Weigh anchor, cut the mooring-ropes and hoist the sails. If the Minoan archers fire at us, we shall fire back.'

While the Egyptians ran to carry out these orders, the king's secretary debated hotly with the officer, trying to stop him firing. Eventually, he managed to convince him that King Minos wished Queen Ahhotep to leave, because her stay in Minoa must remain a state secret.

Uncertain about these arguments, which he had no time to refer to a superior, the officer watched the Egyptian ship move out of the harbour. With the aid of a strong following wind, it sailed quickly away from the Minoan coast.

32

Under the command of Pharaoh Ahmose, the Egyptian army assembled at the Port of Kamose had taken on a proud appearance. Everyone respected the king's authority, yet he remained close to his men. Besides ordering frequent exercises and manoeuvres, he made sure that supplies were delivered regularly and orders followed to the letter. Strict cleanliness was observed in the camp, and the meals were excellent.

Although conditions were as good as possible, no one could forget that a Hyksos attack would come sooner or later, so there was a permanent state of alert. Day and night, many lookouts were on duty, with instructions to alert the pharaoh at the first sign of danger.

Through Rascal and the other carrier-pigeons, Ahmose kept in contact with Moustache and the Afghan, who were in Memphis, helping the resistance there. The Hyksos were still besieging the city, but had made no attempt to take the part that was not under their control.

Ahmose thought often of Nefertari, who had remained in Thebes to carry out the duties formerly performed by Teti the Small. With the aid of Heray and Qaris, the Great Royal Wife must ensure the prosperity of the provinces of Upper Egypt, which provided the soldiers' food. Each morning, she went to the temple at Karnak, where she celebrated the rising of

Amon and implored his protection. The people already loved their new queen, who was both unpretentious and imbued with a sense of responsibility.

Emheb was shown in and bowed to the pharaoh. 'Nothing to report, Majesty,' he said.

'Tell me the truth. Is there anything we can do to improve our warning-system?'

Emheb had regained all his old strength and vigour. 'I cannot see how, Majesty,' he said confidently. 'Every system is fallible, of course, but I have doubled the number of guards at each post. Whether the enemy approaches by river, through the countryside or from the desert, he will be spotted.'

'How is the Minoan behaving?'

'He accepts that he is confined to quarters.'

Ahmose had thought it best to bring Linas to the Port of Kamose, while ensuring that he knew as little possible about the Egyptian army. No doubt he missed Thebes, but he was a guest of a very special kind, and must not be indulged.

'Why do you think Jannas isn't trying to destroy us?' asked Ahmose.

'Because his hands are tied, Majesty. Either the emperor has sent him to spread terror through some far-off country, or else he is in charge of the Delta's security and is preparing an offensive which will sweep away everything in its path. He must have learnt many lessons from his failure last time.'

'But suppose internal disputes are weakening the Hyksos? The emperor is old, and his throne may soon become vacant.'

'I suspect that evil old man will outlive us all!'

Ahmose recognized the characteristic flapping of Rascal's wings as he returned from the oasis at Sekhet-imit, near the border with Libya. The bird landed with his usual neatness; there was a bright gleam in his eyes.

When he read the message, the king realized why Rascal was happy. 'My mother has returned safely,' he told Emheb. 'She and her crew crossed the marshy part of the Delta, followed the desert tracks, and have just reached the oasis.'

'The road is under our control,' said the governor, smiling broadly, 'but even so I shall send some men to meet the queen.'

Laughter and Way-Finder gave the queen a noisy welcome. As soon as they permitted the pharaoh to approach her, Ahhotep and her son embraced.

'Are you well, Mother?'

'Very well. The voyage enabled me to rest after our hurried departure from Minoa.'

'So it was a trap!'

'Not exactly. Minos knows the Hyksos will one day invade his country, but he is afraid of their reaction if he allies himself with Egypt. So I suggested that he should place himself under the protection of the Queen of the Distant Shores.'

'And did he accept?'

'He went up to the cave of mysteries, where the kings of Minoa meditate when they have need of new energy, but he did not return and his potential successors have begun to tear each other apart. Without the help of Minos's secretary, who believes in an alliance between our countries, I would have been held prisoner.'

'Your return is another miracle,' said Ahmose earnestly.

'Good luck has not yet deserted me.'

'So we cannot depend upon Minoa.'

'The Great Island is about to undergo violent upheavals, and who knows what the outcome will be? If the next king does not accuse Minos's secretary of treason, perhaps he will listen to him. To be honest, there is not much hope. Yet my journey may not have been in vain, because the king told me that Jannas and Khamudi, the two most important Hyksos after the emperor, are bitter enemies. They are already virtually at war with each other, each one no doubt hoping to succeed Apophis.'

'So that's why Jannas hasn't attacked us!' Ahmose thought for a moment. 'This knowledge gives us an advantage. Now would be a good time to retake Memphis and gain a foothold in the Delta.'

'We must indeed do both things, but first we must solve the problem of the Hyksos chariots.'

'You have a new plan, haven't you?'

'Before we discuss it, summon the Minoan.'

Linas had a hearty appetite for food and drink, and during his enforced inactivity he had put on weight.

'Majesty, how happy I am to see you again!' he exclaimed as he greeted Ahhotep. 'I dare to think that you will give me permission to return to Minoa.'

'Who are you?'

'But . . . Majesty, you know who I am,' Linas stammered 'I am the son of King Minos, his youngest son.'

'He told me himself that he had lied to me, so that I would not be afraid to leave Egypt. A king would not have sacrificed his son, would he? I did not believe your story, Linas, but I went to Minoa anyway.'

He knelt down. 'I was obeying King Minos, Majesty, but even so I am not just anybody. I am considered one of Minoa's finest ship's captains, and in case of war my ship will be in the forefront of the fighting.'

'You may return safely to your home,' said the queen.

'I thank you, but . . . how?'

'Go to a small port under Hyksos control and join the crew of one of their trading-ships leaving for Minoa. If your new king ever wishes to send me a message, tell him to give it to you. We shall be happy to receive you here again.'

Why had the Hyksos spy not stopped Ahhotep going to Minoa? For two reasons. First, because he had hoped that she would not reach the Great Island, in view of how dangerous the journey was. Second, because he was certain that King Minos would not dare form an alliance with the Egyptians. What he did not know, of course, was that Windswept had turned against Apophis and had betrayed state secrets.

During the queen's absence, there had been no attempts to assassinate Ahmose, and nothing untoward had happened in Thebes. But neither Ahhotep nor the pharaoh could believe the spy had given up.

'Have any senior officers died recently?' asked the queen.

'Yes, an old general of artificers, but he was not the sort of man to be one of Apophis's lickspittles.'

'Surely that is precisely the sort of man Apophis would make use of.'

'But if he really was the lickspittle, Mother, now that he's dead the emperor no longer has a spy here.'

'That is a very fragile theory, Ahmose, and we cannot lay too much weight on it. All the same, it would be a good idea for you to return to Thebes and make detailed inquiries about the general. It will also give you an opportunity to see Nefertari again.'

Ahmose smiled. 'You can still read my thoughts, Mother. As for me, I'm burning to know your plan for fighting against the Hyksos chariots.'

'It involves first of all changing our own methods, and then using the enemy's.'

33

Rascal brought Ahhotep's message to the Afghan and Moustache, who were at the rebels' headquarters in Memphis, a half-ruined and apparently abandoned farm. As it had long ceased to interest the Hyksos, this was where they stored food and weapons from the south before sending them into the besieged city.

The Egyptians knew all the enemy's habits and timetables, and made best use of their weak spots. The commander of the chariot corps had stopped attacking, and confined himself to shows of strength, in the form of large-scale manoeuvres designed to impress the rebels, who were condemned to rot where they stood.

Moustache decoded the message. 'We can't do that! It's impossible – we'd be flayed alive.'

'Is the queen ordering us to attack Avaris?'

'You're not far from the truth! No, not that, but—'

'Then what are her orders?' demanded the Afghan.

'We are to capture a Hyksos chariot and several horses.'

The Afghan stared at him. 'We can't do that,' he murmured.

In silence, the two men downed a whole jar of the local red wine to give themselves courage.

'I suppose,' said the Afghan eventually, 'the queen leaves us no choice in the matter?'

'You know what she's like,' agreed Moustache.

'It's a nice idea, but carrying it out will be rather tricky, particularly as we don't know how to handle horses or chariots – we can't just steal one by driving it away.'

'That's true. So some of the raiding-party will take charge of the horses, which are apparently rather like enormous donkeys, while the others seize the chariot, which will have to be pulled as far as the river. And then we'll have to load the whole lot on board a sailing-boat.'

'I like your summary – it has the advantage of missing out all the critical phases of the operation. Do you think we can politely ask a Hyksos officer to let us examine his chariot? I think your first reaction was the right one: we'll be flayed alive.'

'Orders are orders. And surely we aren't going to disappoint the Queen of Freedom?'

'No, Moustache, you're right about that.'

The two men gathered together their best men to form a raiding-party thirty strong; any larger and they might be spotted. There was no point asking the men if they were volunteering for an impossible mission, because they had done that already. Nevertheless, the plan was heard wihout enthusiasm. Each man realized he had very little chance of surviving this mad venture.

'I suggest three simultaneous operations,' said the Afghan. 'One: the people of Memphis create a diversion by attacking the Hyksos camp closest to the white wall. Two: twenty-five of us remove as many horses as possible from the stable. Three: the other five steal a chariot.'

A hundred questions were fired off, emphasizing the difficulties of the raid. And the local wine flowed in abundance.

Following in the steps of Teti the Small, to whom she paid homage every day, Nefertari was making Memphis more and more beautiful. She had won everyone's heart, even those of the old priests and the most sour-tempered craftsmen. Qaris had become her devoted colleague, and Heray made it a point of honour to present her with proofs of perfect management.

The young queen did not remain shut away in the palace. She travelled all over the countryside, visited houses in the capital, treated rich and poor with equal consideration, and gave help to the sick and the destitute. Her days were long, and sometimes exhausting, but she did not dream of complaining. How could she, when Ahhotep had for so many years risked her very life in the struggle to free Egypt?

Only Ahmose's absence really weighed upon her. Without his peaceful strength, she felt vulnerable. But now, at long last, he was coming back.

Long before he arrived, Nefertari was at the landing-stage, where the people were already celebrating the pharaoh's return. Neither she nor he heard the cheers. In their eyes there was such profound, intense joy that they were alone amid the merrymaking crowds.

They spent such joyful, passionate nights of love together that Nefertari almost managed to make him forget the war. But Ahmose was the pharaoh, and when morning came he owed it to his people to go about his official duties. To worship Amon at Karnak was the first of these, in order to maintain the link between heaven and earth. Next came a meeting with his counsellors, which Nefertari attended and at which her recommendations carried weight. With her detailed knowledge of the strengths and weaknesses of the region, the Great Royal Wife influenced people towards the right decisions.

'How long are you planning to remain in Thebes?' she asked Ahmose, as they enjoyed the gentle evening warmth on the palace terrace one evening.

'Only for as long as it takes me to investigate the death of an old general and find out if he was the Hyksos spy we have been searching for.'

'The Hyksos spy? But . . .'

'My mother believes he was responsible for the deaths of my father and brother.'

'Then that monster murdered two pharaohs – and you might have been his next victim!'

'Be very careful, Nefertari, and take note of any suspicious behaviour.'

Next morning, the king received Heray in his office. While continuing to oversee the harvests and the stocking of the granaries, a weapon of war as essential as the sword, Heray had extended his domain to include the entire Theban economy. He was a man with lively eyes and an easy manner, who got along with everyone. No one would ever forget the time when he had rooted out the Hyksos supporters in Thebes. Still spritely despite his sizeable frame, he had maintained his network of informers, so that nothing escaped him and the capital's safety was assured.

'Heray, have you studied the general's case?'

'In detail, Majesty. He was a Theban who rose through the ranks, mainly because of his skill at training raw recruits. He spent most of his life at the base in the desert, and always displayed fervent support for the struggle against the Hyksos. On his deathbed, he told those close to him to remain loyal to the Queen of Freedom.'

'And you found nothing lurking behind that fine façade?'

'Nothing at all, Majesty. He was a soldier who lived at the barracks and cared for nothing but his soldiers.'

'Did he ever travel to the North?'

'No, never.'

'And no one in his entourage has voiced suspicions about his conduct?'

'No one, Majesty.

'So he was an honest, respectable officer who served his country well.'

'Exactly.'

'Have your informants suggested any likely suspects among the Theban dignitaries?'

'No, Majesty.'

Ahmed sighed. 'Do not let your guard down, Heray.'

'If one single Hyksos supporter still exists in our good city, I shall find him.'

In accordance with Queen Ahhotep's wishes, the pharaoh went to the military base to prepare a vast enclosed training-area and stables. These were destined to house the Hyksos horses which, if destiny favoured the raiding-party, would soon arrive in Thebes.

34

At last the new moon rose, fortunately accompanied by a few clouds.

'Time to go,' decided the Afghan.

'Will you deal with the horses or the chariot?' asked Moustache.

'The horses are more dangerous.'

'Then I'll deal with them.'

'Why you?'

'Because that's how it is.'

'We'll draw lots.'

'There isn't time. I know about donkeys, and the horses are a bit longer and taller, that's all. Just don't fail. Without the chariot, my efforts won't be much use.'

'The chariot without the horses won't be much use, either, remember.'

'It's strange, isn't it? When I joined the rebels I was sure I wouldn't live long. Yet tonight here we are, about to deal the Hyksos invader a terrific blow.'

'You can dream all you like later. Let's go.'

During some highly risky scouting trips, the two men had found a place, away from the main encampment, where some chariots were being repaired. Quite a number of horses were stabled there, too, perhaps because they were sick or tired.

The place had the notable advantage of being less well guarded than the other stables.

Now, at about midnight, there were only ten sentries watching the animals and three guarding the shelter where the chariots were awaiting repair. Lying flat on their bellies in the sharp-bladed grass, the Egyptians watched.

'If a sentry gives the alarm,' whispered the Afghan, 'we're done for. We must kill them all at exactly the same time, and without making a sound.'

'I'm worried that their four-legged friends may sound the alarm, too,' said Moustache. 'Before taking them away, we'd better raid the sleeping-quarters and kill all the other Hyksos.'

They both knew that the slightest slip in carrying out their plan would mean death. But there was no time for debate and, daggers in hand, all the men moved towards their designated targets.

One sentry had just time to let out a cry, though it was stifled almost instantly. Their hearts thumping, the members of the raiding-party froze. Endless seconds went by, but no Hyksos appeared.

The Egyptians converged on the sleeping-quarters and, at Moustache's signal, they poured in. Only the two officers who slept at the far end of the room put up any fight, and the raiding-party were swift and determined. Without a word, they proceeded to the next phase of their mission.

On the Afghan's side, there was no difficulty. He chose the only chariot that still had both its wheels, and he and his four men began dragging it towards the river.

Moustache's task turned out to be a good deal harder. The first Egyptian who approached a horse did so from behind. He was kicked square in the chest and fell flat on his back.

Moustache helped him to his feet. 'Can you walk?'

'I've broken half my ribs, but I'll be all right. But be careful with those brutes.'

'We'll put ropes round their necks and lead them.'

Most of the animals accepted this with more or less good grace, but one neighed and tried to bite, and another reared up, rushed out of the stable and galloped away.

'Let's not waste time here,' ordered Moustache, who was worried that the horses might cause more trouble.

In fact, apparently quite pleased at this unexpected exercise, the rest of them calmly let themselves be led down to the river. On the bank, the Egyptians congratulated each other: only one wounded, and their mission a complete success!

'We still have to get them on board,' the Afghan pointed out.

The gangplank was too narrow for the chariot. The emergency one had to be laid across it and the chariot pushed very slowly so that it didn't fall into the river.

'Now the horses,' ordered Moustache.

The first refused to climb the gangplank, and so did the next.

'Jab them in the backside,' suggested the wounded man, who was not feeling kindly towards them.

'Too risky,' objected Moustache.

'But we can't just leave them.'

'I have an idea.'

Moustache picked out the largest, strongest horse, a white stallion with a steady gaze, who seemed less edgy than the others.

'We're taking you to Thebes,' he told the horse, 'and you will be well treated. The only way of getting there is to board this boat. Show an example by climbing this gangplank. Do you understand?'

He stroked the animal's head and let him sniff his human scent. After a long time, the animal accepted the invitation. A mare calmly followed him, and then the others did likewise.

'You know how to speak to horses,' remarked the Afghan.

'I have so many gifts that I shan't live long enough to use them all.'

As dawn broke over Memphis, the guard was changed at the vast Hyksos camp. Another dismal night when nothing had happened, another dismal morning during which attackers and besieged alike would remain fixed in their positions. Perhaps the commander would order a parade of chariots to impress the people of Memphis and remind them who was the stronger.

The sentry yawned, glad to have finished his watch. He would breakfast on milk and fresh bread, and then sleep until noon. Then have lunch and an afternoon nap. Suddenly, he saw what he thought must be a mirage: a horse, wandering around the camp on its own. He immediately alerted his senior officer, whose eyes were still misty with sleep.

'Look over there, sir.'

'Anyone would think . . . No, that's impossible. Who has let a horse escape? I shall tell the commander immediately.'

Abruptly awakened from his sleep, the commander insisted on checking for himself. What he saw sent him into a violent rage.

'Bring me those responsible for this appalling breech of discipline immediately. And have that horse taken back to its stable.'

A good half-hour later, a white-faced groom returned. 'Sir, the soldiers . . . They're all dead, and the stable's empty.'

'What is this nonsense?'

'The western stable and barracks. There's not a single man left alive.'

The commander went straight there, accompanied by his assistant. The groom had not exaggerated.

'The rebels have dared steal our horses!' bristled the assistant. 'We must warn Avaris.'

'In my opinion, that would be a bad mistake.'

'But, Commander, that is the order. An incident as serious as this—'

'I, you and our subordinates will be accused of incompetence and negligence. At best, we'll be sent to prison. At worst, we'll go to the labyrinth and the bull.'

The force of these arguments shook his assistant. 'Then what do you suggest, sir?'

'Absolute silence. We'll bury the bodies and kill the groom. Then we'll forget the entire incident.'

35

Proud, strong and tall, the Hyksos horses amazed and fascinated the Egyptians. Way-Finder and Young Laughter watched them attentively, and the donkey soon decided that they would not be able to carry heavy loads. An Egyptian word meaning 'the Beautiful' was chosen for the imposing creatures.

At the secret base at Thebes, Ahhotep and Ahmose called a meeting of their general staff. Those present included Emheb, who had been permitted to come to Thebes from the Port of Kamose, leaving Moon in temporary command. At the first sign of danger, Moon would alert the capital.

As they looked at the horses, everyone was full of praise for the Afghan and Moustache.

'They are truly beautiful,' said Qaris. 'I am happy to have lived long enough to see them at close hand.'

'But do not go near them,' advised Neshi. 'Some of them are easily angered. I have given up trying to understand their character.'

'It is no more difficult than that of donkeys,' said Heray. 'We must simply be patient and thoughtful in order to gain their trust.'

'The most urgent thing is for them to start providing us with foals,' said Emheb. 'Even if we succeed in mastering the horses, we shall need many, many of them in order to rival the Hyksos chariot corps.'

'Work has already begun on that,' Moustache assured him. 'From what I have seen so far, the horse likes authority. As Heray said, their masters must establish a friendly relationship with them, so the rule should be one horse to one man. They will learn to know each other and become inseparable.'

'Have you chosen yours yet?' asked the queen.

'The large white male who is watching us, Majesty. He is the one who enabled us to embark and disembark without too much difficulty.'

'Hyksos horses are used to pulling chariots. Why should we not ride them, too?'

'Moustache shall be the Egyptian army's first cavalry officer,' laughed the Afghan. 'He had better try it here and now.'

'What? You want me to climb up there?'

'You've sat on a donkey before, haven't you?'

'In case you haven't noticed, the horse is bigger and taller.'

'That big male has adopted you. He can guess what you want to do. Surely you aren't going to disappoint Queen Ahhotep?'

Stung, Moustache clambered up on to the horse's rump. Not only did the beast refuse to go forward, but it reared. Moustache slid magnificently off and landed on the sandy training-ground, in front of a multitude of guards.

He leapt to his feet in annoyance. 'Hey, White Giant, we're friends, you and I. You've no cause to play nasty tricks on me.'

'Try to find a better sitting position,' advised Ahhotep.

'Near his neck?'

'No, in the middle of his back.'

This time, Moustache managed to sit down. 'Forward, White Giant!'

The horse neighed and set off at a gallop. Caught unawares, Moustache tried to cling on to the horse's neck. The spectators marvelled at its power and its speed, before watching the Egyptian army's first cavalry officer fly unceremoniously through the air.

'Ow! It really hurts,' groaned Moustache, who was stretched out on his belly.

'Behave like a hero,' She-Cat told him as she massaged him gently. 'This ointment will soon relieve the pain.'

'That damned horse has broken all my ribs.'

'It was your fall, not the horse, and you still have a few unbroken ones. No serious injuries.'

'I'm never getting on that monster again.'

'White Giant is magnificent and he is already getting bored with you. You've scarcely begun your apprenticeship, my darling. In two days, you'll ride round the training-ground again.'

'Do you want me dead, She-Cat?'

The way she caressed him proved otherwise. 'There were one or two small problems, but your experience was very instructive. Queen Ahhotep has thought of some improvements which should please you.'

She-Cat was as gifted at healing as she was in the arts of love. A few days later, virtually recovered, Moustache faced White Giant again. Ahhotep had placed a piece of fabric on the horse's back, and he was now equipped with a leather bridle and reins.

'He has accepted this?' gasped Moustache.

'We talked for a long time,' said the queen, 'and tried to find a way for the rider to guide the horse without hurting him. I think we are on the right track, but you will have to perfect the method.'*

Moustache was delighted to find that he could now easily convey his wishes to his mount. He could make him speed up,

---

*Egyptian horses were not shod, and riders did not use a saddle or stirrups.

slow down, turn to the right or the left. The horse responded quickly and clearly enjoyed the exercise.

'You surprise me,' admitted the Afghan. 'I didn't think you'd be able to master this new weapon.'

'While my ribs were healing, I did some thinking.'

'Oh? What about?'

'One rider won't be enough. Others must do what I've done.'

'No doubt,' agreed the Afghan flatly.

'I've noticed a grey horse eyeing you with interest.'

'I like solid ground. Having my feet in the air would make me very uneasy.'

'Emheb and Heray will lift you up easily.'

The two big men promptly did so.

After falling off a few times, the Afghan became the Egyptian army's second horseman.

As there was no activity around the Port of Kamose, the general staff remained in Thebes where they continued to discover the world of horses.

She-Cat healed a mare's sore eye and saw that her remedies worked well on the animals. Young Laughter gradually grew used to the huge creatures. Ahhotep calmed the nervous ones and reassured those that were anxious. She fed them in turn and had long talks with them.

Moustache and the Afghan, who by now were good riders, had moved on to another stage by persuading White Giant and Grey to jump increasingly high obstacles. Several times they headed out into the desert, where the horses loved to gallop across the empty spaces.

But the two men and their mounts hardly constituted an army able to take on the Hyksos chariots. It remained to be seen if the Egyptian carpenters could make chariots like the one spirited away from Memphis.

36

Jannas's body was thrown into a deep ditch, along with those of his assistant, his servants and his bodyguards. Once the house had been hastily cleaned, it became the official residence of the new commander of the war-fleet, an elderly man suggested by Khamudi and duly appointed by the emperor. The man was delighted by his unexpected promotion. He was also a heavy user of drugs, and would cause Khamudi no trouble.

None of the Hyksos officials believed a word of the official story about Jannas's death, but they dared not try to find out the truth. In any case, it was easy to guess: threatened with downfall, Khamudi had got rid of Jannas. Now a single question was being asked: had he or had he not acted on the orders of the emperor?

Apophis had not been seen for several days. Many people thought he must be on his deathbed. Some advocated rallying around Khamudi. Others advised killing him – but then whom would they place on the throne? No one in the army or the war-fleet had a reputation to rival Jannas's. Factions were already forming, ready to tear each other asunder, when news came that all army officers were summoned to the citadel.

One general in the chariot corps, regarded as Jannas's right-hand man, decided to escape. He would leave on a trading-ship – its destination did not matter – would disappear at the first port they came to, and would make sure he was forgotten. But the captain refused to take the unexpected passenger aboard and alerted the port guards, who took him immediately to Khamudi.

'You are a traitor and you deserve to die,' declared the High Treasurer. 'I offer you one choice. If you tell me the names of Jannas's accomplices you will be beheaded, but if you refuse to talk you will be tortured.'

'I refuse to talk.'

'You imbecile, you won't hold out for long.'

Khamudi was right. His face burnt and his limbs lacerated, the general revealed the names of Jannas's supporters in the army. They were arrested in their homes or at the barracks, and were beheaded in front of their soldiers.

The audience chamber at the citadel was as icy cold as ever.

'The purge,' said the emperor in his harsh voice, 'has eliminated many subversives. However, do not think that I have therefore lowered my guard. Any of Jannas's supporters not yet identified will be unmasked and punished. Those who confess here and now will receive my clemency.'

A young captain of footsoldiers stepped forward. 'Majesty, I was wrong to believe what Commander Jannas said. He claimed to have full powers, and I wanted to fight under his command to affirm my belief in the empire's omnipotence.'

'Your honesty has spared you the shame of public beheading. Your throat shall be cut before the Temple of Set.'

'Majesty, I beg you—'

'Cut out the traitor's tongue and take him away.'

Within seconds, the captain's blood poured on to the floor of the audience chamber.

'High Treasurer Khamudi is hereby appointed commander-in-chief of all the Hyksos forces,' announced Apophis. 'He will carry out my orders to the letter. Anyone who refuses to obey him, for any reason whatsoever, will be sentenced to torture.'

Dead drunk, Khamudi stretched out on his bed and tried – with some difficulty – to get his breath back. Never before had he come so close to the edge of the abyss.

If Jannas had been less respectful of the emperor's person, and had taken full powers more quickly, Khamudi would now be languishing in a prison camp. Fortunately, though, Jannas had not been cunning enough. He had made the fatal mistake of revealing his true intentions to the emperor, and Apophis, sensing that he was under threat, had reacted ferociously.

The emperor strongly opposed dividing his forces, and wanted to keep most of his regiments in the Delta and near Avaris. The new commander-in-chief would therefore have to let matters go on much as before, continuing the siege at Memphis and making greater efforts to put down the Hittite rebellion. The Hyksos would burn more Hittite forests, crops and villages, and massacre on the spot any civilians – women, children and old men included – suspected of complicity with the rebels.

There remained Ahhotep and her petty pharaoh. They seemed to be following the same path as the King of Kerma, who was slumbering peacefully in far-off Nubia, content with his harem and his fine food. If Ahhotep was an intelligent woman, she must have realized that she would never enter the Hyksos shrine and that she must be content with the lands she had conquered. The old emperor might endure this state of affairs, weakened as he was by Jannas's downfall, but Khamudi would not put up with it for very long. He wanted to see the rebellious queen helpless at his feet, begging for mercy.

However, there were other priorities, beginning with an expansion of the drugs trade. Khamudi was preparing to offer two new products for sale, one of poor quality and cheap enough for anyone to buy, and the other rare and expensive, reserved for the elite. The profits would ensure that the High Treasurer soon doubled his immense fortune.

With Jannas dead and the emperor growing old, the future lay wide open. But there was still one threat he could not ignore. So Khamudi confided in Yima, his devoted wife.

'What a terrible night!' Tormented by ever-more-terrifying nightmares, the lady Tany had soiled her bed several times, obliging her serving-women to change the linen. Even now she was awake, the empress trembled when she remembered the torrents of flame she had seen engulfing Avaris.

At dawn, she wolfed down some game in sauce and drank some strong beer. She ate and drank so fast that she immediately got stomach cramps, and had to go back to bed.

'The lady Yima would like to see you,' one of her ladies informed her.

'That dear, loving friend. Show her in.'

Yima was made-up to excess and simpering even more than usual. 'You look less tired this morning, Majesty.'

'Alas, I only look it. You were right, Yima. That damned Jannas did put a curse on me. I am so glad he's dead! With your husband in command of the army, Avaris has nothing to fear.'

'You can depend on Khamudi, Majesty. As long as he is alive, the Egyptian will never get near Avaris.'

'That's so reassuring! I hope the emperor has not caused any problems over what happened?'

'He was only too glad to be rid of Jannas and his ridiculous demands.'

'That's good. But we must keep our little secret. No one must know about the part played by our dear Aberia.'

'Have no fear, Majesty. All anyone knows is the official version: that Jannas was murdered by his gardener.'

'Has Aberia received her reward?'

'My husband has been very generous. As for your devoted servant, she would like to provide you with a remedy which might speed your recovery.'

'Go and fetch it quickly.'

The statuesque Aberia entered the empress's bedchamber.

'You, Aberia? You know a potion which will restore my health?'

'It is not a potion, Majesty.'

'Then what is it?'

'Something much more radical.' Aberia held up her enormous hands.

'I . . . I don't understand.'

'The best way of keeping our secret, Majesty, is to silence you once and for all. It seems that you talk in your sleep. That is dangerous.'

Tany tried to struggle to her feet, but Aberia's hands closed round her throat.

Tany was buried in the palace burial-ground. The emperor did not attend the ceremony; he was busy checking the accounts Khamudi had submitted to him.

'Majesty,' said Khamudi, 'permit me to offer you my condolences.'

'No one will miss that old sow, least of all me.'

Thanks to Khamudi, Aberia was rich; and from now only she would work for no one but him. The death of the empress, whose pernicious influence he had feared, took him one step closer to absolute power. But Khamudi did not allow himself that thought in Apophis's presence, for the Emperor of Darkness might have read his mind.

37

Emheb gave Ahhotep his verdict. 'Before taking charge of my good city of Edfu, I plied my trade as a carpenter. Since you wished to be sure no information would leak out, I attended to the Hyksos chariot myself. It's a remarkable piece of work, but very heavy – as it needs to be to carry four soldiers.'

'Then let us lighten it and adapt it to use by only two men,' suggested the queen. 'That will give us greater mobility.'

'Indeed, but the problem of stability will be difficult to solve. And then there is the choice of the right wood, which must be both light and strong. Three kinds seem suitable: tamarisk, elm and birch. We have plenty of tamarisk, but the other two are rather rare. I can use all we have in stock, which will be enough for about a hundred wheels, but then we shall have to go obtain more in the Delta or from abroad.'

Ahhotep's disarming smile wiped away his reservations. He showed her how he planned to bend the wood, by moistening it and heating it until it became pliable enough.

Before long the first two wheels were finished. Each was two cubits in diameter, with four spokes.

'I took the Hyksos wheels as a model,' Emheb explained to Ahhotep, 'but improved on them. Their wheel-spokes are made from two pieces of wood, but I have made mine differently. In particular, I have joined together several

V-shaped pieces, which makes the spokes extremely strong, and have used glues and coatings to harden them.'

Proudly, he ran his hand along an axle four cubits long, which would support the shell of the chariot, and a five-cubit shaft, whose height could be adjusted according to the size of the horses.

'How do you plan to make the chariot floor?' she asked.

'I shall use well-stretched leather strips on a wooden frame. The floor will be strong, but flexible enough to absorb jolting on bumpy ground.'

At last the moment came to try the chariot for the first time. Two horses were harnessed to it; all that was needed was a crew.

'Where will we find two men mad enough to climb into that thing and drive it off at top speed?' wondered Moustache.

'The queen insists that the trials must be held in absolute secrecy,' replied Emheb. 'Of those who know, Pharaoh Ahmose clearly cannot possibly run such a risk, Neshi is a scholar and not used to such exertion, Qaris is too old, and Heray is too heavy. And I am in charge of manufacture. So . . .'

'The Afghan and me?'

'You've faced bigger dangers than this.'

'I'm not so sure about that,' said the Afghan.

'Come on, now, climb aboard. Moustache will drive and you, Afghan, will act as the archer and fire at a straw target. The goal is simple: to score a direct hit while moving as quickly as possible.'

'The future of the war depends on you,' declared Ahhotep, and the pharaoh nodded.

Moustache and the Afghan took their places in the chariot.

In this kind of situation, both men had the same attitude: full speed ahead. When they went in a straight line, the trial was a great success. But at the first turn, taken without slowing down, the chariot tipped over and the two men were flung out.

'I'm not in pain any more,' said the Afghan. 'She-Cat, you're a real sorceress!'

'My wife is in charge of the battlefield doctors,' said her proud husband, who had also recovered well. 'Anyway, you aren't an emergency any more.'

'When are you going to try again?' asked She-Cat.

'There's no hurry, my darling, and—'

'Yes there is: we have no time to lose. Making a better chariot than the Hyksos ones will take a lot of trials, and you do not have the leisure to be lazy.'

'But we were injured, and—'

'All you had was some bruising, which has already healed. You're both perfectly healthy, so you can certainly take a few more falls.'

She-Cat's prophecy proved accurate.

During the months that followed, Emheb made repeated adjustments to make the chariot as effective a weapon as possible. He used more coatings and adhesives, fixed the rear of the shaft more solidly into the bar under the platform, and made a better harness from a wide strip of fabric covering the horse's withers, another narrower one under its belly and a third, lined with leather, against its chest so that the animal was not hurt. He lightened the shell still further, and left it open at the rear. Its frame consisted of several curved wooden bars and its thin walls were covered with leather. The same material reinforced the parts of the chariot that were exposed to friction and the joins between the different sections.

Each day, Ahhotep feared she would receive bad news from the Port of Kamose. But the pigeons always brought the same message: 'Nothing to report.'

The rebels at Memphis sent an astonishing message. According to rumours from Avaris, Jannas had been murdered by one of his servants, and Khamudi, who had been appointed supreme commander, was to carry out a purge and reorganization of the Hyksos army. If this was true, it meant that a rebel network, however tiny, had been recreated inside the enemy capital and was managing to communicate – no doubt with great difficulty – with the besieged city.

'The death of Jannas would explain why the Hyksos are playing a waiting game,' observed Ahmose.

'It is all the more important that our chariots are a success,' said Ahhotep. 'Horses take a long time to breed, and we have only a few pairs. We shall have to steal more from the enemy, and hope that our chariots work well – which is not always the case!'

'I shall see to it,' promised Emheb.

Moustache and the Afghan had lost count of their attempts, some of which went better than others. A particular success was that they had learnt how best to handle the reins. The driver wrapped them round his waist, so that simply turning his body to right or left made the horses turn in that direction, while leaning back made them slow down or stop, depending on how steeply he leant.

Inside the shell, Moustache had installed leather pockets containing arrows, spears, daggers and leather straps for emergency repairs.

'This time,' he confided to the Afghan, 'I can tell it's going to go right.'

'You've said that lots of times!'

'Gee up, my lads, full speed ahead!'

Given their heads, the horses galloped off. Although the ground was uneven, the chariot did not slacken speed. It safely negotiated the first turn, round a boundary stone, then the second, which was very tight because of a rut. The chariot remained perfectly balanced.

The Afghan fired five arrows at the straw figure of a man. Every one hit the target.

Moustache turned for a second run, which was as successful as the first.

'We have succeeded,' the queen told Emheb, who was almost weeping with happiness. 'Work is to begin immediately on making more chariots and training more drivers.'

38

After smoking plenty of opium, the officer in charge of port security at Avaris flung himself on top of the young Egyptian girl he had selected for his pleasure, but he had beaten her so badly that she was unconscious.

'Wake up, you idiot! I can't have any fun with a dead woman.'

He slapped her several times, but there was no response. Too bad for her. She would be thrown into a mass grave with all the other whores.

The Hyksos emerged from his official residence to urinate over the edge of the quay, taking care not to fall in the water. Suddenly, he was surrounded by ten pirates belonging to Khamudi's personal guard. He thought he must be having a bad dream.

'Follow us,' one of them ordered him.

'There must be some mistake.'

'Are you in charge of port security or not?'

'Yes, but—'

'Then follow us. The High Treasurer wants to see you.'

'It's been a hard day, and I . . . I'm very tired.'

'If necessary, we'll help you walk.'

Khamudi had taken up residence in Jannas's office, at the heart of the largest barracks in Avaris. He had changed the furniture and had the walls painted red. On the work-table lay papyri giving the names of men who had supported Jannas, soldiers of all ranks and regiments. Khamudi examined the cases one by one, and set his accusatory official seal upon almost all of them. Only a truly thorough purge of the army would enable him to command the Hyksos troops without fear of betrayal.

When the latest suspect was brought before him, Khamudi said, 'You have a good deal of explaining to do.'

'I do my work well, High Treasurer. For me, the port's security is a sacred duty.'

'You were a friend of Jannas, were you not?

'Me? Oh no, my lord, I hated him.'

'You were often seen with him.'

'He was giving me orders, that's all.'

'That may be true.'

The suspect relaxed a little.

'I have summoned you here for another reason, which is just as serious,' Khamudi went on. 'There was a young Egyptian girl in your bed.'

'That is so, my lord, but—'

'Last night there was a different one, and the night before that yet another.'

'Well, my lord, I am a man of strong appetites and—'

'Where do these girls come from?'

'I meet them, and—'

'Stop lying.'

The accused squirmed. 'Since the harem was closed down, a man has to find ways of getting by. So I . . . I've found ways.'

'You have set up your own little harem and you hire out your girls to others, don't you?'

'Several of us do benefit, but it's because of the closure – I'm sure you understand, my lord? In a way, I'm providing a service.'

'I am the High Treasurer, and no trade can begin on Hyksos soil without my prior knowledge. Defrauding the state is a very serious crime.'

'I will pay any fine, my lord.'

'I want to know how you have organized your operation and the location of all the closed houses in Avaris.'

The officer talked for some time. Khamudi was delighted. Now he could take control of this prostitution and make substantial profits from it.

'You have cooperated fully,' he conceded, 'so you deserve a reward.'

'And I am not a suspect any more?'

'Not at all, now that the facts have been established. Come with me.'

The officer did not really understand the High Treasurer's meaning, but he followed him without hesitation. Khamudi led him to the barracks gate where Aberia dealt with the Hyksos officers and soldiers convicted of conspiring with the criminal Jannas.

'You are now not a mere suspect,' explained Khamudi, 'but guilty of treason and are therefore sentenced to deportation to a prison camp. I wish you a good journey.'

The man tried to run, but Aberia seized him by the hair, making him cry out in pain, then threw him to the ground and broke one of his legs.

'You still have one leg to walk with. And I advise you not to fall behind on the journey.'

This was the third time in a month that the guards had raided the weapons store at Avaris port. Fifty of the workforce had been arrested, and nobody knew what had become of them.

One of the team in charge of making and repairing chariot-wheels was called Arek, a vigorous young man born of a Caucasian father and an Egyptian mother. He had seen his elder brother leave in a convoy of men, women and children, accused of having plotted with Jannas. Rumour had it that those who survived the march were thrown into a camp from which no prisoner ever emerged alive.

Convinced that the emperor's madness would become more and more murderous, Arek had joined the rebel movement, passing on all he knew to a man who delivered sandals. When necessary, the merchant went to Memphis with supplies of sandals for the Hyksos troops, and afterwards, taking a thousand precautions, he contacted the Egyptians.

Although he felt very alone, Arek lived for one hope. According to the sandal-merchant, the Queen of Freedom was no mirage. She had raised an army which had more than once defeated the Hyksos. Thanks to her, one day Egypt would defeat the darkness.

Apart from the scraps of information he could offer the sandal-merchant, Arek devoted himself to an dangerous, delicate task: damaging the chariot-wheels. He made deep cuts in the spokes or the rim so as to weaken them, then disguised the cuts with varnish. When the chariot travelled at high speed, an accident was inevitable.

Suddenly he heard shouts and the sounds of running feet.

'It's the guards,' a colleague warned him.

'Stay where you are and do not try to run away,' ordered the imperious voice of the lady Aberia.

The workers obeyed. The guards herded them together with blows in the back from their staves, and drove them to where Aberia stood. At her feet lay a warehouseman, covered in blood from his appalling wounds.

'This criminal was plotting with Jannas,' she said. 'He must have had an accomplice among you. If you do not denounce him immediately, I shall have all the members of this man's family executed.'

Aberia forced the unfortunate man to his feet.

'He has had his eyes put out!' exclaimed a workman in horror.

A guard knocked the insolent man unconscious and dragged him out of the workshop.

The tortured man staggered towards his colleagues. 'I swear to you . . . I haven't got an accomplice.'

'All you need do is touch the guilty man and your family will be spared,' promised Aberia. In fact, she had already sent them to the camp at Tjaru.

The blind man reached out. His fingers brushed the face of Arek, who dared not breathe. The dying man's fingers closed on the shoulder of the man next to Arek, a Syrian, who cried out in fear.

39

Two happy events occurred on the same day. First, Nefertari gave birth to a son, who received the same name as his father, so that the dynasty of the moon-god might continue the fight. Second, Emheb informed Ahhotep that the first regiment of Egyptian chariots was ready for battle.

Ahmose had been training with Moustache and the Afghan, in order to master the new weapon. Obstinate, serious and precise, he was now fully the equal of his teachers. The last trials in the desert had pleased him greatly.

Ahhotep rocked the baby, who would be suckled by his mother for three months before being entrusted to a wet-nurse.

'Majesty,' said Nefertari, 'will you do me the honour of giving my son the secret name he will bear if he proves worthy of it?'

'May he become the founder of a new dynasty, which will witness the reunification of the Two Lands and the re-establishment of the rule of Ma'at over Egypt. May his secret name, the completeness of his being, be Amon-hotep, "Amon is at peace".'

The queen had no time to lavish more affection on her grandson, for Rascal had arrived from Memphis and was awaiting her on the sill of her bedchamber window.

The news he had brought necessitated an immediate meeting of the general staff.

'We now have a source of information within Avaris itself,' said the queen. 'It reaches the rebels in Memphis, who pass it on to us.'

'Are we sure, Majesty, that the information is true?' asked Neshi sceptically. 'We must take care that we are not deceived by lies spread by the emperor.'

'That warning is important,' agreed the queen, 'but I tend to believe what we have been told: confirmation of Jannas's death, the appointment of Khamudi to lead the Hyksos armed forces, and the fear that reigns in Avaris. Jannas's supporters are being ruthlessly pursued, arrested and executed.'

'Is Khamudi planning to attack us? asked Emheb.

'Our informant speaks only of a terrifying purge, in which not even the highest officers are being spared.'

'It's almost as if the invaders are withdrawing,' said Qaris, 'and their barbarity is gnawing away at them from the inside.'

'Surely this is a new sign from destiny?' suggested Heray. 'The time has come for us to go on to the offensive.'

Moustache and the Afghan nodded in agreement.

'Does any of you disagree?' asked Ahhotep.

Each man was conscious of the weight of his own silence.

'Then the Council of Pharaoh is unanimous,' concluded the queen. 'But it is he who must make the decision.'

'Let us make ready to leave Thebes,' declared Ahmose.

Now fully recovered from the birth of her son, Nefertari was walking in the palace gardens with Ahhotep. The Great Royal Wife was both overflowing with happiness and overwhelmed with anguish as she thought about the intensification of the war.

'Once again, Nefertari, you will be solely responsible for

Thebes,' said Ahhotep. The battle will be terrible, and no one can predict the outcome. Like his father and his brother before him, Ahmose will fight in the vanguard, for his example will be vital to ensure the unity of his men and stem their fear. We are about to defy the darkness. It is possible that neither I nor my son will return from the front, so I must take measures which affect you directly.'

Nefertari made no futile protests. She had to face reality as clear-headedly as Ahhotep did.

'I scarcely had time to be young,' Ahhotep went on, 'which I hope will not be the case for you. But if destiny proves merciless, you will have no right to show any sign at all of weakness. Come with me.'

In a chariot driven by Ahhotep, the two women went from the palace to the temple at Karnak, where Pharaoh Ahmose and High Priest Djehuty were waiting for them. Despite the seriousness of the moment, Nefertari enjoyed the unexpected ride and the novel sensation of speed.

Once the purification rites had been carried out, the quartet crossed the open courtyard to the shrine where the pharaoh's coronation had been celebrated. Nefertari was surprised to find a stele there.

Ahmose summarized its inscription. 'At the request of Queen Ahhotep, I grant to Great Royal Wife Nefertari the title of Wife of God and the office of Second Servant of Amon. She will govern the Temple of Karnak with the High Priest. To enable her to do this, she will receive gold, silver, clothing, pots of ointment, fertile fields and servants. May this institution endure and prosper, may it enchant the spirit of Amon and maintain his goodwill towards the land beloved of the gods.'

Nefertari bowed to the king. 'You clothed me when I had nothing, you made me rich when I was poor. This fortune belongs to the temple; it is in the service of the creative power that gives the temple life.'

Ahhotep embraced the new Wife of God, who would take her place if she fell to a Hyksos sword.

The next day, at dawn in order to avoid the worst of the heat, Ahhotep led Ahmose, Nefertari and a few soldiers of the Royal Guard across the Nile and into the desert, to test the chariots on the desert tracks. Once again, the chariots proved both stable and manoeuvrable.

Ahhotep halted at the opening to a valley protected by hills. She said, 'The true riches of Egypt are the builders who create it. While my son and I fight the Hyksos, you, Ahmose-Nefertari, shall found a craftsmen's village here, the Place of Truth.* The men must work in secret, far from prying eyes and ears, and create the ritual objects we need. Within them will be written Ma'at, the righteousness of the work. Gather together the men you believe worthy of this work, put them to the test, initiate them according to the ancient rites, and accept no one who is not of good character. The oldest Theban goldsmith shall be your assistant. Here is the offering he has created for Pharaoh.'

The queen hung round Ahmose's neck a pectoral combining gold, cornelian, lapis-lazuli and turquoise. It depicted the king standing in a boat, flanked by Amon and Ra. Both gods were holding vases from which celestial energy was gushing. As this energy impregnated the king's being, it would enable him to carry out his office.†

'And now,' said Ahhotep, 'we may leave for the Port of Kamose.'

Qaris came to see the queen. 'Majesty, the man arrived an hour ago. I thought it fitting to give him a room in the palace,

---

*In Egyptian *Set Ma'at*; its modern name is Deir el-Medina. We encountered the brotherhood in the four volumes of *The Stone of Light*.
†This pectoral was found in Ahhotep's tomb at Dra Abu el-Naga (western Thebes).

but under guard. I have taken him wine and a dish of hare, and he is asking for more.'

'Which man do you mean?'

'The Minoan, Linas. He has returned.'

Ahhotep agreed to see him, and Qaris went and fetched him. Linas had not changed.

'Did you have a good crossing, Commander?' asked Ahhotep.

'No, Majesty, a very bad one. The sea was rough, and the winds chancy. If I were not a good sailor the ship would have sunk, and that would have been a great pity, both for myself and for you.'

'Does that mean you bring good news?'

'Permit me to give you two presents: this battleaxe, decorated with griffins, and this dagger, depicting a lion racing after its prey. The handle is shaped like a bull's head, the symbol of King Minos.'*

'Are you saying that he is still alive?'

'Indeed, Majesty. He eventually returned from the cave with an answer from the oracle, and he showed no mercy to those who had tried to seize his throne. He wishes you to have the strength of the lion and the magic of the griffins to triumph over your enemies.'

'Am I to understand that it is not a question of *our* enemies?'

'Everywhere Minoans go, they shall declare that the Queen of Freedom is waging war on the emperor, who is incapable of defeating her. Minoa recognizes you as Queen of the Distant Shores, places herself under your protection and will send the Hyksos no further tributes or assistance.'

*They were also found in Ahhotep's tomb.

40

He was the last one left. The last senior officer who had fought at Jannas's side in all the provinces of the empire. He had been heaped with honours, but he lived modestly in his official residence, with just two servants.

All his old army comrades had been executed or deported to the prison camps, whose existence he had only just discovered. Horrified, he had shut himself in his house to get drunk.

So the High Treasurer was sending loyal Hyksos warriors to end their days in prison camps! Why was the emperor yielding to the whims of this sick-minded man, who was guided solely by his own rapacity?

He himself must have been forgotten, no doubt because of his age – he was fifty-seven. So should he not try to avenge Jannas and his comrades? He would request an audience with Khamudi, on the pretext of denouncing traitors who were so far undetected. As soon as he was face to face with the monster, he would strike.

Although it was rough and ready, his plan might succeed.

The officer called to his servant, to bring him some flavoured wine. When she did not reply, he left his living-room and found her in the hallway, lying on her back with her tongue lolling out of her mouth. Next to her lay her husband, who had also been strangled.

Aberia emerged from the shadows. 'I have not forgotten you, my friend.'

The old emperor spent most of his time in the secret room, at the centre of the citadel where cold and darkness reigned. It was there that Khamudi came, each morning, to give him his report and the list of appointments.

'Have you wiped out all Jannas's supporters?' asked Apophis.

'The purge is under way, Majesty. We are hunting down the traitors without mercy.'

'That is good, Khamudi. Do not relax your efforts for a moment. Can you believe it? That man Jannas demanded full powers! He forgot that, like any other Hyksos, he owed me absolute obedience.'

'Thanks to the lady Aberia, we are even arresting conspirators who thought they were safe.'

'That's good. Purge and deport: those are our two priorities. Once Avaris and the Delta contain only faithful servants of Apophis, the Hyksos order will have been re-established.'

'I have some good news from Memphis, Majesty, where your plan is proving its worth. According to the commander besieging the city, the Memphites are at the end of their strength. He asks if you wish him to launch a new attack.'

'No. He must continue to let them rot, I want those rebels to die in their own filth. Then we shall burn the city. Decay, Khamudi, that is the true law of life.'

'The news from Anatolia is satisfactory, too. As you ordered, our army is killing civilians and rebels, and is retaking one village after another. In the mountains, the reconquest is slow but sure. Soon there will be not a living soul left in Anatolia, and the Hittites will have been eradicated.'

'Jannas was wrong to demand an attack on several fronts. In the event of success, our soldiers would have become idle. It is good that they should fight and kill.'

'There is still Ahhotep, Majesty. It appears that she has given up the fight, which is probably why there has been no word from our spy.'

'There has been. Here is his latest message: "Whatever happens, I shall fulfil my mission."' Suddenly, the rasping voice became even more sinister, as if it was rising up out of dark depths to which Apophis alone had access. 'Ahhotep is approaching, I can feel it. She is coming towards us because she thinks she is capable of defeating us. The disasters that have already struck her are not enough to halt her. She will know more despair and suffering. Come, Ahhotep, come closer. I am waiting for you.'

'Majesty, there is information from Elephantine,' Qaris told Ahhotep, whom he found contemplating his model of Egypt. 'The annual flood will be ideal: it will reach about sixteen cubits.'

This was the last, and oh-so-important, detail that Ahhotep needed before giving the signal for departure. Using the strength of the current, the Egyptian fleet, made up of new war-boats launched from the boatyard at Thebes, would soon reach the Port of Kamose, where it would join up with the main body of the troops. Sailing onward with the aid of the Nile, it would make for Hyksos territory.

The queen gazed at the model with emotion. 'This was our first state secret,' she recalled. 'I was nothing but a head-strong little girl and you, the wise, cautious steward of a decrepit little palace, were gathering information on the enemy and trying to believe that a few rebels still existed. You showed me this model, on which the last free space was the city of Amon.'

'You ought to have been discouraged, Majesty, but instead that realization increased your strength tenfold. Thanks to you, we have lived in dignity and hope.'

Ahhotep thought of Seqen, Kamose and Teti the Small. For

her, they were not shades but living allies who continued to fight at her side.

'The model has changed a great deal,' observed Qaris. 'You have liberated the South of the country, Majesty, and part of Middle Egypt.'

'You and I both know that that is still not enough. The next battle will be decisive.'

'You have horses and chariots now, Majesty.'

'They are not enough, either, Qaris. And we have no experience of fighting on level ground, army against army.'

'Do not give in, Majesty. Even if you are defeated, even if Thebes is destroyed, even if we all die, you will have been right. Pharaoh must reign over the Two Lands, celebrating the union of Upper and Lower Egypt. Outside that harmony, that brotherhood of Set and Horus, no happiness is possible.'

The steward had rarely spoken so forthrightly, and his words swept away Ahhotep's last traces of hesitation.

The atmosphere at the palace and on the quaysides of Thebes was effervescent. Despite his weight of years, Qaris saw that nothing was forgotten to ensure the comfort of Queen Ahhotep and Pharaoh Ahmose. He checked everything, from the quality of the bedlinen to the sharpness of the razors.

As for Neshi, he refused to place his trust in any of his assistants. Some people called him 'the Star of the Two Lands' because of his exceptional mind, but he showed scant care for his reputation, and threw all his efforts into the preparations for departure. He examined each shield, each spear, each sword; equally carefully, he examined the moringa pods, which were dropped into jars of water to purify it, and were also used to clarify jars of oil. Nor did he overlook a single mat or kilt. Fortunately, She-Cat and her assistants packed and loaded the remedies and ointments themselves.

Far from this bustle, Ahmose and Nefertari gazed at the

Nile, which was rising and taking on a reddish tint. After embracing his son for a long time, Ahmose had taken his wife to the riverbank, to savour a last moment of intimacy in the shade of a tamarisk, before launching himself into a venture from which he had little chance of returning alive.

Not far away, hidden in a thicket of papyrus, the Hyksos spy planned to take advantage of this opportunity. The king was unarmed, and his guards were posted a long way off so as not to disturb him.

If he crept along the bank and struck very quickly, the spy would not be seen. With great meticulousness, he went over every move he must make; his victims must have no chance of sounding the alarm. The slightest mistake would be fatal to him. Hesitating, he took one last look around.

Once again, his caution saved him from disaster. Well hidden near the royal couple was a soldier, alert and dangerous. And stretched out under the low branches of the tamarisk, his eyes bright and alert, Young Laughter was protecting the royal couple. The spy instantly abandoned his plan.

41

'The stars of Sah* have risen,' declared High Priest Djehuty. 'Osiris is reborn in the celestial light.'

Twenty new war-boats cast off, including *Shining One of Memphis*, *Offering* and *Fighting Bull*. They were followed by *Septentrion*, which attacted great interest because she was carrying horses. All the vessels flew Ahhotep's standard, showing the full moon's disc in its ship.

At the prow of the *Septentrion*, the queen held the golden Set-headed sceptre. Near her stood Ahmose, dressed in a leather corselet and wearing the White Crown of Upper Egypt and a leather corselet. When he raised aloft the Sword of Amon, the priests of Karnak roared out the sacred song composed in his honour: 'When he appears, Pharaoh is like the moon-god amid the stars. Accomplished in government is his arm, happy are his steps, firm his tread, lively his sandals; he is the sacred symbol upon whom rests the Divine Light.'

After entrusting the sword to the Queen of Freedom, Ahmose took his place at the steering-oar, which had been brought all the way from Elephantine, and the fleet set off towards the Port of Kamose, aided by a strong current.

*

*The constellation of Orion.

'We are almost there,' said Emheb.

Housed in vast cage-like structures, each comprising two stalls which were partially open to the air, the horses had shown no distress during the voyage. When the fleet halted at the Port of Kamose, they were able to exercise, watched dubiously by Moon and Ahmes.

'Are you sure you can control them?' Moon asked Moustache and the Afghan.

'We've trained intensively,' replied Moustache. 'There won't be any problems.'

Moon wanted to see the chariots, which were stowed securely on another cargo-boat and guarded by archers.

'Will our chariots be as effective as the Hyksos ones?'

'Probably more so,' replied the Afghan. 'Emheb has greatly improved upon the one he used as a model.'

The halt had to be a short one, for they could not let the flood rise too far.

As the fleet was to about leave, a strange wind arose. It was swirling and icy, like a winter gale.

'This will seriously hamper our manoeuvrability,' said Moon worriedly.

'It is the emperor,' said Ahhotep. 'He is trying to delay us by unleashing the evil breath of the dying year.* Let us call upon Amon, the master of the winds, and ask him to protect the fleet.'

On the deck of each vessel they laid dozens of offertory bags containing incense, powdered galenite, dates and bread. Then Ahhotep raised her sceptre towards the sky, which had grown threatening, to win the favours of Set.

The wind dropped, and the clouds dispersed.

In this seventeenth year of his reign, Ahmose gave the order for the army of liberation to depart for the North.

*

*The new year began with the flood, approximately at the beginning of July.

The Theban soldiers who had taken part in the raid on Avaris under Kamose's command were greatly moved when they revisited landscapes that were engraved for ever in their memory. The others were venturing into an unknown world which was, none the less, the land of their ancestors.

Thanks to the strong current, the fleet made swift progress. Ahhotep expected to join battle with the enemy at any moment. But the emperor had abandoned the area between the Egyptian front and the outskirts of Memphis. The only soldiers there were Hyksos mercenaries who terrorized the villagers and stole most of their harvests to send to Avaris.

'Majesty,' ventured Emheb, 'we cannot abandon these unfortunate people. If we do, the mercenaries will kill them all.'

To stop or slow the fleet would be fatal, so Ahhotep entrusted a message to Rascal: the three last vessels were to halt and their footsoldiers were to liberate several villages. Once the Hyksos were wiped out, the peasants would be given weapons and, under the command of a Theban officer, would spread the rebellion throughout Middle Egypt.

Neshi was still checking the weapons: straight and curved swords, in imitation of Hyksos weapons, for hand-to-hand combat, bronze-headed spears, light, stabbing daggers, clubs, easily handled axes, bows of various sizes, wooden shields strengthened with bronze, breastplates and helmets. The equipment was of better quality than ever before, but would it be as good as the enemy's?

As the fleet approached its first major objective, an acid test for the army, hearts began to beat faster. Even those who, like Emheb and Ahmes, were used to fierce fighting knew that the next battle would be completely different.

If they were defeated, Egypt would not survive.

The Hyksos officer directing the siege of Memphis was in a foul mood. The heat did not agree with him and, worse still, the annual flood had forced him to alter the deployment of his forces. Soon the Nile would flood the land and much of Egypt would turn into a shallow inland sea.

He had already had to move the horses from several stables on low ground. The animals were being held in an enclosure, ready for evacuation to the north. Only a single chariot unit remained operational and, like the others, it would soon take shelter in the fortress of Taremu, near the sacred city of Iunu.

A soldier came up to him and saluted. 'Artificer officer reporting, Commander.'

'What is it now?'

The artificer was excited. 'We could use the flood to take Memphis once and for all. If we station our archers on pontoons, the river will lift them up to the walls, and they will easily wipe out the defenders. My men will destroy a part of the walls, and our footsoldiers will pour into the city through the breach.'

'It would be a delicate operation, and it isn't in accordance with the orders I've received.'

'I know, sir, but the defenders are at the end of their strength. And the emperor will hardly reproach you for capturing Memphis. Our men want to end this siege, and success should be worth promotion for you.'

Pillaging this rat-hole and then razing it to the ground, at last leaving this camp where he was dying of boredom, achieving total victory . . . The commander let himself be tempted. He would explain to Khamudi, the new commander-in-chief, that the desperate Memphites had made a fatal mistake in attempting a mass break-out.

The order was given to deploy boats side by side, so as to form a sort of wall in the canal closest to the white wall. Next, the pontoons would be placed in the water and the river allowed to do its job.

The last strip of land still accessible to chariots would be flooded within the next few days. So the chariots had been gathered together in the widest section, before being loaded on to cargo-vessels destined for Taremu.

The commander summoned his subordinates and revealed his intentions to them.

A sentry interrupted the meeting.

The commander glared at him. 'What is the meaning of this insolence, soldier?'

'Sir, there are chariots in sight.'

'What nonsense is this?'

'It is not nonsense, I assure you, sir.'

So Khamudi had at last sent reinforcements. But what use would they be during the time of the flood? Angrily, the commander left his tent to have frank words with whoever was in charge of this useless regiment.

The sentry had forgotten to say that the chariots were coming not from the north but from the south.

The astounded commander was the first man to die in the battle of Memphis. An arrow fired by Moustache, who was securely balanced on the platform of a chariot driven by the Afghan, lodged square in the middle of the Hyksos' forehead.

42

The Egyptians could not have wished for better fighting conditions. The Hyksos' horses were gathered on one side, their chariots on the other, their boats moored and unable to manoeuvre, their soldiers busy with domestic tasks. The men commanded by Moustache and the Afghan took instant advantage of the situation, and their skilled archers killed many Hyksos.

This swift and significant breakthrough eased the task facing Emheb's footsoldiers, while the sailors commanded by Moon and Ahmes attacked the enemy vessels. Once the effect of surprise had passed, the emperor's men attempted to regroup, but their units were too isolated from each other.

At the height of the battle, as the Sword of Amon flamed in the pharaoh's hand, the rebels emerged from Memphis and came to the Thebans' aid. Realizing that none of them would emerge unscathed from the fight, the Hyksos fought ferociously. But the Egyptians sensed imminent victory, and cut them down one after another.

'Memphis is free,' Ahmose told his troops, 'and we have captured a considerable number of chariots and horses. But before we celebrate our success let us think of our dead, of all those who have given their lives for Egypt.'

At the sight of the many corpses strewn across the ground

or floating in the canals, Ahhotep felt almost as much grief as if the army had suffered a defeat. War was one of the worst depravities in the world, but what other way was there of defeating the Emperor of Darkness?

Rather than withdrawing into her thoughts, Ahhotep made sure that none of her faithful companions had been wounded or killed. Only Moon was wounded, in the arm. Treated by She-Cat, who hardly knew where to turn, he refused to rest even for a moment, so anxious was he to know the extent of his losses.

Gathering together the least exhausted soldiers and the chariots, Emheb formed a front line north of Memphis, in case the Hyksos reserve troops counter-attacked. If that happened, the apparent victory would be transformed into a disaster. Moustache, the Afghan, their soldiers and horses got their breath back. They, too, knew that they were in no condition to fight off a Hyksos attack.

Evening fell. An oppressive calm hung over the Memphis plain.

'This place is very difficult to defend,' commented Ahhotep.

'The white wall of Memphis will be a valuable ally,' replied Neshi. 'Let us shelter our chariots and horses inside the old city.'

'No one shall sleep until it has been done,' ordered Ahmose.

The Egyptians consolidated their new positions at the edge of the land the Hyksos considered sacred, at once so close and so inaccessible. Although this breathing-space was welcome, it could not last long. Everyone was already thinking about the next objective: Avaris. That was the battle they must win. If they failed, all their sacrifices would have been in vain.

'Our men are ready,' Ahmose told Ahhotep. 'They are afraid, but nevertheless they are ready to attack Apophis's lair. They are aware of the enormity of the task, and no man will flinch in the face of his duty.'

'Marching on Avaris would be madness,' said Ahhotep.

'Mother, we cannot simply give up!'

'I said nothing about giving up. There is a reason why the emperor did not send reinforcements to Memphis: he wanted to find out what we are really capable of. He has tried for a long time to lure us on to his own ground, in the hope of entrapping and defeating our entire army. No, Ahmose, we are not ready.'

'But we must strike into the Delta!'

'Yes, indeed we must, but only when we decide the time is right. After Kamose's raid, the Hyksos will certainly have taken measures to repel any naval attack, and our chariot corps is still too small. We must adapt the Hyksos chariots we captured, make them lighter, and then train men to drive them. Besides, we cannot defeat the emperor with material weapons alone. You and I must go to Saqqara, so that your royal power may be confirmed.'

Young Laughter greatly enjoyed the chariot ride to Saqqara. As he watched attentively, Ahhotep and Ahmose gazed in wonder at the immense burial-ground, which was dedicated to the ancestors who had been reborn into the Light. Pyramids and houses of eternity bore witness to their presence, and their words continued to be passed on, through the radiance of the hieroglyphs and architectural forms.

Dominating the site and seemingly guarding it was the step pyramid of Djoser, built by the masterbuilder Imhotep, whose fame had endured through time. It was a true staircase to heaven, enabling the pharaoh's soul to commune with the stars, then to come back down to earth as the embodiment of the harmony on high.

The pyramid reigned at the heart of a vast ritual space, surrounded by a curtain wall. The king and his mother saw that there was only one entrance and that it was – to all appearances – eternally open.

'That's strange,' said Ahmose. 'Why have the Hyksos not destroyed this shrine? They must know that the royal soul is regenerated here in mystery, away from human eyes.'

'I am quite sure they do,' nodded the queen, 'but the emperor found himself confronted with such power that his evil magic failed.'

The pharaoh made to step through the narrow gateway, but Ahhotep held him back.

'Apophis is undoubtedly still trying to do us harm. If he has left this monument intact, without even destroying the gateway, he must have discovered a way of blocking its radiance.'

'You mean he has locked the regenerative energy inside?'

'That is what I fear. He must have made this gateway impossible to pass through, by placing a curse upon it. So no pharaoh will now be able to feed upon the ancestors' inheritance.'

The queen prayed for a while, calling upon her dead husband and son.

'The curse must be broken,' she told Ahmose. 'I shall do it, for I think I know the name of this gateway.'

'Mother, I—'

'My death does not matter. It is you who must live, to reunite the White Crown and the Red.'

Ahhotep walked forward very slowly. When she reached the stone gateway, she was halted by a blast of icy breath. Then it seemed to her that the uprights were as hot as burning coals, and that they were crowding in on her, trying to crush her. She could not take another step.

'Gateway, I know your name. You are called "Righteousness Gives Life". Since you are known to me, open.'

An intense light began to shine from the beautiful white stone, and the icy wind disappeared.

Ahhotep told Ahmose to follow her, and walked across the narrow space between the sturdy columns. Laughter lay down on the threshold, in the posture of Anubis, and guarded the gateway to the world of the Invisible.

Guided by the spirits of Seqen and Kamose, the queen sensed that the emperor's curse had not been completely destroyed.

When she emerged from the colonnade, she saw several carved cobras on the top of a wall, ready to rear up and strike from the stone. Were they about to attack Ahmose?

She said to them, 'Your task is to open the way of Pharaoh and to cover his enemies with your fire. Have you forgotten the spirit that devised you and the hand that created you? I know your name, O royal serpents: you are the first flame.'

The queen and the snakes stared fixedly at each other, and then the sculptures returned to stone.

Exhausted but serene, Ahhotep could at last gaze upon the great open-air courtyard before the step pyramid. It symbolized the whole of Egypt, over which her son had been called to reign.

43

Apophis now devoted all his time to one of two activities. Either he watched the suffering and death of those he sent to the labyrinth or the bull's arena, or he shut himself away in the secret room and lit a lamp. Its flame glowed with a disturbing greenish light, and in it he witnessed scenes visible only to him.

The High Treasurer had to wait impatiently upon the emperor's pleasure in order to give him the alarming information he had received. 'Majesty, the rebels have retaken Memphis! The regiment besieging the city has been wiped out.'

'I know.'

'Our mercenaries in Middle Egypt have been wiped out, too.'

'I know.'

'Majesty, we must accept that Ahhotep and her son have a formidable army.'

'I know,' said Apophis again. 'The queen has even succeeded in breaking my curse on Saqqara. Now Ahmose is a true war-chief.'

'What are your orders, Majesty?'

'To wait. Although she is still hesitating, Ahhotep will come to us.'

'Should we not attack her before she reaches Avaris?'

'Absolutely not.'

'Forgive me for pressing the point, my lord, but these Egyptians can no longer be taken lightly.'

Apophis's icy gaze stabbed right through Khamudi. 'Do you really I would make such a foolish mistake? Ahhotep is a fitting adversary for me, because I have allowed her to grow. There is a power in her, *the* power I must destroy. If I had acted sooner, she would not have got beyond the borders of Thebes. Now she thinks she is as strong as I am. The flame tells me that her hope for freedom has never been so intense, and it is that very hope which is leading the Egyptians towards the abyss. I am going to inflict on them a defeat so terrible that they will never recover from it. And it is at Avaris, before my citadel, that they will suffer that defeat. Once Ahhotep is dead, not a single one of her countrymen will dare take up arms against me.'

Mad with rage, Khamudi smashed a low table and trampled it underfoot.

'Calm yourself, darling,' begged Yima.

He hurled the remains of the table out of the window. 'The emperor is too old to rule,' he declared through clenched teeth.

'Hush, please! Someone might hear.'

'You're the only one who can hear me, and you aren't the sort of woman who'd betray me, are you?'

She simpered. 'Of course not, my love. And I shan't hide my deepest thoughts from you. You are rid of Jannas now, so don't delay any longer.'

Khamudi was surprised. 'What exactly do you mean?'

'You know as well as I do.'

Memphis was coming back to life. Gradually, the survivors were growing used to the fact that there would be no more Hyksos attacks. Now they could leave the city without fear of being killed, had enough to eat and had begun to talk about the future. With the footsoldiers' help, priests and stone-cutters worked to repair the least badly damaged temples.

The soldiers were relieved not to have to march on Avaris immediately. They awaited a decision by the Council of War, which was meeting at the palace, itself badly damaged during the siege.

'The king's power has been confirmed at Saqqara,' Ahhotep told the council, 'but there is still a danger dogging our steps: our lack of *heka*. Without that magical force, which has helped us to overcome so many obstacles, we stand no chance of defeating the Hyksos forces massed in the Delta. So we must gather the *heka* where it shines forth in its purest form, at Iunu.'

'From what the Memphite rebels have told us,' said Neshi, 'I very much fear that Iunu is out of our reach.'

'Why?'

'Because it is in the area controlled by the fortress of Taremu, the largest in the Delta after Avaris.'

'We know how to deal with fortresses,' Ahhotep reminded him.

'This one is different, Majesty: it has thick walls twenty cubits high, and gates too strong to be broken by battering-rams.'

'Are the monuments of Iunu intact?'

'The emperor has written his name upon the leaves of the sacred tree,' said the mayor of Memphis, 'and so has taken his place in the line of pharaohs. That is why the shrine of Atum is still standing – but it is guarded by Hyksos.'

'In a certain way,' said Neshi sadly, 'the tree has made Apophis immortal. Besides that, he has probably destroyed the source of the *heka*.'

'Before we give up hope,' said Ahhotep, 'we must check this for ourselves.'

*

Mounted on White Giant and Grey, Moustache and the Afghan had gone on a scouting expedition to Taremu. They returned safely, but their news was not good. Built on a promontory beyond reach of the flood, Taremu looked impregnable. Two war-boats blocked the canal linking it to Iunu.

'Our swimmers will damage them so badly that they will eventually sink,' said Moustache.

'And there will be no problems with the Hyksos foot-soldiers at Iunu,' added the Afghan. 'Our chariots will win through.'

'The fortress is bound to send reinforcements to Iunu,' Emheb pointed out. 'Then the emperor will be alerted, thousands of Hyksos will converge on Iunu, and we'll be crushed. We stand no chance of sucess unless we take Taremu.'

'Precisely. So our carpenters must set to work at once,' said Ahhotep. 'Why look elsewhere for the weapon we need when it exists in our own tradition?'

Although he knew of the Egyptian army's victory at Memphis, the commander of Taremu was concerned only with matters of supply. The fortress was temporarily housing a huge number of horses, which had to be fed, and two chariot regiments, which caused a difficult problem of over-crowding. Fortunately, the flood had begun to recede. In a few days' time, his inconvenient guests would be leaving.'

'Commander,' shouted a sentry, 'enemy boats in sight!'

Astonished, the commander climbed to the top of the highest guard-tower.

It was true. Dozens of vessels flying the Queen of Freedom's standard were coming up the canal leading to Taremu's landing-stage. The rebels must have destroyed the guard-boats. Not that that would do them any good. When they reached the high walls, the Egyptians would present perfect targets for the Hyksos archers. Then the great gate would open, and the chariots would charge out and kill all the rebels as they fled.

And the commander of Taremu would have the honour of bearing Queen Ahhotep's head to the emperor.

44

The Egyptian boats halted, out of range of the enemy.

To the Hyksos commander's astonishment, the enemy's best archers were armed with large bows, with which they were able to shoot down many of the Hyksos stationed on the ramparts.

The soldiers of the artificer corps disembarked, carrying enormous wooden beams. Under cover from the archers, and with only light losses, they reached the great gate. The commander smiled. No battering-ram would ever break it down.

But the Egyptians did not even try. On the contrary, they used the beams to bar the gate, trapping the Hyksos inside. Then other footsoldiers arrived, bearing very long ladders mounted on wheels. The archers on the boats began to fire more rapidly, enabling their comrades to raise the ladders against the walls.

Alarmed, the commander ordered all his men to the ramparts. But the ramparts were narrow, and the first attackers were already reaching the tops of the wheeled ladders.

Big-Feet, prisoner number 1790, was the longest-surviving inmate of the camp at Sharuhen. The only thing keeping him alive was the will for revenge. Since death would not take him, he would make the Hyksos pay for the theft of his cows.

218

For several weeks, convoys of deportees had been arriving continuously. They were mostly Egyptians from the Delta, but some were a new category of prisoner, discovering the horrors of the camp for the first time: Hyksos soldiers.

The Hyksos huddled together and avoided the eyes of the women, children and old men who were dying of hunger and suffering at the whims of their torturers. Like them, the former soldiers now had a number branded into their flesh.

One night, an officer approached Big-Feet, who was sleeping on some planks, a vital protection against the mud.

'1790 – you didn't arrive yesterday! What is your secret for surviving in this hell?'

'I will never accept injustice. You, or others like you, stole my cows.'

'Well, my honour and my reason for living were stolen from me.'

'Why are you here?'

'There was a purge. My comrades and I believed that Commander Jannas represented the future. The emperor had him murdered.'

'One Hyksos fewer. Good.'

'There's better news than that, as far as you're concerned. Queen Ahhotep has freed Memphis and captured the fortress of Taremu. Soon she'll attack Avaris.'

Big-Feet wondered if he was dreaming. Then he understood. 'You're lying to torture me, aren't you? You filth! You think it's funny to give me hope again!'

'Don't lose your temper, my friend. It is absolutely true. Now the emperor wants me dead and your queen does, too, so my only chance is to escape.'

Big-Feet was stunned. 'No one can escape from here!'

'I and the other Hyksos will kill the guards. You seem a good fellow, which is why I'm telling you. You can either follow us or rot here in this pigsty.'

Big-Feet wanted to believe the man was telling the truth;

but he did not follow when he and his comrades tried to force the gates of the camp, because he was sure they would fail.

He was right. Cut to pieces, the would-be escapers' bodies were thrown to the pigs.

The chariots and horses captured at Taremu meant that the Egyptians boasted twice as many as before. Now the chariots had to be made lighter, and drivers and archers trained so that they would be fit to fight the Hyksos at Avaris.

As the floodwaters receded, a vast plain was uncovered. Training began immediately, while Ahhotep and Ahmose went to Iunu, which was at last free.

Emptied of its priests and the craftsmen who had formerly worked in the temple workshops, the old city seemed almost dead, sleeping in an oppressive calm. How could it possibly provide *heka*?

All his senses on the alert, Laughter led the queen and the pharaoh to the great Temple of Atum and Ra. Its monumental doorway was closed, so they followed the outer wall round to the little gate of purifications, which had been crudely walled up. A soldier removed the bricks, and Ahhotep and Ahmose went inside.

They saw a gold-tipped obelisk, standing on the primordial mound that had emerged from the ocean of energy when the universe was born. Then they found the sacred tree of Iunu, the huge-branched persea on whose leaves were preserved the names of all the pharaohs.

In accordance with ancient ritual, Ahmose went down on his left knee, his right leg stretched out behind him. He offered the Sword of Amon to the persea tree, so that the Invisible might imbue it with power.

The Wife of God examined the leaves. She was so astonished by what she found that she checked again. This time, there could be no doubt.

'Apophis lied,' she said. 'His name is nowhere on the

leaves of the sun's tree. The persea refused to preserve the memory of that tyrant, so the *heka* of Iunu has not been defiled.'

As Ahhotep wrote the ritual names of Pharaoh Ahmose on the leaves, the Sword of Amon became a ray of light so intense that the king had to close his eyes.

'Come and stand beside me,' said his mother.

She performed the rite of Sechat, who brought the gods' words to life, and Ahmose performed that of Thoth, who passed on their message. As they did so, the young pharaoh's names began to radiate light.

In his heart, he heard the voice of Atum, the indissoluble bond of being and non-being, totality preceding time and space, the first matter from which everything had originated. And the link was recreated with his predecessors, whose protecting magic entered his breath.

'There is more we must do,' said Ahhotep. 'The temple does not yet vibrate as it should.'

Continuing her exploration, she entered a huge shrine. There lay the pieces of two large acacia-wood boats.

'The ship of day and the ship of night,' she murmured. 'If they no longer sail, the rhythms of the cosmos are disturbed and darkness invades the earth. That is why the emperor was able to impose his law.'

Patiently, Ahmose assembled both boats. At the prow of the ship of day stood an Isis made of gilded wood; while Nephthys stood at the prow of the ship of night. Facing each other, the goddesses stretched out their hands to pass across the gold disc that embodied the regenerated light. But there was no disc: Apophis had stolen it and destroyed it.

However, on the ground lay the Amulet of Knowledge,* which the queen hung round her son's neck.

*The *siat*, a word formed from the root *sia*, 'to know intuitively, to be wise'.

'Stand between Isis and Nephthys,' she told him. 'Like every ruler of Egypt, you are the son of the light who returns to the ocean of energy with the evening sun and is reborn in the east with the sun of morning.'

A serene smile lit the goddesses' faces, and they filled the pharaoh's spirit with *heka*.

After Ahhotep and Ahmose had left, a gold disc appeared in the hands of Nephthys, who passed it to Isis in the secrecy of the temple. The ships of day and night had begun to sail again.

45

Far, far from Egypt, the Nubian kingdom of Kerma enjoyed a prosperity which its king, Nedjeh, relished more every day. After trying to get the better of the Hyksos in southern Egypt while proclaiming himself their ally, and then waging war against Queen Ahhotep, Nedjeh now contented himself with his golden existence.

The King of Kerma, once so warlike, had given up fighting. He remained within his kingdom with its rich agriculture, and had grown fat on delicious food. He rarely left his palace, which was built in the Egyptian manner, its windows and doors arranged so as to ensure a constant flow of cool air. He ate five meals a day, sweetened with favours dispensed by the magnificent women of his harem. None of the women allowed her disgust to show, for the old despot's anger still made his subjects tremble. Anyone who displeased him died instantly, their skull smashed, and joined the huge pile of bones in Nedjeh's future tomb, which was even bigger than the tomb of a Theban king.

'You again!' growled the fat man when Ata, head of his security guards, approached the soft bed the king was reclining on.

'My lord, we cannot go on like this. Ahhotep's soldiers, in alliance with the Nubian tribes that betrayed us, make it impossible for us to set foot outside Kerma.'

'That is nothing new, so keep calm.'

Ata was tall, thin and edgy. Nedjeh was always reproaching him for not being able to stand still, but he was a good officer and kept good order in the city.

'Kerma is a warrior kingdom and must regain its pride,' he insisted.

'Those are dangerous dreams. Forget them and make the most of life. I am beginning to tire of some of my women, and I shall graciously give them to you. They will calm your nerves.'

'For too long we were cut off from the outside world and knew nothing of events there,' said Ata. 'I have put an end to our isolation.'

The king frowned. 'What have you done?'

'My best men risked their lives to cross Egyptian-controlled territory and reach Avaris by way of the desert.'

'I did not give permission for anyone to do anything so foolhardy!' thundered the king.

'You must approve of what I did, my lord. You were right to play a waiting game, but it is now time to re-establish our links with the Hyksos and take back the territory we lost.'

'You have lost your mind, Ata!'

'My messengers informed the emperor that Kerma is taking up arms against Egypt again.'

Nedjeh was stunned. 'How dare you!'

'You must approve of what I did,' repeated Ata.

'You are very much mistaken!'

'Then too bad for you.' Ata plunged his sword into Nedjeh's belly as he lay there appalled at this crime of insolence.

The king rose to his feet with menacing slowness. 'I shall crush you, you vermin!'

Ignoring the deadly blade, Nedjeh walked towards Ata, who recoiled in disbelief. How could the fat man still move? Snatching up a bronze lamp-stand, he hit him savagely on the head.

Nedjeh stood still for a moment, then began to move forward again, his face dripping blood. Ata struck again; and this time the king fell. Ata could inform the people of Kerma that they had a new ruler.

'Taremu has fallen,' Khamudi told the emperor, who was huddled in a crudely carved armed chair.

'It does not matter.'

His ankles swollen and painful, his jowls more pendulous than usual, his voice tired, Apophis no longer left the secret room at the heart of the citadel. Only Khamudi had access to it.

'Majesty, the fall of Taremu led to the fall of Iunu.'

Now, thought the emperor, Ahhotep knows that the sacred tree refused to accept my name and that I do not belong to the line of pharaohs. She must die.

'We must not remain passive any longer, Majesty. The queen is winning too many victories. I propose to attack her at once. On the Delta plains our chariots will rout the Egyptian army.'

'Allow her to come right up to the capital,' ordered Apophis. 'My plan is unfolding stage by stage, and it is here that Ahhotep will fall into my hands, here and nowhere else. The more vainglorious her futile victories make her, the more vulnerable she will be.'

'Majesty, I—'

'That is enough, Khamudi. I need to rest. Inform me when Ahhotep reaches the city gates.'

Khamudi's rage knew no bounds. How could he make that senile old man see reason, face up to reality? True, at one time Khamudi had himself opposed deploying the Hyksos forces on more than one front, but the situation had changed completely. Ahhotep and Ahmose's army had just seized a fortress reputed to be impregnable, and had violated the Hyksos shrine.

It was clear what they planned to do: destroy all the Hyksos strongholds in the Delta, one by one, and attack Avaris only when it was isolated. To wait for them would be suicidal. Now that they had made the mistake of venturing on to level ground, the Hyksos chariots could attack and annihilate them. But a chariot attack could not be launched without the emperor's explicit order.

While he was pondering what Yima had said, Khamudi was informed that messengers from the Prince of Kerma had arrived. Good, he thought. He would be able to to take out his temper on the Nubians, whom Ahhotep had reduced to the state of sheep.

'My lord,' said a military-looking young man, 'we bring you greetings from the Prince of Kerma.'

'That coward who does nothing but eat and fornicate?'

'Nedjeh is dead, and Prince Ata is not at all like him. Leading the warriors of Kerma, he will break out of the chains that have bound us for so long.'

'Do you mean he intends to fight the Egyptians?'

'To begin with, he will reconquer all Nubia. Then he will seize the South of Egypt, on condition that you agree not to hinder his onward march.'

Khamudi did not have to think for long. 'I agree.'

'Majesty, Egyptian scouts have been spotted,' said Khamudi.

'At last, she is here! Come, Ahhotep, come to me.' The hatred that filled the emperor's eyes made them impossible to look at.

'Should you not go to the Temple of Set to unleash his rage against the enemy?'

'Ahhotep knows how to ward it off. But you are right: we must not neglect that valuable ally. A fierce storm will strike the Egyptians, and lightning will destroy part of their fleet.'

Khamudi helped the emperor to his feet and led him out of the palace. On the threshold, Apophis got into a travelling-chair. He did not notice the discreet signal Khamudi gave to the leader of the Cypriot guards.

Obsequiously, Khamudi supported Apophis again when he got into the boat that would take him across to the islet where the Temple of Set stood.

'These oarsmen are not members of my personal body-guard,' remarked the emperor.

'No, Majesty, they are my men.'

'What does this mean, Khamudi?'

'That I am taking power.'

'You have lost your head, like Jannas!'

'Jannas bided his time too long. I shall not make the same mistake.'

'You are a only little man, my friend, and you always will be, despite your vanity, your wealth and your sordid scheming.'

Apophis's voice and gaze chilled Khamudi's blood, and he felt his limbs becoming paralysed.

Delving deep into his rage, he drove his fist into the emperor's face, breaking his nose and tearing his lip. With loathing, he plunged a dagger into his heart. As the old man collapsed on to his side, Khamudi seized Apophis's dagger and stabbed him in the back.

Wide-eyed, he stepped away from the corpse.

'Keep on rowing,' he ordered the crew.

When the boat reached the islet, he told them, 'Take this corpse to the altar of Set and burn it.'

'He's still moving!' exclaimed a sailor in terror.

Khamudi grabbed an oar and hit the emperor ten, twenty, a hundred times, until he was no more than a bloody, broken puppet.

Apophis's right hand rose slightly. Hysterical now, Khamudi realised that the old man was wearing protection: at his throat the *ankh*, the cross of life, attached to a gold chain, and on the little finger of his left hand an amethyst scarab on a gold ring. The High Treasurer tore them off and trampled on them.

The old man's hand fell back, motionless at last.

'Quickly, take him and burn him!'

The smoke that rose above the Temple of Set smelt of plague.

46

'It is done,' Khamudi announced to Yima.

'So are you Emperor of the Hyksos now?'

'I am. From now on, everyone will have to obey me without question.'

'That is wonderful, wonderful! But . . . my love, you're covered in black dust and it smells dreadful. Go and wash, quickly, and I'll pour you some of our best wine. And I . . . I am Empress!'

Leaving Yima to dreams of grandeur which were becoming reality, Khamudi hastily summoned all the senior officers and dignitaries to the citadel's audience chamber.

'Emperor Apophis has died,' he said. 'I had the sad privilege of carrying out his last wishes: that his body should be burnt on the altar of the Temple of Set, and that I should succeed him in order to maintain the greatness of the empire.'

There was no one left capable of opposing his seizure of power. Through his purges of the army and his complete control of the Hyksos economy, he had eliminated all his rivals. Everyone therefore bowed before the new emperor, who felt his chest swell with pride. This was more intoxicating than all his drugs put together!

Walking rather unsteadily, as though he were drunk, Khamudi entered Apophis's private apartments. The former emperor's guards had been killed that very morning by

Khamudi's Cypriots, and he had ordered Aberia to send all Apophis's servants to Sharuhen. A clean sweep: that was the watchword, and it also applied to objects. Every memory of the tyrant must disappear, with the exception of the Minoan paintings, whose freshness pleased Khamudi.

Yima ran from one room to another, weeping, laughing, kissing one servant girl and slapping the next, lying down on a bed, getting up, demanding a drink, forgetting her cup, taking quantities of drugs and shrieking as she ripped up her old dresses.

'We have succeeded! I am Empress! Empress, just think of it!'

She threw her arms round her husband's neck, but he pushed her away and said, 'We have work to do. The purge must continue, and you must investigate everyone who works in the citadel. If there is the slightest suspicion about any of them, Aberia must get rid of them.'

Leaving his wife to her own devices, Khamudi summoned the senior officers of the army and war-fleet. He was determined to prepare a counter-attack which would enable him to retake Taremu, Iunu and Memphis, while the new Prince of Kerma's Nubians poured into Upper Egypt. Forced to fall back to Thebes, Ahhotep would be caught in the crossfire.

Khamudi wanted her alive. For her, he would invent hitherto unknown tortures, so that she would die as slowly as possible, in unbearable agony.

Lost in his thoughts, the new emperor bumped into the elderly man he had appointed to command the fleet.

'Egyptians, my lord!'

'What do you mean, "Egyptians"?'

'They are here!'

Why was this imbecile repeating the lie he had told Apophis to induce him to leave the citadel? 'Return to your post immediately.'

'You don't understand, my lord! The Egyptians are attacking Avaris!'

'Don't talk nonsense. Our lookouts would have spotted them long ago.'

'No, because they did not come from the south.'

'That's impossible!'

'We await your orders, my lord.'

The Hyksos would be expecting an attack similar to the one led by Kamose. So Ahhotep had proposed doing something totally different: attacking Avaris in several different ways and places at the same time. It meant first destroying all the lookout posts, then throwing the entirety of the Egyptian forces into the battle.

The Afghan and Moustache saw to that, while the queen strengthened the guard around Ahmose. If the Hyksos spy was still active, he would try to kill the pharaoh in order to halt the forward march. More than ever, Young Laughter was on his guard.

'There is Avaris,' said Emheb with emotion.

At last Ahhotep set eyes upon the capital of the Empire of Darkness!

Like his mother, Pharaoh Ahmose was impressed by the extent of the site, the size of the naval base and trading-port and, above all, by the vastness of the citadel. No fortress could compare with it.

When the Egyptian troops saw the countless Hyksos war-vessels, and the chariots lined up on the eastern bank, they were afraid. Everyone had prepared themselves for this moment, but no one had imagined that the enemy would be so terrifying.

'We are walking into a massacre,' predicted Neshi, white-faced.

'What do our two most intrepid officers think?' asked Ahhotep.

'Neshi is right,' nodded Moustache.

'For once,' admitted the Afghan, 'my colleague here isn't wrong.'

'It would be better to fall back than to suffer a crushing defeat,' advised Emheb. 'I know that you have never retreated, Majesty, but no one will criticize you for it.'

Moon's silence showed that he agreed with his colleagues.

But in her son's eyes the queen saw very different intentions.

'Look at the Hyksos,' said Ahmose. 'They are running about in all directions like frightened animals. Our attacking deployment is excellent, and it will compensate for our shortfall in men and weapons. Every man to his post immediately. When the drums beat, all our units are to act according to the agreed plan.'

Khamudi had not crumbled; quite the contrary. He was so enraged at the prospect of the Egyptians attacking Avaris that he ordered his officers even more fiercely to regain control of their soldiers. Were the Hyksos not superior to their enemies? Was Avaris not impregnable?

The real battle was about to begin, and it absolutely must be won. Fired by their new commander's determination, the Hyksos organized themselves. The chariot-drivers and their crews leapt into their vehicles, the sailors rushed to their positions, and the archers took their places in the citadel's towers.

The Egyptian flagship, the *Golden Falcon*, entered the canal that led to the citadel's landing-stage, followed by several other vessels. It was the fatal mistake Khamudi had been hoping for! Imitating his elder brother, Ahmose was trying to seize the ports – but they would soon become graveyards for the Egyptian boats.

But the *Golden Falcon* halted halfway along the canal, while other ships entered the northern canal to attack the

Hyksos vessels from the rear, to the heady beat of the drums.

This unpleasant surprise was followed by a much worse one: out of the flagship came a chariot, drawn by two horses and driven by the pharaoh himself, wearing the White Crown of Upper Egypt. On the vehicle's sides were painted Hyksos, bound and kneeling.

'They have managed to build a chariot!' gasped Khamudi.

'Not one chariot, my lord,' a horrified general corrected him. 'Hundreds of them.'

At top speed, the Egyptian chariots thundered down on the Hyksos.

47

Ahhotep firmly believed that only combined and surprise actions would give the Egyptians a chance of victory.

The flagship and her escort vessels acted as a lure for the Hyksos war-fleet, which – wrongly – thought they would be easy prey. A fierce battle commenced, during which other Egyptian vessels approached along the northern canal and cut the enemy fleet in half. Meanwhile the naval footsoldiers commanded by Emheb and Ahmes used fortified barges to attack and board the heavy Hyksos vessels, catching them completely off guard. On both fronts, the Egyptians' enthusiasm and mobility enabled them to fight the opponent on an equal footing.

There remained the main arena, on which the outcome of the battle of Avaris would depend. Whose chariots would gain the upper hand?

At first taken aback by the Egyptian attack on level ground with two-man vehicles, the Hyksos chariot commander sent a regiment up the line to sweep away everything in its path.

On an order from Ahmose, the Egyptians swerved aside and fired on the enemy's flanks. Most shots reached their targets. Horses fell, causing absolute chaos in which many Hyksos were wounded or killed. Like a swarm of hornets, Pharaoh's chariots rushed at their opponents, which were slower and less manoeuvrable. The archers killed the enemy drivers. Uncontrolled, the horses crashed into each other and caused confusion which spread to other driverless teams.

The Egyptians observed the orders to avoid head-on confrontation with the Hyksos, and to attack them from the side and the rear. As expert charioteers, Moustache and the Afghan had a fine hunt in prospect. Surrounded by the chariots that Ahhotep had ordered to protect him, Pharaoh Ahmose fired arrow after arrow.

Amid the appalling cacophony of neighing horses and men screaming in pain, the Hyksos found themselves surrounded. The Egyptians encircled them, and gave no quarter.

Then a new wave of Hyksos chariots began a counter-attack. Ahhotep watched anxiously, afraid it might turn the tide of the battle. Would the exhausted Egyptians manage to contain it?

But the new chariots' wheels were those Arek the storeman had weakened, and most gave way as soon as the chariots picked up speed. So those which ought to have changed the the course of the battle added to the rout in their own ranks, which were now unable to defend themselves.

Urged on by Ahmose, the Egyptian chariot troops, both men and horses, redoubled their efforts. Spears and arrows rained down murderously.

Things were not going well on the flagship. After repelling two boarding-parties, the Egyptian sailors were beginning to yielding to weight of numbers. It would take a bold breakthrough by Moon to avert the worst. He pulled back from the northern canal, which enabled several Hyksos boats to regroup and retake control of this route to Avaris.

She-Cat heated a knife in the fire and cauterized a deep sword-cut in the Afghan's flank. Although made of stern stuff, he could not repress a moan of pain.

'You were lucky,' she told him. 'It looks bad but it isn't serious.'

'What about me?' complained Moustache. 'Don't I get any treatment?'

'All you have is scratches.'

'But I'm covered in blood and I almost died a hundred times!'

'First I must treat the serious cases. You and the other survivors must help me.'

There were countless wounded, and She-Cat and her staff were overwhelmed with work, but the Egyptian chariots had just won their first great victory. But there was no celebration in the ranks, because the citadel was still intact, defying them with its massive bulk.

The time came for reports, which Ahhotep and Ahmose listened to attentively in the flagship's cabin.

'A quarter of our chariots have been destroyed,' said Neshi, 'but we have captured a great deal of equipment. Our soldiers acquitted themselves admirably. First thing tomorrow, we must train new drivers to replace the dead. Fortunately, the countryside around here is lush, so the horses will be well fed.'

'I've nothing to add,' said Moustache, and the Afghan nodded.

'How is your wound, Afghan?' asked the queen anxiously.

'It will keep me out of the front line for a few days, Majesty, but I can still train the new charioteers.'

'Ten boats were sunk or badly damaged,' said Moon, 'and there were heavy casualties among the sailors and foot-soldiers aboard them. Fortunately, the Hyksos fleet was hit much harder than our own, but it is still large and has massed in the northern canal. I would advise against renewing battle immediately, because our men are exhausted.'

'I shall need time to organize supplies,' said Neshi, and that is not likely to be easy. Our brave men must have proper food and sleeping-quarters.'

'Our mobile ladders cannot be used,' said Emheb. 'The citadel's walls are too high and, unlike at Taremu, the Hyksos archers are perfectly protected by the crenellations. They are out of range, and will kill any soldiers who try to get near the walls.'

Ahhotep agreed that these arguments were valid. Despite their bravery, the Egyptian troops had been only half successful.

'I am very worried,' confessed Neshi. 'There must still be many thousands of Hyksos in the east of the Delta, and yet more in Syria and Canaan. The emperor will summon them to the rescue of Avaris, and we shall be overwhelmed.'

'Withdrawal is out of the question,' said Ahmose. 'We must take Avaris, no matter what the cost.'

'Indeed we must, Majesty,' agreed Emheb, 'but it will be a long siege, very long.'

'We all need to rest and reflect,' said Ahhotep.

What a strange night! Although the starry sky was that of Lower Egypt, the black earth, the canals and the fields still belonged to the Emperor of Darkness.

Ahhotep thought of Kamose who, with only slender resources, had launched the first attack on Avaris and had succeeded in pillaging its trading-port. Had it not been for the Hyksos spy, he would have caused much more serious damage. But he, too, would have been powerless in the face of this citadel, which seemed to scorn Ahmose's army.

Until now, each time the army had encountered an obstacle the queen had found a way to overcome it or to go round it. This time, the obstacle seemed insurmountable. Nevertheless, Ahhotep had known since she was a girl that, when no way through existed, you must create one.

Allowing her thoughts to wander among the stars, the eternal dwelling-place of Pharaohs Seqen and Kamose, she went toward Ahmose's tent, to check that all the guards were on the alert. During the battle the Hyksos spy had been unable to make any move, but he might try now.

All was well. The king's bodyguard was made up of his most loyal men, and ensured that he had the best protection possible. Young Laughter, lying in the doorway of the tent, slept with one eye open. Moreover, all the king's food and drink was tasted by two volunteer cooks, so the spy could not poison the pharaoh.

The ships of night and day were sailing again. Ahhotep watched the passing of the old sun to the new, and its rebirth in the east, after it had vanquished the serpent of darkness in the lake of flame.

By dawn, the queen's decision was made. Either the army of liberation would take Avaris, or it would be annihilated.

48

Thanks to the drugs Khamudi had had distributed, the Hyksos soldiers were not afraid of the Egyptians. Some felt their anxieties vanish, others felt capable of fighting ten enemies at once. Some of the lower-quality drug had even been distributed among the city's population, so that they would not give way to panic.

It was clear that Ahhotep and Ahmose were interested in only one objective: the citadel. But they had no means of getting inside it. The siege would crumble, and the reinforcements from the Delta and Canaan would inflict a decisive defeat upon them.

From the top of the main watchtower, Khamudi observed the enemy. They were doing something very strange. The archers and ship's soldiers were embarking on the war-boats, which, one by one, were entering the canals and the lake of Avaris. At the prow of the flagship stood Pharaoh Ahmose, easily recognizable because he wore the White Crown.

They want to destroy my fleet, thought the new emperor, the better to encircle Avaris.

'Find me a first-rate archer,' he ordered the officer standing nearest him. 'Have him take a light boat with two good oarsmen to within firing range of that insolent little king.'

*

The boat commanded by Ahmes, son of Abana, had been renamed 'He Who Appears in Glory at Memphis' since the liberation of that great city. Ahmes and his skilled archers had ravaged the enemy ranks, thus making it easier to board their ships. Already, two Hyksos vessels had fallen into the hands of the Egyptians.

As he looked around, Ahmes spotted a light boat. On board were three bare-chested men, two of them oarsmen rowing fast.

Suddenly the oarsmen slowed their pace. When the third man stood up and took an arrow from his quiver, Ahmes saw that he was looking towards the flagship. The pharaoh! The Hyksos archer wanted to kill the pharaoh, whose White Crown was glinting in the sun!

Ahmes drew his bow and fired; he scarcely had time to aim. The shot grazed the head of the Hyksos, who was so shocked and afraid that he dropped his weapon. Abandoning his comrades, he threw himself into the water.

As a precaution, Ahmes killed the two oarsmen. Then, enraged at the thought that this vermin could have harmed the king, he dived in, too.

Swimming with a powerful, rhythmic overarm stroke,* he soon caught the Hyksos. He punched him hard on the back of the neck before dragging him to the bank and throwing him on to his back like a sack of grain. Although only semi-conscious, the prisoner made a grab for Ahmes's dagger. Ahmes held him down, cut off his hand and then knocked him out properly.

'Commander Ahmes, son of Abana, I award you the gold collar for bravery,' declared Pharaoh Ahmose, hanging a slender collar about the officer's neck.

*This stroke, a form of the crawl, was used as early as the Old Kingdom.

Ahmes's reputation was steadily growing in the Egyptian army, which had seized several Hyksos boats. Soon the fight would begin again, intense and murderous.

Ahmes bowed. 'May I request a favour, Majesty?'

'Speak.'

'Will you grant me the honour of commanding your personal bodyguard, so that I may be the first to protect you in all circumstances?'

'After what you have just accomplished, I grant your request willingly.'

Queen Ahhotep raised her eyebrows. What if Ahmes was the Hyksos spy? What if his brave deed had been a deception, designed to win the pharaoh's trust? As head of Ahmose's bodyguard, he would always be close to the king, and sooner or later would have the ideal chance to kill him.

She shook her head. These suspicions were absurd. Ahmes had served in the army since he was a youth and had risked his life a hundred times, fighting the Hyksos in an exemplary fashion. Nevertheless, she would warn her son to be on his guard.

'We shall now question the prisoner,' decided Ahmose.

The Hyksos' wounds had been treated but he was terrified, and dared not raise his eyes to look at the king.

'Tell me your rank and station.'

'Leading archer in the regiment of the lower citadel.'

'Describe the interior to us,' ordered Ahhotep.

'I was never allowed inside. All I know is that it houses enough soldiers and supplies to hold out for years.'

'Who gave you the order to fire on Pharaoh?'

'Khamudi – Emperor Khamudi.'

'Don't you mean Emperor Apophis?'

'No, Apophis is dead – or, rather, the High Treasurer killed him, and his body was burnt. Now Khamudi is the emperor.'

'If you want us to spare your life, go and tell him that the pharaoh has been seriously wounded.'

'Oh no, Majesty!' cried the Hyksos. 'Khamudi would never believe me! I'd be thrown into the labyrinth or the bull arena.' He told them in detail about the ordeals and tortures so beloved of the former and the present emperor alike, and begged, 'Kill me now.'

'When we have won this war,' decreed Ahhotep, 'you shall become the servant of Ahmes, son of Abana.'

All the workers in the weapons storehouses of Avaris had taken cheap drugs and were dreaming dreams in which they were impervious to Egyptian arrows and spears.

All except Arek, who could hardly contain his delight. At last the Egyptians were attacking Avaris! Khamudi might be another fearsome brute, but the death of Apophis had weakened the Hyksos.

After the chariot-wheels, Arek had secretly weakened the bows: when they were drawn, the wood would snap. This was much easier than his work on the wheels, but it was also more dangerous, because he was not authorized to be in that storehouse. So he had to wait until his colleagues were asleep to unbar the door and work through the night.

'What are you doing there, my little man?'

Arek froze.

It was the gravelly voice of his overseer, whose resistance to drugs was unbelievable. 'This evening I noticed that you did not take any drugs, and that interested me. You have no right to be here.'

'I . . . I wanted a bow.'

'That is theft. And the theft of a weapon in wartime is a crime.'

'Forget it, and I'll do the same for you.'

'I haven't anything wrong! You're coming with me to the citadel to explain yourself to our new emperor. If you have anything to hide, he will make you confess it. And he will thank me.'

Arek leapt forward, knocked him down and ran out of the storehouse. The overseer shouted to the guards patrolling the quayside. At once a terrible burning sensation tore through Arek's shoulder as a spear hit him. Ignoring the pain, he threw himself into the canal.

He could not swim, but at least this death was gentler than torture.

49

Yima clung to her husband's arm, her eyes unfocused and her gait unsteady. 'Are we really safe, my Emperor?'

'You have taken too much of the drug,' commented Khamudi.

'But we must combat fear. Here, no one is afraid of the Egyptians any more, because you are omnipotent, the country's sole master. And I am helping you. With the aid of my friend Aberia, we shall execute all the traitors.'

'That's an excellent idea. If you have no proof, choose a suspect at random, assemble those close to him and kill him in front of them. Everyone must understand that Khamudi is invulnerable.'

Delighted at the prospect of such fun, the empress went off to join Aberia, while the emperor called a meeting of his generals.

'The battle is beginning to rage on the canals and the lake,' one of them told him. 'Contrary to what we thought, Ahhotep and Ahmose are not interested in the citadel. Their goal seems to be to destroy our fleet. They will not succeed in doing so before our reinforcements arrive. Unfortunately, it is no use sending out raiding-parties to kill the pharaoh, because he is very wary and no longer shows himself in the open.'

'Change the guard every three hours. Fill the watchtowers and battlements with archers,' ordered Khamudi.

The Flaming Sword

*

While Ahhotep, Emheb and Moon were directing the naval battle and taking care to prolong it as much as possible, Ahmose was far from Avaris, on the road used by supply caravans. Guarded by Laughter and Ahmes, he was carrying out his mother's plan: to cut the trading-route and prevent Hyksos reinforcements from Canaan and the eastern Delta reaching Avaris. He had already captured several consignments of food, which provided his soldiers with a feast.

Now the chariot regiment commanded by Moustache was engaging its Canaanite counterpart, while the Afghan and his men fought the Hyksos from the Delta. Maintaining contact with them through Rascal and the other carrier-pigeons, Ahmose was able to hurry to wherever his troops were in difficulty.

Although outnumbered, the Egyptians made good use of their greater mobility. Under the burning sun, the Sword of Amon flashed out such intense brilliance that every soldier felt filled with inexhaustible energy.

Not the seasons, the months, days, nights, hours or anything else counted now. All that mattered was the battle of Avaris in which, little by little, the Egyptian war-fleet was gaining the upper hand. In She-Cat's absence Ahhotep took charge of the wounded, most of whom demanded to return to the front. Now they were so close to their goal, no one would give in, although the proud citadel still looked down haughtily on the fierce fighting.

'We have sunk their best boats,' announced Emheb. 'At last we have a marked superiority in numbers.'

Rascal chose this moment to perch upon Ahhotep's shoulder. As usual, she lavished caresses upon him before reading the precious message he bore.

The queen thought constantly of her son, fervently hoping that he really was protected; she could never forget the battle

Christian Jacq

in which her husband had been betrayed and murdered. But they had no other choice. Unless Ahmose could block the Hyksos reinforcements' way, the Egyptian army would be crushed.

Emheb could not hide his anxiety. 'Is there any news, Majesty?'

'The reinforcements from Canaan have had to retreat.'

'What about those from the Delta?'

'They have fallen back, too, but our chariot regiments have suffered severe losses. Pharaoh asks us to send him more men and equipment.'

'It would be possible, but we would be very much weakened here. If the Hyksos tried to break out of the citadel, it would be a very close-run thing.'

'Then, Emheb, we must finish off their war-fleet.'

At the sight of Ahhotep's sceptre, which symbolized the power of Thebes, the Egyptians forgot their exhaustion and their wounds. On both the lake and the canals, their vessels rushed to attack the enemy. And despite a bad spear-wound in his leg, Moon cut off the hands of the last Hyksos captain, who had fought to the death.

'Majesty, ought we not to try to break out?' suggested a Hyksos general.

'Absolutely not!' said Khamudi angrily. 'Do you not understand that that is exactly what the Egyptians are waiting for? We no longer have a single boat, Ahhotep has blocked all the canals, and Avaris is surrounded. In other words, our chariots would fall into a trap. We are safe only inside the citadel.'

The general and his fellow officers all wondered what had happened to the thunderbolt of war, which was supposed to ravage everything in its path.

'Is there at least some news of our troops from Canaan and the Delta?' fumed the new emperor.

246

'No, Majesty, but they will be here soon.'

'Have our links with the North been cut?'

'It would appear so, my lord. No messengers can now get though to Avaris. Nevertheless, you may be certain that our men will swarm down on the Egyptians like locusts.'

To calm his nerves, Khamudi attended a mass execution. With great pleasure, Aberia strangled the supposed traitors one after the other.

Each day, the Queen of Freedom shared her soldiers' meals, which were of dried fish or pork, garlic, onions, bread and grapes, washed down with small beer. After the privilege of spending time with her, every man felt his courage renewed.

'The Hyksos couldn't eat this,' laughed a footsoldier, 'because they are forbidden to eat pork. Me, I'm dreaming of a good meal of roast pork with lentils.'

'Thank you, soldier,' said the queen. 'You have given me an excellent idea for sending a message to Emperor Khamudi.'

The soldier gaped, and his comrades all began to tease him. The queen prepared a pigskin water-bag, into which she slipped an inscribed tablet.

'Boat coming!' shouted a Hyksos lookout.

Immediately, the citadel's archers took up their positions, and a deluge of arrows rained down upon the war-boat, which did not respond.

'Cease fire,' ordered Khamudi.

The boat ran fast to a quay to the north of the citadel, and halted.

'It's one of ours,' said an archer, 'but there's no one aboard.'

'Look, at the top of the mainmast!' urged his neighbour.

From it there hung a wooden effigy of a man dressed in a black breastplate and with a water-skin on its head.

'It must be a message from the enemy,' said an officer.

'Go and fetch it,' commanded the emperor.

'Me, my lord? But—'

'Are you daring to argue?'

Faced with either being tortured to death or else falling beneath a rain of Egyptian arrows, the officer chose the second. Climbing across from the top of the ramparts with the aid of a rope, he was utterly astonished still to be alive when he reached the top of the mast and retrieved the strange effigy.

Safe and sound, he reappeared before Khamudi. 'Do not touch this water-skin, Majesty. It is a horror – it's made of pigskin!'

'Open it.'

The officer took out the tablet, and laid it on a crenellation in disgust. Ahhotep's message informed Khamudi that he could no longer count on getting help, because his troops had been halted by Ahmose.

'Throw that thing away.'

The officer obeyed.

'You stink of pig – you are impure. Bring me a cloth for my hands, quickly!'

Using the cloth so as not so soil his hands, Khamudi grabbed the water-skin, put it over the officer's head and pushed him off the battlements.

50

The fighting had ground to a halt again. From the safety of his citadel, Khamudi still sneered down at Ahhotep and her forces. As for Ahmose, he could not continue his offensive. In the months – no, years – to come, he would have to be content with consolidating the new front and barring the road to Khamudi's hoped-for reinforcements.

The queen sat beside Way-Finder, gazing at the magnificent sunset in all its many-coloured splendour. The donkey was tired after a long day carrying weapons and provisions, and was glad of this quiet moment. Suddenly, as she sat there Ahhotep realized the truth.

Once the Egyptian camp was soundly asleep, she summoned Moon, Emheb and Neshi.

'Avaris is impregnable because of Apophis's magic,' she said, 'but until the citadel has been destroyed all our efforts will come to nothing. It is my responsibility to destroy it by honouring the ancestors. Without them, Ahmose will not win the war, and will never unite the Red Crown and the White. I must leave at once.'

Moon was horrified. 'Leave? I don't understand, Majesty.'

'I am going to the Isle of the Flame, where I shall implore the ancestors to come to Pharaoh's aid. Continue to prosecute the siege while I am away.'

'How many soldiers will you need?' asked Neshi.

'Two oarsmen.'

Emheb was outraged. 'It's too dangerous, Majesty,' he protested.

Ahhotep simply smiled.

'Are we to tell the king?' asked Neshi anxiously.

'Of course. If I have not returned in twenty-eight days' time, ask him to fall back to Thebes. Amon shall be our final bulwark.'

Using the network of waterways, Ahhotep's boat crossed vast stretches of the Delta populated by goats and sheep kept for their wool. Civets ran away as they approached the landing-stage, watched by wild bulls half hidden in the tall grass. Everyone had to be constantly on the alert for hippopotami, which had to be left undisturbed, or crocodiles, which could be driven off by thrashing the water with oars.

The boat sailed on a shallow lake, bursting with fish such as Nile perch, grey mullet and silurids. The queen and her oarsmen smeared their skin with ointment to avoid being bitten by the swarms of mosquitoes.

Little by little, the papyrus thickets grew thicker until they were impenetrable.

'We cannot go any further in this boat, Majesty,' said one of the oarsmen. 'We must build you a raft.'

The two men laid bundles of papyrus on a frame of interwoven branches, and bound the whole thing up with ropes.

'Wait for me here,' said the queen. She drove a long pole down into the mud, then pushed hard on the pole, thus moving the raft forwards.

Alone, she entered a dark, hostile forest. Hundreds of birds and small predators lived in this perpetually flooded area, where the vegetation was more than three times the height of a man. Ibis, hoopoes, lapwings and woodcock bred here, despite attacks by civets and wild cats.

Suddenly, she saw a net stretched between two posts, and poled the raft to a halt.

Someone was watching her.

'Show yourself,' she commanded.

There were four of them. Four naked, bearded fishermen.

'Well I'll be damned!' exclaimed the oldest. 'It's a woman! A woman, here!'

'She must be a goddess,' said a red-haired fellow, 'unless . . . You wouldn't by any chance be that Queen of Freedom, the one all the Hyksos want to kill?'

'And you wouldn't by any chance be their allies?' asked the queen.

'Absolutely not. It's their fault that we're starving to death.'

'Then take me to Buto.'

The fisherman froze. 'That is a sacred place and no one can enter it. There are monsters there, and they devour the unwary.'

'Then take me near the place, and I shall go in alone.'

'As you wish, but it's very dangerous. The place is infested with crocodiles.'

'My cornelian staff will keep them at a distance.'

Impresssed by the queen's calmness and confidence, the four men helped her into a papyrus boat and skilfully steered it into a maze which could only be negotiated by those who knew it intimately. At the end of the day they stopped by a low mound or bank, and ate an evening meal of grilled fish and bitter-tasting papyrus stems.

'The Hyksos tried to explore these marshes,' said the red-haired man, 'but none of them came out alive. We shall sleep now, and tomorrow we'll set you on your way to Buto.'

When they awoke, one of the fishermen had disappeared.

'It's Loudmouth, an odd, half-crazy fellow,' said the redhead. 'He's stolen fish from us before now – a fine thing to do!'

After several hours of arduous travel, the thickets began to open out. The forest disappeared, giving way to a lake across which ran a narrow strip of land.

'All you have to do is cross it to reach the island of Buto. We shall wait a while for you here. But you must realize that you won't be coming back.'

Armed only with her cornelian staff, Ahhotep hurried towards the resting-place of the spirits of the first kings of Egypt and those of their divine ancestors, the Souls of Pe and Nekhen, the two mythical cities built in their honour on the island of the first morning of the world.

The queen walked with a light step. The birds had fallen silent, and the water was incredibly clear.

Then she saw it. An island, planted with tall palm-trees sheltering two shrines guarded by statues, the first group representing falcon-headed men, the second men with the heads of jackals.

At the instant Ahhotep stepped into this sacred place, a flame flared up from its centre. She stopped, and the flame changed into a cobra crowned with a gold disc.

Ahhotep was in the presence of the Eye of Ra, the Divine Light.

This was where the impossible marriage was accomplished between water and fire, earth and sky, time and eternity.

'I have come to seek the aid of the Souls,' said the queen. 'You who have brought together that which was scattered, you who have accomplished the Great Work, permit Pharaoh Ahmose to wear the Double Crown, upon which the Eye of Ra shall rest to light his way.'

A long silence began. When it was as deep as the *Nun*, the ocean of primordial energy, the voices of the ancestors sounded in Ahhotep's heart. Her cornelian staff was now topped by a rearing gold serpent, wearing the Double Crown.

The queen would have liked to stay on the island and enjoy

for a little longer the peace that reigned there, but harsh battles still awaited her.

She retraced her steps across the strip of land. When she came within earshot of the papyrus forest, she heard shouts and the sounds of a struggle. The water was red with the blood of the three fishermen.

Loudmouth appeared, leading a patrol of Hyksos with their black helmets and breastplates. He had guided them through the labyrinth of foliage.

Ahhotep had no chance of escape.

51

To run like a terror-stricken animal towards the island, which she had no hope of reaching, and to be felled by an arrow in the back as she fled. That was a fate unworthy of a queen. So Ahhotep turned to face the Hyksos.

'It's her,' shouted Loudmouth, 'it's really her, the Queen of Freedom!'

She gazed at him with such contempt that he took fright and hid behind a soldier.

When they saw the beautiful queen walking composedly towards them, the Hyksos drew back. They felt sure her poise must conceal a curse against which their swords would be powerless.

'She's unarmed,' cried Loudmouth, 'and she's only a woman! Seize her!'

The soldiers pulled themselves together. Taking her prisoner would earn them a fabulous reward.

When they were only a few paces from their prey, a dolphin leapt gracefully nearby and swam towards the strip of land.

Its eyes called to Ahhotep. She dived into the water.

'Catch her! Go on, catch her!' roared Loudmouth.

But the Hyksos soldiers did not dare try, because the weight of their breastplates would have drowned them, so the traitor leapt in and set off alone in pursuit of the queen.

With a movement of supreme elegance, the dolphin ripped open his face with its sharp dorsal fin, which it used to slice open the fragile bellies of crocodiles.

As the Hyksos hurled their swords and daggers at her, the queen clung on to the dolphin, which towed her away to the south. Without a guide, the emperor's soldiers would never find their way out of the papyrus forest alive.

The dolphin was nicknamed 'Sun-Disc', and as if by magic he always saw that the nets of the fishermen who were his friends were well filled. He brought the queen to where the two Egyptian oarsmen were waiting for her.

Like Tany, Yima loathed Egyptian art, especially pottery. She refused to allow into the capital anything but egg-shaped Hyksos jars of the Canaanite type, narrow-mouthed and with two handles. Each year, Avaris took delivery of more than eight thousand of them. The most beautiful ones, which were covered with a bright-pink glaze, were reserved for the military aristocracy.

Despite the official ban on making traditional pottery, one old craftsman had dared to use his wheel. Reported by the wife of a Syrian officer, he had just been strangled by Aberia in front of his colleagues. They had become slaves, and realized that the same fate awaited them before long.

'There's to be a meeting tomorrow morning at the lame man's house,' said the dead craftsman's son.

The only people living in most of the Hyksos houses where the enslaved potters worked were the wives and children of officers who were in the citadel or campaigning in Anatolia. 'A meeting at the lame man's house' – the lame man was the father of Arek, the storeman who had killed himself to escape torture – had a special meaning: they would no longer bear the humiliation and intended to rid themselves of their tormentors.

First thing the following morning, the empress once again summoned all the former potters to a small square in Avaris. Behind her stood Aberia and some guards.

'You have not learnt your lesson, you obstinate ruffians! What madman left an old-style pot outside the house of the rebel who was executed yesterday? Unless the culprit confesses, you will all die.'

Intoxicated by her new power, Yima rejoiced. After these, she would kill some more craftsmen.

'I did,' confessed the old man's son.

'Step forward.'

Head lowered, hesitant, the guilty man obeyed.

'You know the fate that lies in store for you.'

'Have pity, Majesty!'

'You sicken me, you band of cowards! Do you think your Queen of Freedom is going to save you? Well, you're very much mistaken. The reinforcements will soon be here, she will be taken prisoner, and I shall torture her with my own hands.'

The potter fell at the empress's feet. 'I am sorry, Majesty. Have pity!'

Yima spat on him. 'You and your accomplices are lower than the beasts.'

The potter suddenly leapt up and slit the empress's throat with a shard of glass hidden in his right hand. Blood instantly soaked the front of her dress. While he finished her off, his colleagues rushed at the guards. Taken by surprise at this violence from men they had regarded as sheep who were incapable of fighting, the guards were slow to react. Since they had nothing left to lose, the craftsmen struck and struck again.

Directed by Aberia, however, the guards soon regained the upper hand and immediately put all the rebels to the sword.

'You look as stupid dead as you did alive,' commented Aberia, looking down at Yima's body.

*

As soon as Ahhotep returned, to great acclaim from her soldiers, Emheb entrusted a message to Rascal so that he could alert Ahmose. The legend of the Queen of Freedom had just acquired a new chapter.

'The Souls of the ancestors are protecting us,' she declared. 'Ahmose now belongs to their line. So that you shall have no doubts, and so that Emperor Khamudi is aware of the punishment that awaits him, let us approach the citadel.'

Emheb frowned. 'Majesty, what exactly are you planning to do?'

'Have a platform built.'

Artificers carried out the order, but the queen was not satisfied. 'Move it closer to the citadel.'

'We cannot, Majesty. You would be within range of their arrows.'

'Khamudi must understand clearly what I have to say to him.'

To avoid digging a new grave in the palace burial-ground, which was small and overcrowded, Khamudi had Tany's grave reopened. Yima's body, still in the bloodstained dress, was thrown on top of her predecessor's, then they were covered with earth again.

She had been a great help to Khamudi, who had enjoyed the perverse games she had so cunningly devised. But today, as supreme commander of the Hyksos, he was not displeased to be rid of her. A hundred craftsmen had been beheaded as a reprisal, and Aberia would now be at the emperor's side at all times, so as to ensure his safety.

'My lord, the Egyptians are about to attack the citadel,' an officer warned him.

Khamudi ran up the steps to the highest tower, taking them four at a time. The attackers had indeed assembled, but at a good distance from the ramparts. All except Ahhotep, who was standing on a platform not far away, brandishing a staff made of cornelian.

'Look, Khamudi,' she said loudly and clearly, 'look closely at the cobra-goddess of Buto, who wears the Double Crown. You try to deny the truth, but your reign is already at an end. If you have even a little intelligence left, surrender and beg Pharaoh Ahmose for mercy. If you do not, the anger of the Eye of Ra will utterly destroy you.'

'Give me a bow!' demanded the emperor, mad with rage.

Ahhotep's eyes did not leave the killer as he aimed at her.

'Majesty, step back!' begged Emheb.

The queen continued to hold high the cornelian staff. At the moment he drew his bow back to its furthest extent, the wood split and the bow fell apart.

The Hyksos and the Egyptians both understood what it meant: that the Eye of Ra was protecting Ahhotep and the pharaoh.

52

The Afghan and Moustache exchanged glances. They were numb with weariness. This was the third attack by Canaanite chariots that they had repulsed in less than ten days.

Utterly exhausted, they and their soldiers wondered how they could still find the strength to fight. As for the horses, they had acquitted themselves admirably, responding to their drivers' smallest instruction. An intimate understanding had developed between man and beast, enabling them to survive in the most desperate situations.

'What are our losses?' asked Pharaoh Ahmose anxiously.

'They're miraculously light,' replied the Afghan. 'Only ten dead – and thirty enemy chariots have been put out of action.'

'With respect, Majesty,' ventured Moustache, 'you should not expose yourself to danger so much.'

'With an archer like Ahmes covering me, I am not afraid of anything. And I must take part in the fighting. Why should my men risk their lives for a coward who merely looked on?'

At sunset, a scout returning from the east of the Delta brought them some good news. Several areas had risen up against the Hyksos, and everywhere rebels were damaging chariots and stealing horses. Fully occupied in trying – and failing – to re-establish order, the enemy was in no position to retake the offensive.

'We must support the rebels,' decided the king. 'Two hundred men are to go to their aid, so that they can continue to cause as much disruption as possible.'

Since Ahhotep had returned unharmed from Buto and ridiculed Khamudi, each soldier in the army of liberation regarded her as a protecting goddess who, with the aid of the Eye of Ra, could extricate them from even the worst danger. But the enemy's resources were still vast and the citadel of Avaris remained impregnable.

'The men are physically exhausted,' said She-Cat, who had herself grown thin through long nights spent caring for the wounded. 'If they do not take some rest, they will collapse where they stand.'

'After the punishment we've just inflicted on the Canaanites,' said Moustache, 'the enemy can't be much fresher than we are.'

Ahhotep received Neshi, who had just returned from the Northern front.

'Tell me what is happening – in plain words,' she said.

'The situation is not wonderful, Majesty. Since we began intercepting the caravans, we have plenty of good food, but our troops are exhausted. The rebellion rumbling on in the east of the Delta looks very promising, and many of the Canaanites' chariots have been destroyed, but time is not on our side, and the fact that the citadel is easily holding out ensures that our enemies remain united.'

Unfortunately, he was right. And the information the queen had just received from Elephantine made things look even worse. The new Prince of Kerma, Ata, had recaptured villages controlled by the Egyptians and was advancing down the Nile. The garrison at the fort of Buhen and the Nubian tribes loyal to Ahhotep were trying to halt him. War was raging between the Second and First Cataracts.

If Ata won, first Elephantine would be threatened, then

Edfu and eventually Thebes itself. And not even one regiment could be spared to go to the rescue.

'What do you suggest we do, Emheb?' asked Ahhotep.

'The volunteers who reached the walls of the citadel were killed by archers or by slingshots. A massive attack would be suicidal. There is nothing we can do, Majesty.'

'Then we must wait until their food and water run out.'

'The Northern front may collapse before that happens,' predicted Emheb.

'Then we must find another way.'

The weary governor withdrew into his tent.

The Egyptian scout was dying from wounds to his belly and forehead. Without the drugs administered by She-Cat, he would have been in terrible pain and unable to speak. But his expression was almost peaceful, and he was proud to be able to deliver his report to the King of Egypt.

'The gods protected me, Majesty. I succeeded in crossing the Canaanite lines. Things are serious, very serious . . . Thousands of Hyksos soldiers will soon arrive from Anatolia to join the Canaanites. Horde and hordes of chariots and footsoldiers will thunder down on us.'

The scout's body tensed, his hand gripped the king's, and the light faded from his eyes.

Pharaoh wandered round the camp for a long time, after entrusting Rascal with an urgent message informing Ahhotep of the situation.

So this was the end of the road. All those people dead, all that suffering, all that heroism, would end beneath the chariot-wheels of the invader, whose repression would be terrifying. Nothing whatsoever would remain of Thebes. Khamudi would complete Apophis's destruction.

The pharaoh gathered together those close to him, and told them the truth.

'Do you wish to strike camp first thing tomorrow morning, Majesty?' asked the Afghan.

'No. We shall stay here,' declared Ahmose.

'But, Majesty, not one of us will escape!' protested Moustache.

'It is better to die as warriors than as fugitives.'

Rascal knew that he had brought very bad news, and remained at a distance from Ahhotep, who did not even think to stroke him.

'It is over,' she told Emheb, Neshi and Moon. 'Alongside the Canaanite chariots, the troops from Anatolia will attack first Ahmose, then us. The pharaoh will hold out for as long as possible, to cover our retreat to Thebes.'

'If we retreat, the Hyksos will pursue us and destroy us,' said Moon, 'so why not attack the citadel with all our forces? If we must die, Majesty, I should like to do so without regrets.'

'It is more important to protect Thebes,' said Emheb.

'Could you not persuade the king to combine our forces?' suggested Neshi. 'Together, we would be much stronger.'

'I shall give you my decision tomorrow morning.'

Whatever it did, the Egyptian army would be wiped out. And yet Ahhotep had gone to Buto, had heard the voices of the ancestors and received the Eye of Ra.

The queen raised her eyes to the night sky and begged her protector, the moon-god, Ah, for help. It was the fourteenth day of the waxing moon, when the eye was made complete again, caught, and put back together by the gods Thoth and Horus. It shone forth in his ship, encouraging all forms of growth. No, her celestial companion could not abandon her like this!

Refusing to believe in disaster, the queen spent all night thinking about the deeds of those who had fought for freedom. When dawn came she had still not heard the voices of the ancestors.

Suddenly there was a terrifying roar. The sun, which had only just risen, vanished. The sky became blacker than ink, incredibly strong winds carried away the tents and attacked the walls of the citadel.

And, added to this fury, there was an earthquake.

Several days' voyage away, in the Mycenean islands, the volcano on Thera had erupted.*

*Thera is also known as Santorini.

53

'Majesty, it is raining rocks!' exclaimed Neshi.

It was true. Pieces of pumice stone from the volcano, carried along by the wind, were falling on Avaris, and black ash veiled the sky. Terrified, the Egyptians ran about in all directions.

'Calm the horses,' ordered Ahhotep.

For his part, Way-Finder brayed imperiously, urging his fellow donkeys to remain calm.

Little by little, the stones stopped raining down, the wind dropped and the black veil disappeared. With the return of the sun, Ahhotep saw that the Egyptian camp had been laid waste and that there were many wounded. Nevertheless, a broad smile lit up her face. What the Egyptians had suffered was nothing compared to the damage inflicted on the citadel.

Deep cracks had torn through the walls and many of the battlements had collapsed, dragging hundreds of archers down with them. Where the great gate had stood, there was a gaping hole.

'Assemble the footsoldiers and the chariots,' the queen ordered Emheb.

An entire wall swayed and fell, its stones and bricks coming apart with a great crash. The army gazed at the incredible sight. All that stood before them now was a ruin.

'Thanks be to Set for his help,' said Ahhotep. 'He has just placed his fury and his power at the service of freedom. Attack!'

Still covered in ashes, both footsoldiers and archers rushed to attack the disembowelled monster.

Khamudi gazed in shock at the results of the earthquake. Whole rooms had disappeared, roofs and ceilings no longer existed, and countless corpses strewed the great inner courtyard.

'We must organize our defences,' urged Aberia, who had a slight head wound.

'It would be useless. We must escape.'

'And abandon the survivors?'

'They will not hold out for long. Let us go to the strongroom.'

Khamudi hoped to seize Apophis's treasures, above all the Red Crown of Lower Egypt, but blocks of stone barred his way.

He summoned the commander of his personal bodyguard, a Cypriot with a moustache, and told him, 'I shall drive back the attackers to the north of the citadel. You are to gather together the survivors and deal with the south. The Egyptians have not won yet. If we manage to contain their first assault, they will lose heart.'

Bloody hand-to-hand fighting broke out. Determined to hold off the Egyptians, the Hyksos took up station in the intact corners of the citadel and formed pockets of resistance which were difficult to stamp out.

For long hours, Ahhotep urged her soldiers not to weaken. Despite the favourable circumstances, victory was far from won.

'Majesty, the pharaoh is coming,' said Emheb.

How good it was to hear the sound of chariot wheels!

By great good fortune, the earthquake had severely affected the Hyksos' Canaanite and Delta troops, but not the Egyptians. Hoping that the citadel would be shaken by the anger of heaven and earth, Ahmose had headed for Avaris. The result filled him with joy.

Immediately taking command, the king broke down the enemy defences one by one. All that remained for him to conquer was a hall of arms, the least damaged part of the citadel. When he entered it, the king did not see the Cypriot with the moustache step out behind him, ready to bury an axe in his back.

Swift and accurate, an arrow fired by Ahmes, son of Abana, sank into the Cypriot's neck.

After again receiving the gold award for bravery, together with three female prisoners who were to become servants in his household, Ahmes proudly reread the hieroglyphic text written by Neshi on the trophy he held most dear: '*In the name of Pharaoh Ahmose, gifted with life: an arrowhead brought back from defeated Avaris.*'

In the eighteenth year of Ahmose's reign, the capital of the Hyksos Empire had expired.

Several carrier-pigeons left for the South, bearing the wonderful news, while Egyptian scouts were charged with spreading it throughout the cities of the Delta, where the rebellion was intensifying.

'But,' lamented Emheb, 'there is no trace of Khamudi.'

'He has fled, the coward,' said Moon contemptuously.

'As long as he is alive,' said Ahmose, 'the war will continue. Khamudi still has a powerful army, and he will be bent on revenge.'

'His men will soon learn that Avaris has fallen,' said Ahhotep, 'and the defeat will dishearten them. Our most urgent task is to free the Delta completely and to recruit more men. First, though, we must carry out the will of the ancestors. I am convinced that the Red Crown is hidden here. We must take the citadel apart stone by stone if necessary.'

Units of soldiers at once set off on the hunt.

As the men left, Ahhotep heard the Afghan calling from outside the palace. 'Majesties, come and see, I beg you.'

When they found him and Moustache, both men looked shaken and horrified. The place was a strange garden, littered here and there with bricks from the fallen palace walls. Before the first arch, which was covered with climbing plants, stood around fifty large jars.

'I removed the lids,' said the Afghan. 'Inside are the bodies of children and tiny babies. Their throats have been cut.'

Hundreds of other jars were heaped up in the garden. During the siege of Avaris, Khamudi had done away with all those who could not fight.

'Down there, in front of the thicket of tamarisks, is the body of a man almost cut in two,' said Moustache.

'This must be the evil labyrinth,' said the queen. She was certain that the Emperor of Darkness had dreamt of throwing her into this death-trap, with its deceptively pleasant appearance. 'Burn it.'

Not far away, an animal bellowed. Emheb went to investigate, and found a wild bull shut up in an enclosure whose door was blocked by rubble.

'Set it free,' ordered Ahhotep.

'But, Majesty, it is dangerous,' warned Moon.

'The bull is the symbol of Pharaoh's power. Apophis put a spell on this one to turn it into a killer. We must bring it back into the realm of Ma'at.'

As soon as the entrance was unblocked, spears, swords and arrows were pointed at the animal, which fixed its eyes on the queen.

'Do not go any closer, Majesty,' urged Emheb. 'He could easily run you through with one toss of his horns.'

The huge creature pawed the ground.

'Be calm,' Ahhotep told it. 'No one will force you to kill any more. Let me offer you peace.'

The bull was on the point of attacking.

'Lower your weapons,' ordered the queen.

'This is madness, Majesty!' protested Moon.

In one quick movement, the queen laid the Eye of Ra against the bull's forehead. Instantly a look of intense gratitude appeared in its eyes.

'Now,' she told it, 'you are truly free. Go now.'

Immediately, the bull rushed out of the fortress towards the marshes.

'There are still Hyksos at large,' warned Neshi. 'One of our footsoldiers has been seriously wounded in the ruins of the throne room.'

The Afghan and Moustache were the first there, daggers in hand. A flame attacked them from the back of the room, burning the Afghan on the wrist.

'There is an evil being in here,' said Moustache.

'The Eye of Ra will blind it,' promised Ahhotep, who had entered the chamber just behind them. She pointed her cornelian staff at the place from which the flame had sprung.

In the chaos of bricks and rubble, the faces of the two griffins had been spared. They struck down anyone who approached the emperor's throne.

Protected by the Eye of Ra, Ahhotep covered the eyes of the evil spirits with a cloth. Then Emheb coated them with plaster to render them harmless.

'Smash the throne into a thousand pieces and block the noses of all the intact statues,' ordered the queen. 'The emperor must have cast a spell upon them so that they would spread evil vapours.'

'Majesty,' said Neshi excitedly, 'we have found a strongroom.'

Fearing one of Apophis's traps, Ahhotep had a fire lit at the foot of the door. When the metal bolts melted, the door opened with a creak.

In the strongroom lay the Red Crown of Lower Egypt.

54

Big-Feet was worried. There had not been a single convoy of new deportees for more than a month.

Around him, people continued to die. Since becoming the camp's official gravedigger, Big-Feet had received an additional weekly food ration. Being clever with his hands, he repaired the guards' sandals, and they were no longer wary of this walking skeleton, whose continued survival amazed everyone.

'I have two children and an old man to bury,' he told the head guard, a bearded Persian. 'Look, my pickaxe is broken. May I take another one?'

'Dig with your hands!'

Big-Feet was trudging away resignedly when the guard called him back.

'All right, all right, get one from the hut.'

Among the tools were several bronze branding-irons, which were used to burn each prisoner's number into their skin. Big-Feet stole one, and hid it in a corner of the camp. If he came out of this hell alive, he would have evidence of his sufferings and would gaze upon it each day while giving thanks to destiny.

After finishing his painful task, he returned the pickaxe to the guard.

'There haven't been any new people for a long time,' he commented.

'Does that bother you, 1790?'

'No, but . . .'

'Clean up this pigsty and get out of my sight.'

From the man's bitter tone, Big-Feet realized that all was not going well for the Hyksos. Had the Queen of Freedom won some significant victories? Was the empire beginning to disintegrate?

Now, more than ever, he must not despair. Today his stale bread would taste better.

Pharaoh Ahmose stood for a moment in the Hyksos' emperor's former throne room, for the first time wearing the Double Crown, the union of the Red Crown of Lower Egypt and the White Crown of Upper Egypt. Then he went out to his troops, so that they could see the two crowns reunited. They cheered loud and long.

Ahhotep stood several paces behind him, trying to hide her tears of joy. But her son made her come forward.

'We owe this great victory to the Queen of Freedom. May the name of Ahhotep become immortal and may she be the benevolent mother of a reborn Egypt.'

The queen thought of Seqen and Kamose. They were here, close beside her, and they were sharing this moment of intense happiness.

But the victors of Avaris had no time to rest, for the citadel must be transformed into an Egyptian military base. The first task for the prisoners they had taken, women included, was to purify the houses that were still standing, by burning herbs and other cleansers. Then the prisoners were placed in the service of Egyptian officers and assured that they would be freed one day if they behaved well.

While the artificers began demolishing the parts of the fortress that were damaged beyond repair and restoring those worth preserving, the queen arranged for the soldiers who had died in combat to be buried. She was outraged to discover that the Hyksos had buried their dead in the courtyards of the houses or in the houses themselves, and that many of the tombs in the palace burial-ground contained nothing but large quantities of drugs. There was no trace of stelae or offerings, nor the inscriptions of eternity that ought to have been recited by a servant of the *ka*. Cut off from their traditions and their rites, the Egyptians of Avaris had lived through terrible times.

Before an army could be created to liberate all the cities of the North, the Temple of Set must be purified. Ahhotep went there by boat with the pharaoh, guarded by Young Laughter and Ahmes. As nothing untoward had happened during the many battles the king had fought in, reason said that he no longer needed to be so closely guarded. But the war was not over, and Ahhotep refused to let him run even the slightest risk, for he must establish a new dynasty.

'According to my latest information,' said Ahmose, 'the Prince of Kerma's advance has stalled, so there is no need to send troops to help Buhen and our Nubian allies.'

The pharaoh and his mother were astonished by the insignificance of the temple, which was a shoddy brick building, utterly unworthy of a divine power.

On the altar, which still stood intact amid the oak trees, lay Apophis's scattered remains, which had been torn apart by vultures. There was also a deep ditch, filled with sacrificed donkeys.

'What a sinister place!' said the pharaoh. 'We must eradicate all traces of this shrine to evil.'

Ahhotep agreed. 'Here we shall build a great temple dedicated to Set, he whom the emperor failed to enslave, he who gave us his strength when we had sore need of it. May Horus and Set unite and be at peace within the being of Pharaoh.'

*

Scarcely had Aberia driven the chariot into the fortress of Sharuhen when the two horses collapsed, dead from exhaustion. Khamudi was glad to have his feet on the ground again, after a difficult journey during which he had constantly been afraid they would be intercepted.

Everywhere, they had seen the damage done by the earthquake: trees had been uprooted, farms destroyed, huge cracks ran through the fields, and the ground was strewn with the bodies of hundreds of Hyksos who had been killed in the accompanying storm. But, to the emperor's great relief, the fortress of Sharuhen seemed almost intact.

'What is the extent of the damage?' Khamudi asked the commander, who came to greet him.

'Just some cracks in one wall, Majesty, and we are repairing it. But a few horses went mad and trampled some footsoldiers, and several men who were on watch on the ramparts were carried away by the storm.'

Khamudi ordered the commander to set aside the best rooms in the living-quarters for himself, and others for Aberia, and to bring him food and wine. The rooms were far removed from the luxury of the palace at Avaris, but Khamudi knew how to be patient until he once again enjoyed surroundings worthy of him. Famished, he wolfed down some grilled mutton, duck and goose, and drank a jar of white wine.

When he had finished his meal, he summoned the commander again. 'I have decided to bestow a great honour upon Sharuhen,' he said. 'I am making it the capital of my empire. Summon all the officers to my throne room.'

He was still free, he mused, still invincible. He had, after all, succeeded in getting rid of Apophis and seizing supreme power.

'The Egyptians were in no way victorious,' he announced to the officers. 'Faults in its construction meant that the citadel at Avaris could not withstand the earthquake and the storm. All the enemy did was invade a ruin. You may be sure that I shall not make the same mistakes as my predecessor. Our army is still the best, and it will crush the rebels. Ahhotep and the pharaoh do not know that we have an immense reserve of troops in Anatolia, all of whom I shall order to return forthwith. We shall begin by retaking the Delta, then we shall raze Thebes to the ground. My reign will be the greatest in Hyksos history and my fame will exceed that of Apophis. Prepare the men for battle and have no doubt that we shall triumph.'

The officers withdrew, all but five of them.

'What do you want?' demanded Khamudi in surprise.

'We have just arrived from Anatolia,' replied a Syrian general, 'and we bring very bad news. That is why we, the surviving generals, preferred to speak with you in private.'

'Surviving? Surviving what?'

'We no longer control any territory at all in Anatolia. King Hattusil I formed an enormous Hittite army and defeated us. In addition, our bases in the north of Syria have been destroyed, and Aleppo has fallen. The few regiments that still exist are surrounded, and there will be no survivors.'

Khamudi was speechless for a long time. Then he said, 'You must have fought badly, General.'

'All our provinces rebelled, my lord – even the civilians took up arms in the end. The Hittite rebels were very effective fighters, and all they needed was a man like Hattusil to bring them together.'

'A defeated Hyksos is unworthy to obey me. All you incompetent generals shall be taught your place: the prison camp.'

55

Left to their own devices by the emperor, the soldiers, mercenaries and security guards in the Delta no longer received clear orders. With their means of communication cut, they were unable to offer coordinated resistance, and were perpetually harried by the rebels and by Ahmose's raiding-parties.

When the Egyptian army entered the eastern Delta, it encountered only weak opposition from a demoralized enemy. The towns of Lower Egypt were liberated one after another, in a climate of inexpressible celebration.

In the ancient city of Sais, where the goddess Neit had spoken the seven words of creation, a wrinkled old woman collapsed not far from Ahhotep, whom everyone was eager to approach. The queen immediately had her carried to a bedchamber in the palace, where She-Cat examined her.

With a glance, the Nubian woman gave the queen to understand that the poor old woman's body was worn out. Nevertheless, she opened her eyes and managed to speak; there was such pain in her voice that Ahhotep was almost overcome.

'The Hyksos took away my husband, my children and my grandchildren to torture them.'

'Where are they?' asked the queen gently.

'In a death-camp at Tjaru. Anyone who dared speak of it

was deported as well. Save them, Majesty, if there is still time.'

'You have my word.'

At peace at last, the old woman died a gentle death.

The pharaoh was as deeply moved as his mother. 'A death-camp? What does that mean?'

'Apophis travelled further along the path of evil than any demon of the desert, and I fear we shall find unspeakable horrors. I am leaving for Tjaru at once.'

'But the area around it is still controlled by the Hyksos, Mother. Khamudi is undoubtedly regrouping large forces in Syria and Canaan, we must prepare for another major battle.'

'You must prepare for it, Ahmose. I gave my word that I would act as quickly as possible.'

'Listen to me for once, I beg you. Do not take any risks. Egypt needs you too much – and your son does, too.'

The pharaoh and the queen embraced.

Ahhotep went on, 'Tjaru is at the very edge of the Hyksos area, and I shall take Moustache and the Afghan, and two chariot regiments. If we cannot take Tjaru ourselves, we will wait for you.'

'Hold out? Hold out? That's wonderful,' said Tjaru's commander furiously. 'Hold out with what and with whom? Khamudi seems to have forgotten that since the fall of Avaris our position is the furthest forward in the whole Hyksos empire.' He had grown used to living comfortably within the shelter of the fortress's walls, and had no wish to undergo the rigours of a siege.

Standing at the end of the trade route from Canaan, and within reach of the many canals that crossed the Delta in the direction of the Nile valley, Tjaru was both a trade-control post and a place where goods were stockpiled. It was built on the isthmus that had formed between Lake Ballah and Lake

Menezaleh, at the centre of a landscape which alternated between desert and broad expanses of greenery.

'Let us not give up hope, sir,' urged his second-in-command. 'The emperor is rebuilding his army, and a counter-offensive is bound to come soon.'

'But in the meantime we are in the front line. Is there any news from the Delta?'

'Nothing good. I fear the pharaoh and Queen Ahhotep may have retaken all of it.'

'To be defeated by a woman – what shame for the Hyksos!' The commander stamped in rage, but only hurt his heel on the flagstones.

'The men are to be put on permanent alert,' he ordered. 'Archers on the ramparts, day and night.'

Nervously, the commander reviewed his men and inspected the reserves of weapons and food. He could hold out for several weeks, but what was the point of resisting if he was going to get no help? He was as distrustful of Khamudi as he had been blindly obedient to Apophis, because the new emperor was a dishonest money-maker and drugs-seller with not a scrap of military experience.

'The Egyptians are coming, Commander,' said his second-in-command in a quavering voice.

'Are there many of them?'

'Yes, sir. And they've got chariots – hundreds of chariots – and ladders on wheels.'

'Every man to his post.'

'A fine beast,' commented the Afghan as he gazed at the fortress of Tjaru. 'But compared to Avaris it's almost a toy.'

'Don't fool yourself,' said Moustache. 'That beast is sturdy and knows how to defend itself.'

Ahhotep asked, 'Have any Hyksos troops been seen in the area?'

'No, Majesty. It looks as though Khamudi has abandoned

Tjaru to its own devices, in the hope that it will slow down our advance towards the north-east. The fortress probably has enough supplies to withstand a long siege.'

'We must free the prisoners as quickly as possible,' said Ahhotep.

'We could try an assault, but we would lose a lot of men,' said the Afghan. 'Before we do that, let us study the terrain in detail and identify the fortress's weak points.'

'I cannot wait so long,' said the queen.

The plan she outlined made Moustache and the Afghan extremely nervous. But how could they prevent the queen from carrying it out?

'What? Alone?' asked the commander in astonishment.

'Queen Ahhotep stands alone before the great gate of the citadel,' confirmed his assistant, 'and she wishes to speak with you.'

'The woman's mad! Why haven't the archers killed her?'

'A queen, alone and unarmed . . . They didn't dare.'

'But she's our worst enemy!'

The men have lost their minds, thought the commander, and he rushed off to chain up this she-demon himself before she could put a spell on the whole garrison.

The great gate had been opened a little way, and Ahhotep was already inside the fortress. A fine gold diadem, a red gown, and eyes filled with intensity, honesty, perception . . .

The commander was enchanted. 'Majesty, I—'

'Your only chance of survival is to surrender. Your emperor has abandoned you, and the army of liberation is coming. No fortress has held out against it, in the South or the North.'

The commander could arrest Ahhotep and deliver her up to Khamudi, who would make him a wealthy general. She was here, at his mercy. All he had to do was give the order. But the Queen of Freedom's eyes forced him to acknowledge the truth of what she had said.

'I have been told,' she went on, 'that there is a camp here, containing deportees.'

The commander looked down at his feet. 'The lady Aberia opened it, on Khamudi's orders. It is nothing to do with me.'

'What happens in this camp?'

'I don't know, Majesty. I am a soldier, not a prison guard.'

'The Hyksos soldiers shall become prisoners of war and will be employed in rebuilding Egypt,' decreed Ahhotep, 'but not the torturers. Gather together immediately all the torturers who have worked in the camp. If a single one is left free, I shall regard you as one of them.'

56

The queen could not even weep. After so many years of struggle, she had thought she knew everything about suffering, but what she found at Tjaru tore her heart into pieces.

She had managed to rescue only fifty deportees, including ten women and five children, some of whom would not survive their injuries and starvation. One little girl died in her arms. Everywhere on the ground lay corpses, half eaten by rats and birds of prey.

The only two prisoners who could still talk, spoke haltingly, often incoherently, about what Aberia and her henchmen had done to them.

How could human beings, even in the service of a terrifying monster, have behaved like that? Ahhotep would not hear any explanations; only the facts counted. To have forgiven the torturers would have been so terrible a crime against the gods that it would have led inevitably to a repetition of these same horrors. So the queen had them executed on the spot.

As soon as he arrived, Pharaoh Ahmose saw that Tjaru was a fine prize: horses, chariots, weapons, provisions. But he was horrified when he learnt how Ahhotep had taken it.

'Mother, you ought not—'

'The commander says there is another camp, larger than this one, at Sharuhen, a fortified city. That is where Khamudi has taken refuge.'

The war in Canaan had been going on for over two years, and Big-Feet was still holding on. It was no longer Egyptians from the Delta who were being thrown into the camp, but Hyksos soldiers guilty of desertion or of retreating in the face of the enemy. Tortured by Aberia, they died quickly.

At least Prisoner 1790 now had some rumours to be happy about. Step by step, and despite their ferocity in battle, the Egyptian army was finishing off the Syrian and Canaanite troops. The fortified town of Tell Hanor, whose governor enjoyed killing dogs for sport, had surrendered. Sharuhen was now isolated.

Big-Feet went over to a Phoenician youth with only one arm. 'Did you lose your arm in the war, youngster?'

'No. Aberia cut it off because I hid from the Egyptian chariots.'

'Are they still a long way away?'

'They'll be here soon. We can't hold them back any longer.'

Big-Feet breathed deeply, in a way he had not done for a very long time for fear of shattering his fragile body.

'My lord,' said the commander of Sharuhen, 'the war is lost. All our strongholds have been taken, and we have not a single regiment left. If you wish, Sharuhen can still resist for a little longer, but in my opinion it would be better to surrender.'

'A Hyksos dies with his weapons in his hands!' snapped Khamudi.

'As you command.'

The emperor withdrew to his apartments, where Aberia, who was hated by the garrison, had taken refuge. At night, she enjoyed satisfying Khamudi's whims.

'Arrange for our departure, Aberia.'

'Where are we going?'

'To Kerma. Prince Ata will give me a welcome worthy of my rank and he will place himself at my service.'

'You have no great fondness for black men, my lord.'

'They will be better warriors than this rabble of cowards, who have dared let themselves lose the war. The Egyptians will make the fatal mistake of believing that I have been defeated. We shall take a boat to the Libyan coast, then follow the desert tracks. Select a reliable crew, and load the boat with as much gold and drugs as you can.'

'When are we leaving?'

'At dawn, the day after tomorrow.'

'Once the boat is ready, I shall have one small formality left to undertake,' said Aberia greedily. 'I shall close the camp myself.'

Ordinarily, the torture ended at nightfall, just before the prisoners' miserable daily meal, so Big-Feet was astonished to see Aberia and her men enter the camp at dusk. What new torment had she invented now?

'Come here,' she ordered the one-armed Phoenician.

The prisoners looked at the torturer who ruled this hell.

'In a few hours,' she said 'the Egyptians will enter Sharuhen and this camp. We cannot, you will agree, leave it in such a untidy state, which would damage my reputation. You and your laziness are the cause of the untidiness, and I must eliminate that cause.'

She put her arm round the young soldier's neck and snapped it.

While the guards were busy restraining a Libyan who had tried to run away, Big-Feet dug up the branding-iron he had hidden.

With her foot, Aberia forced the Libyan's face into the mud and held it there until her victim had stopped breathing.

Very slowly, Prisoner 1790 went towards her. 'Am I to bury the bodies?'

The idea amused her. 'Dig me a large grave, and do it quickly.'

Aberia was taller than Big-Feet and could easily have killed him with a single blow of her fist. Neither she nor any of the guards would ever have imagined that submissive, broken Big-Feet was capable of rebelling. It was precisely that supposition that enabled him to do what he did.

'This is for my cows,' he said calmly, and he plunged the bronze branding-iron into Aberia's right eye. She roared with pain. Big-Feet struck again, thrusting his weapon into Aberia's mouth so savagely and so deeply that it pierced right through her neck.

Stunned for a moment, the guards raised their swords to kill Prisoner 1790. But the Hyksos prisoners, sensing that this was their one chance to escape, hurled themselves at the guards.

Before leaving the camp, Big-Feet picked up a sword and cut off Aberia's enormous hands. 'Now,' he murmured, 'I have won my war.'

Great Royal Wife Nefertari reread the message brought by Rascal to old Qaris, the steward: Sharuhen, the last pocket of Hyksos resistance, had been conquered.

'Ahhotep is victorious!' exclaimed the old man. He could not help thinking of the young girl who, more than forty years before, had been the only one to believe in the liberation of Egypt.

'I am taking you to the temple,' said Nefertari.

'Of course, Majesty, of course. But the chariots make me a little nervous.'

'Would you prefer a travelling-chair?'

'Majesty! I am only a steward and—'

'You are Thebes's memory, Qaris.'

The good news spread very quickly. Already people were busily preparing an immense celebration for the return of Queen Ahhotep and Pharaoh Ahmose.

High Priest Djehuty stood on the threshold of the temple. His face was grave, showing not a sign of joy. 'The door of the shrine of Amon is still closed, Majesty. This means that the war is not over and that we have not yet won the final victory.'

57

After informing King Hattusil I that Egypt had been freed from the Hyksos yoke and that he hoped to develop better relations with Anatolia, Pharaoh Ahmose sent troops to occupy Syria and Canaan, in order to discourage any would-be invaders. A special secretariat would govern the region, and the use of carrier-pigeons would ensure that the king was kept informed of all that happened there.

There was only one dark cloud: the disappearance of Emperor Khamudi, who, according to witnesses, had left Sharuhen by boat.

'He has no hope of finding allies in the north or in the Delta,' said Ahmose. 'Either he has left for the Mycenean islands, hoping to hide there until his death, or he is plotting ways of taking his revenge.'

'To raise the question is to answer it,' said Ahhotep. 'But there is one other possibility. He may have tried to reach Kerma, the last enemy we must confront. Thebes may be filled with celebration, but our work is not yet done.'

While Ahmose was joyfully reunited with his wife and son, Ahhotep consulted the latest reports from Nubia. It was true that Prince Ata was not advancing, but the civil war was continuing unabated. There could be no doubt that this running sore was the reason why Amon had put the Egyptians on their guard.

'Is there no news of Khamudi?' she asked Neshi.

'Nothing,' he replied. 'Perhaps he lost his way in the desert.'

'We should not assume as much. Hatred will have enabled him to find his way again.'

Neshi bowed, then changed the subject. 'Majesty, may we hope to be honoured with your presence at the banquet this evening?'

'I am tired, Neshi.'

Ahhotep spent the night at the Temple of Karnak, communing with the statue of Mut. She had received so much from the Wife of Amon, the mother of the living souls and the keeper of the divine fire, that she owed her the tale of those taxing years of war, at the end of which Ahmose at last wore the Double Crown.

To no one but Mut could Ahhotep confide that she longed for silence and solitude. 'Pharaoh no longer needs me,' she told her. 'He has become an excellent leader in his own right, and inspires respect and trust.'

An angry gleam appeared in the statue's stone eyes.

'If you grant me rest, O Mut, incline your head.'

The statue did not move.

The first contact between Ata, Prince of Kerma, and Khamudi, Emperor of the Hyksos, was icy.

'Your presence honours me, my lord, but I would have preferred to see you at the head of thousands of soldiers.'

'Do not worry, Ata, they exist. Everywhere my reputation holds firm. As for the Egyptians, they tremble at the very thought of speaking my name. As soon as we have reconquered Nubia and destroyed Elephantine, my supporters will rise up and join us. Of course, I shall march at the head of our army.'

'You are not a Nubian, my lord, and my warriors obey only their prince.'

Khamudi took the insult without flinching. 'What is your plan, Prince?'

'To recapture the villages the Egyptians stole from us, then retake Buhen. Otherwise it will be impossible to begin the conquest of southern Egypt.'

'You know nothing of fortresses, Ata. I do.'

'Then your counsel will be invaluable.'

'First we must clear a path to Buhen, and mere attacks by raiding-parties will not be enough for that.'

'What do you suggest, my lord?'

'Give me a map of the region and we shall talk again. For the moment, I wish to rest.'

A tall, strongly built steward showed Khamudi to spacious, comfortable rooms in the palace of Kerma. Khamudi's attention was caught by the look in the steward's eyes: a drugged look.

'What is your name, steward?' he asked.

'Tetian, my lord.'

'You smoke herbs, do you not?

The tall fellow nodded.

'I have brought something better – much better. If you want the finest drugs, listen to me. You have the look of a warrior, not a servant. Ata has ordered you to spy on me, hasn't he?'

'That is so, my lord.'

'Why did you accept such humiliating work?'

'We do not belong to the same tribe. One day, mine will take its revenge and govern Kerma.'

Khamudi smiled. 'Why wait, Tetian? Strike immediately, and we will fight the Egyptians together. You will kill many hundreds of them, and your people will be at your feet.'

'I shall kill many, many hundreds, and I, Tetian, shall be admired by everyone.'

'First, my friend, taste the promised marvels.'

For a whole night, Tetian took the best drugs Khamudi had brought. Next morning, he went to see Ata as arranged, to deliver his report.

'Have you won Khamudi's confidence?' asked Ata.

'Yes, my prince.'

'What are his real plans?'

'To take command of our army and invade Egypt. And also he has entrusted me with a mission.'

'What mission?'

'To kill you.'

Ata had no time to defend himself. The dagger thrown by Tetian pierced his heart. Kerma had a new prince.

In view of Amon's warning, Ahhotep took the Nubian affair very seriously. Some people thought a simple expeditionary force would be enough to put down the rebellion, but the queen disagreed, and had persuaded her son not to treat this last obstacle lightly.

So Ahmose was leaving for the Great South with almost the entire army of liberation. Moon, Emheb, Neshi, Moustache, the Afghan and all the other heroes of the war were in the party, as were Ahmes, son of Abana, and Young Laughter, both of them still charged with protecting the king. Only Way-Finder was to be left behind. The old donkey was at last enjoying a well-deserved retirement.

On the quayside, where the last of the party were embarking, the atmosphere was gloomy.

'So Queen Ahhotep isn't coming?' asked the Afghan.

'No, she needs rest,' replied Moustache, who was as downcast as his friend.

A young sailor summed up the general opinion: 'Without her, we may well be defeated. The Nubians are much more frightening warriors than the Hyksos. The queen would have known how to destroy their magic.'

'There are ten times more of us than of them,' pointed out the Afghan.

'There were ten times as many Hyksos, too,' said the sailor, 'but they weren't commanded by the Queen of Freedom.'

There was a sudden hubbub at the far end of the quay, accompanied by cries of joy.

Ahhotep appeared, carrying her cornelian staff, wearing her fine gold diadem, and dressed in a green gown woven for her by Nefertari. As soon as she was aboard the flagship, the fleet set off with all speed.

58

The first halt Ahhotep ordered took the Egyptian fleet by surprise. Why were they stopping at Aniba, which was a long way short of Buhen?

Only a hundred men, twenty of them quarrymen, disembarked, together with donkeys laden with water-skins and provisions. They set off for the diorite quarry that had been opened by Pharaoh Khafra, builder of one of the three pyramids on the plateau of Giza. Solemnly reopening the quarry, Ahhotep inaugurated a long-term programme: once Nubia had been pacified, it would be covered with temples in which the divine powers would come and dwell. By producing Ma'at,* the temples would lessen the risk of conflict.

When the fleet reached Buhen, the fortress's commander, Turi, welcomed Pharaoh's army with immense relief. Forgetting protocol, he spoke to the queen and her son without concealing his anxiety.

'You have arrived just in time, Your Majesties, for there have been dramatic events in Nubia, and the balance of power has changed. Khamudi has allied himself to the new Prince of Kerma, a man named Tetian, who murdered his predecessor and stirred up tribes which had been peaceable until then. Our defensive arrangements have been thrown into disarray. It

*In ancient Egyptian it was possible to 'say', 'do' or 'produce' Ma'at.

seems that the warriors of Kerma have never been more ferocious – even when they are mortally wounded, they go on fighting. According to my scouts, they have just crossed the Second Cataract and are charging towards Buhen. My men and I are afraid. Fortunately, a sculptor has fashioned a work which preserves hope.'

He showed them a painted lintel on which were depicted Pharaoh Ahmose, wearing the Blue Crown of war, and Queen Ahhotep, wearing the vulture-shaped wig symbolic of Mut. Mother and son were worshipping Horus, the region's protector.

'To work,' ordered the king. 'We must prepare for a fierce battle.'

Khamudi congratulated himself on having brought sufficient drugs to turn the warriors of Kerma into veritable killing-machines. Tetian was a madman, but a notable leader of men, with no fear of danger. Handling the slingshot as ably as the bow or spear, he enjoyed only extremely savage battles in which he killed as many as possible of the enemy, most of them too paralysed with fear even to fight.

Urged on by Tetian and Khamudi, the army of Kerma had killed all the Egyptian troops and their Nubian allies, laid waste many villages housing supporters of Pharaoh, and seized trading-boats, which had then been converted into warships.

The next objective was Buhen. If he could force back that bolt, Khamudi would open wide the doorway to Egypt.

'My lord, a messenger wishes to speak with you,' his assistant told him.

'Where is he from?'

'He says he is from Buhen.'

Khamudi smiled. An Egyptian soldier ready to sacrifice his life to kill the Hyksos Emperor? What a clumsy trick!

'Bring him to me.'

The man was a young Nubian, and was clearly afraid.

'So, my lad, you wanted to kill me, did you?'

'No, my lord, I swear I did not. Someone gave me an urgent message to deliver to you. He promised that in exchange you would give me gold, a house and servants.'

'What is his name?'

'I don't know, my lord.'

'Show me this message.'

'Here it is.'

The moment the young Nubian slipped a hand into his kilt, Khamudi's assistant pinned him to the ground, fearing that he was about to draw a dagger. But the only thing he was hiding was a small Hyksos scarab covered with coded writing, whose key Khamudi knew.

So Apophis's spy was still alive! And what he suggested made Khamudi rejoice.

'Am I to have what was promised to me, my lord?' asked the messenger.

'Do you want to know what the writer of this message advises me to do?'

'Oh yes, my lord!'

'To keep the messenger's mouth shut, kill him.'

'The Nubians of Kerma have chosen to fight us head-on,' said Ahmose as he watched the enemy boats approaching, laden with warriors in red wigs, gold earrings and thick belts. 'Order our archers to take up their positions.'

An officer ran up. 'Commander Ahmes, son of Abana, is called to the rear.'

'Why?' asked Ahmes in surprise.

'Commander Moon wishes to consult him urgently.'

Ahmose gave his agreement, and Ahmes went off just as the fighting was about to begin.

Only the presence of the Queen of Freedom reassured the Egyptian soldiers, even though they outnumbered the enemy and were better armed, for the roars of the warriors of Kerma chilled their blood. Ahhotep gave the order to beat the drums to drown out the din. And when the first attackers, unaware of the danger, fell beneath the Egyptian arrows, everyone realized that they were only men.

Tetian had only one idea in his head, for it had been drummed into him a thousand times by Khamudi: he must smash Pharaoh Ahmose's skull with his club.

While the battle was unfolding, Tetian swam at top speed. He scaled the prow of the flagship as fast as if it were a palm-tree, determined to kill anyone who got in his way. In his drug-induced fever, he could already see the pharaoh dead, his face covered in blood. Once deprived of its leader, the enemy army would fall apart and Egypt would be defenceless.

His eyes filled with madness, Tetian found himself on the deck of the flagship. But the prow of the *Golden Falcon* was empty.

'Where are you, Pharaoh, where are you? Come and fight with Tetian, the Prince of Kerma!'

'Drop your weapon and surrender,' demanded Ahmes.

Roaring like a wild animal, Tetian charged at the archer, who shot him in the forehead. Despite the wound, the Nubian managed to club Ahmes down.

She-Cat's operation had been perfectly successful. Ahmes was now endowed with a little toe made from wood and painted the colour of flesh, which replaced the one crushed by Tetian's club.

The Prince of Kerma's body had been added to those of his defeated warriors, and thrown on to an immense bonfire. For his latest exploit, Ahmes had received yet another gold award for bravery, plus four servants and a priceless gift: a large arable field at Elkab, his native town, where he would spend his old age.

Not for one moment had he believed that Moon wished to consult him. It was just a trick to get him away from the pharaoh. So he had asked the king to go to the poop of the flagship, while he awaited the inevitable attack by a killer.

Summoned by the king, Moon confirmed emphatically that he had not asked to see Ahmes, but it was impossible to interrogate the officer who had brought the message, because he had been killed during the battle.

'Only one boat managed to escape,' said Moon, 'but Khamudi was aboard it.'

59

After Ahhotep had distributed food to the communities hit hardest by the demands of Ata and Tetian, the Egyptian army travelled up the Nile towards Kerma. It met no resistance.

When the fleet reached the rich grain-producing basin of which Kerma was the capital, the soldiers prepared to fight again. Given the Nubians' well-known bravery, there would have to be more fighting before Khamudi could be unearthed from his lair.

The flatness of the terrain would enable the chariot regiments commanded by the Afghan and Moustache to launch the first attack, as soon as the last boats from Kerma had been disabled. But those boats were moored at the quayside; there was not a single sailor aboard.

'Be careful,' advised Moon. 'It is probably a trap.'

An old man came forward, a staff in his hand, and raised his eyes towards the pharaoh and the queen, who were standing at the prow of the *Golden Falcon*.

'I am an envoy from the Council of Ancients,' he declared, 'and I hand you the city of Kerma. Please spare its people, who long for peace after so many years of tyranny. May Egypt govern us without enslaving us.'

Queen Ahhotep was the first to step ashore on to the soil of Kerma.

Emheb looked around suspiciously. Part of the army had

disembarked, the archers remaining on full alert. But the old man had not lied, and the anxious inhabitants of Kerma were huddling in their homes, awaiting the pharaoh's decision.

'We shall grant your request,' announced Ahmose, 'on condition that Khamudi is delivered up to us.'

'When he fled here, he ordered us to take up arms and make all the people of Kerma join the fight, women and children included. We refused, and he insulted us. What right had that evil-hearted man to talk to us in that way?'

'Did he run away again?'

'No, he is still here.'

'Take us to him,' ordered Ahmose.

With its monumental gateways, bastions and its cross between a temple and a castle, Kerma looked very fine. The old man slowly climbed the staircase that led to the top of the palace.

The last emperor of the Hyksos would have no further opportunities to attack Egypt. Impaled on a long post, carefully sharpened by a grinning rubbish-collector, Khamudi was transfixed in a final cry of hatred.

The door of Amon's shrine had opened of its own accord.

Pharaoh Ahmose presented to the dawn sun the flaming sword with which he had vanquished the darkness, then he handed it to Queen Ahhotep who, as Wife of God, entered the shrine and laid it on an altar. It was Great Royal Wife Nefertari's responsibility to tend the altar flame so that the unity of the Two Lands would henceforth shelter Egypt from invasion.

'I worship you, O One of many manifestations,' chanted Ahhotep. 'Awake in peace. May your gaze light up the darkness and give us life.'

To Amon, Mut and Khonsu, the Sacred Three of Karnak, the pharaoh made the offering of Ma'at, the righteousness from which Ahhotep had never departed and thanks to which it would be possible to rebuild an Egypt worthy of many happy years.

'I have an important promise to keep,' Ahhotep reminded her son.

The whole court moved on to the place where the young Princess Ahhotep had met a surveyor, now long dead. He had permitted her to touch the Sceptre of Set for the first time without being struck by a thunderbolt, in the hope that the queen would one day give Egypt back her true borders.

The place was deserted, the land registry offices threatening to fall into ruin.

'Why have they not been restored?' Ahhotep asked Qaris.

'I ordered it several times, Majesty, but the workmen would not work here. They say the place is haunted.'

With the sceptre of power in her hand, Ahhotep took a few steps forwards. At once she had a strange sensation, as if the land refused to be conquered.

In one corner of the dilapidated buildings grew a tamarisk tree. Only two of its branches still had flowers on them. At its feet lay a heap of dried wood. Detecting a seat of negative energy, the queen went towards it. Hidden in the wood were torn, bloodstained clothing, tufts of hair and fragments of papyrus covered in magical incantations and words, including the name of Apophis.

Ahhotep placed the end of the sceptre on this cursed construction. A red light shot out of the eyes of the beast of Set, setting fire to the wood. Despite the efforts of his spy, Apophis was at last truly dead.

So the queen was able to survey the stretch of ground reserved for the land registry. Beginning the very next day, an official in charge of fields, an archive-keeper and specialist scribes would work there. The land of Egypt would once again attract the love of the gods.

Then the court moved on, to a vast ploughed field.

Nefertari sprinkled powdered gold there, ensuring that seed sown throughout Egypt's provinces would be fertile.

The true order had at last been re-established. At its summit ruled the gods, the goddesses and the glorified spirits whom the king and queen represented on earth; it was their responsibility to appoint a tjaty, judges charged with applying the law of Ma'at, and officials responsible for each sector of the community of the living.

'We shall begin by rebuilding the temples,' said Ahmose. 'The curtain walls will be rebuilt, the sacred objects placed in the shrines, the statues erected in their proper places. The circulation of offerings will be restored and the rituals of the mysteries shall be celebrated once more.'

'Where is this boat taking us?' Ahhotep asked her son curiously.

'It should be you who closes our former secret base, Mother. Also, I have a surprise for you.'

Ahhotep remembered the days of anguish when her husband, Seqen, had gathered together the first soldiers of the army of liberation, to the north of Thebes. Today the barracks was deserted, the palace disused and the temple abandoned. In a few years, the sandstorms would have covered over the whole of this base, where hope had been born. Hundreds of men trained here had lost their lives on the fields of battle; others had suffered serious wounds and could never forget the terrible battles in which they had fought.

But Egypt was free. Future generations would forget the blood and the tears, for Pharaoh was rebuilding happiness.

With her sceptre, the queen closed the mouths of the temple and the palace. This time, the war really was over.

When she returned to the boat, she saw a broad-shouldered man standing on the quayside next to the king and Ahmes, son of Abana. Young Laughter was lying down peacefully.

'This is the Master of the Place of Truth, the craftsmen's

village,' said Ahmose. 'He wished to present you with his Brotherhood's first great work, here in this very place where the clash of weapons has faded away.'

The Master laid his precious burden on the ground. It was covered with a white cloth, which he gently removed, revealing a perfectly cut cube of stone.

'We extracted the raw stone from a deep valley, lost in the mountains,' he explained. 'It is a lonely place, dominated by a pyramid-shaped peak in which there dwells a cobra-goddess who demands silence and punishes liars and people who say too much. With copper chisels and wooden mallets, we created this plinth, on which our future works shall rest, on condition that Your Majesty consents to give it life.'

The pharaoh handed his mother the white club, the Illuminator, with which he consecrated offerings. Ahhotep struck the stone, which instantly flamed like the Sword of Amon. Then the rays of light became concentrated inside the stone cube, which the Master covered with its cloth again.

'May this Stone of Light transform matter into spirit,' declared the queen, 'and may it be faithfully passed on from one Master to the next.'

60

Although he had murdered two pharaohs, the Hyksos spy had not succeeded in killing the third. But the army of liberation would have achieved its goal even if he had succeeded, for its true heart was Ahhotep.

At first he had been amused by her. He would never have believed her capable of such deeds, and he had wanted to know just how far she could go. At each new stage, he had been convinced that she would go no further. And yet, no matter what blows destiny struck her and what terrible sufferings she had to bear, she continued determinedly, as if nothing could make her turn aside from her path.

He admired her, and probably even more than that. She had benefited from the favour of the gods, with the death of Apophis and the eruption of Thera. Today the Hyksos empire had been annihilated and the Two Lands reunited.

But the spy had promised to carry out his mission. And he would keep his word.

This reborn Egypt was much more fragile than it thought. By killing Ahhotep, he would destroy its foundations. During the coming festivities, he would choose the best opportunity to prove to the people that the Queen of Freedom was not immortal. Deprived of the person who had given it back its life, Egypt would sink into chaos. And the Emperor of Darkness would finally have triumphed.

The Flaming Sword

*

In the presence of Ahhotep, Pharaoh Ahmose celebrated the start of the twenty-second year of his reign by opening the famous quarries at Tura, where the most beautiful limestone in the land was extracted. Two stelae, carved and placed at the entrance to the galleries, commemorated the event.

Six humped oxen drew a wooden sledge, bearing the first block for the future Temple of Ptah at Memphis. The ox-herd who gently urged the animals along was none other than Big-Feet, who had recovered well. He had become the owner of a farm and an estate where many cows grazed, and he employed prisoners of war who had neither killed nor tortured Egyptians.

Everywhere people were restoring and building. Little by little Memphis, the white-walled city, was regaining its former splendour. Gold and silver were once more arriving from Asia and Nubia, copper and turquoise from Sinai; and from Afghanistan came lapis-lazuli, the symbol of the celestial vault and the primordial waters.

Who but the Afghan – like Moustache, he had been promoted to the rank of general in the reserve forces – could have been appointed overseer of imports?

'Still determined to go back home?' his friend asked him. 'Here you're rich and heaped with honours, the women run after you, the wine is excellent and the climate is wonderful.'

'I miss my mountains.'

'You know, Afghan, I can understand almost everything, but that. . .'

'Don't forget you have to climb a snow-covered slope to prove to me that you're a real man.'

'Instead of that, look at this lapis-lazuli and tell me if it's worthy of being taken to the temple.'

'It's magnificent.'

The ways of trade were picking up again. At Memphis and Thebes, the royal workshops had set to work once more, as had the land registry, weights and measures, waterways and census offices. The principle of the redistribution of wealth was once again applied under the aegis of Ma'at, the guarantor of stability and social cohesion.

The royal fleet sailed towards Abydos.

Despite his great age, Qaris wanted to be present at the ceremony during which the memory of Teti the Small would be honoured. Pampered by Emheb, who was soon to return to his good town of Edfu, and by Neshi, who had grown increasingly careworn since the tasks of government had accumulated on his shoulders, the old man could remember every episode in the war of liberation.

'What an incredible life we have lived!' he said to Emheb. 'Thanks to Ahhotep, we are nourished with hope and we have created a future where once it did not exist.'

Heray brought them some cool wine and cakes.

'Your responsibilities haven't made you lose any weight,' commented Neshi.

'Qaris and I did not have the good fortune to be in the front line, as you were. At Thebes we were often anxious, and anxiety makes you hungry. Look at the Afghan and Moustache: since they stopped cutting Hyksos into pieces, they have put on weight.'

'We have arrived,' Moon informed them.

'You look worried,' said Heray in surprise.

'The journey was not easy. The Nile sometimes has whims which demand extreme watchfulness. I did not even have time to taste that wine.'

'You will catch up,' predicted Emheb.

Nefertari was particularly anxious to venerate her husband's grandmother, whose popularity had never declined. Worshipped in Thebes, she must also be so at Abydos, in the sacred domain of Osiris.

So the king did 'what no king had done before', in the words of the ritual, for Teti the Small. A shrine and a small pyramid were built, surrounded by a garden, and a service of offerings was set up with a staff who would each day nourish the dead woman's *ka*, which was present among the living. Housed, fed, clothed and endowed with lands and animals, the priests would have no other care but to carry out their duties impeccably.

A large stele was raised depicting Ahmose, sometimes wearing the White Crown of Upper Egypt, sometimes the Double Crown, consecrating offerings before Teti the Small.

In the treasury set aside for her mother, Ahhotep laid the fine gold diadem she had so often worn, which had protected her from so many dangers.

For the spy, this ceremony was much too intimate an occasion. He would not strike until they were back at Thebes, so that Ahhotep's brutal death would have the greatest possible impact.

It looked very much as if Heray, Qaris and Neshi were plotting something.

'What are you talking about?' Ahhotep asked.

'Nothing important, Majesty,' replied Neshi.

'Is that true, Qaris?'

The old steward hesitated. 'In a way . . . Well, from a certain point of view . . .'

'You have never been able to lie to me,' said Ahhotep with a smile.

'Permit me to keep the secret, Majesty.'

'Is this plot restricted to the three of you, or do others also know of it?'

'All the most senior officials do,' confessed Heray, 'and the order comes from very, very high up.'

'In that case,' said the queen with amusement, 'it is pointless to question you any further.'

Ahhotep joined her son in the cabin of the flagship, whose door was guarded, as ever, by Ahmes and Young Laughter.

'Surely, Mother, the strict guarding of my person can be relaxed now?'

'The general staff believe that the officer who brought the false message from Moon, and who was killed during the battle, was the Hyksos spy. I disagree.'

'Even supposing that the spy is still alive, surely his sole aim is be forgotten?'

'He murdered your father and your brother. To leave those crimes unpunished would be to bow before the ghost of Apophis. So long as the criminal remains unidentified and still able to do harm, how can we truly know peace?'

61

Once again, the Temple of Amon at Karnak was alive with the sound of hammers and chisels. In accordance with his plan for extending and developing the temple, Ahmose was overseeing the installation of new offertory tables, which were copiously laden each morning. The king opened the eyes, mouths and ears of the divine statues with the worshipful staff. Then, using gold ewers and vases, the priests performed the rites with calm solemnity, carefully purifying the food so that its immaterial aspect would recharge the statues with positive energy.

For each member of the Sacred Three, a large cedar-wood boat had been made, covered with gold leaf. The boats would sail on the sacred lake and be borne in procession during festivals.

'I have taken two new decisions,' Ahmose told Ahhotep. 'The first is to build a new temple at Thebes to house the secret form of Amon and to worship his *ka*. The temple is to be called "Inventory-Maker",* in other words the one which reveals the Number, the true nature of the gods.

The second decision concerns you, Mother. It is time that you were honoured as you deserve to be.'

'So that is what the plot was all about!'

*Ipet-sut, the Temple of Luxor.

'I asked those close to us to keep the secret, it is true, for a great ceremony is being prepared.'

'But this is far, far more than I deserve.'

'No, Mother, it is not. Without you, Egypt would no longer exist. And it is not only your son who sets great store by this celebration. Pharaoh does, too.'

The great day had arrived.

In the open-air courtyard of the Temple of Karnak, all the notables of Thebes and even other Egyptian cities were present at Ahhotep's triumph. Outside, a huge crowd was already gathering, eager to cheer the queen, who had never flinched in the face of adversity.

Ahhotep regretted having given in to Ahmose, for she did not seek honours. Like the many, many soldiers who had died for Egypt's freedom, she had only done her duty.

Ahhotep remembered that Teti the Small, in all circumstances, had been immaculately dressed and made-up. To do her honour, the queen therefore placed herself in the hands of two palace maids who handled the combs, alabaster detangling-needles and face-paint sticks with special skill. Using exceptionally fine cosmetics, they made the queen more alluring than a young beauty.

With as much respect as emotion, Qaris crowned Ahhotep with a gold diadem. On the front was a raised braid and the cartouche of Ahmose on a background of lapis-lazuli, flanked by two sphinxes. Round the queen's neck he put a broad collar made up of many rows of small gold pieces, some representing lions, antelopes, ibex and uraei, others geometrical figures such as spirals or discs. It was fastened by a clasp in the form of two falcon's heads.

The old steward added a pendant, made up of a gold chain and a gold and lapis-lazuli scarab which embodied the soul's perpetual regeneration and its never-ending metamorphoses in the celestial paradise. All that was left was for Qaris to adorn the queen's wrists with fine gold, cornelian and lapis-lazuli bracelets. Far from being simple objects with an aesthetic purpose, they depicted scenes confirming the pharaoh's sovereignty over Upper and Lower Egypt. The earth-god, Geb, enthroned him in the presence of Amon. And the vulture-goddess, Nekhbet, Holder of the Royal Title, recalled the queen's vital role.

Deeply impressed, the old steward stepped back. 'Forgive my forwardness, Majesty, but you are as beautiful as a goddess.'

'My damned back,' complained Moustache. 'It's still hurting! Couldn't you rub it for me, She-Cat?'

'The ceremony starts in less than an hour, I haven't finished dressing, and you've just put on your ceremonial robe. Do you really think we have time for that kind of thing?'

'It really hurts! If I can't stay standing up and be present at Ahhotep's triumph, I shan't ever recover.'

She-Cat sighed. 'Just a moment. I'll fetch you some pills to take the pain away.'

Moustache looked at himself in a mirror. He had never in all his life looked so splendid, what with the golden collars rewarding his exploits, his broad belt and his fine sandals.

'I forgot,' said She-Cat. 'I gave them to the Afghan for the pain in his neck. You two aren't very wonderful for war-heroes!'

The Afghan's house was next door to Moustache and She-Cat's. Moustache rushed round there.

'My master is in the bathing-room,' said the maid.

'Don't disturb him. I'll manage on my own.'

Moustache went into the room where his friend kept weapons, kilts and medicines. After rummaging through a linen chest in vain, he happened on a box containing little pots of ointment and a curious object which he examined in astonishment.

It was a scarab. Not an Egyptian scarab, a Hyksos one, bearing the name of Apophis. Clearly, it had often been used as a seal. On its back were signs written in a coded script.

'Are you looking for something?' asked the Afghan, who appeared in the doorway, still dripping water.

With fury in his eyes, Moustache brandished the scarab. 'What does this mean?'

'Do you really need an explanation?'

'Not you, Afghan. Not you! It's not possible!'

'Everyone has his own battles to fight, my friend. There is one thing you don't know: it was Egypt that ruined my family, by trading with a rival tribe. I swore to take revenge, and the oath of a man of the mountains cannot be retracted. The Hyksos gave me my chance. Apophis ordered me to infiltrate the rebels, and I succeeded beyond my greatest hopes. Two pharaohs to my credit, Seqen and Kamose, do you realize? What other spy could boast as much?'

'But you fought alongside me, you took insane risks, and you killed dozens of Hyksos!'

'That was unavoidable. I had to make sure that I was trusted totally and that no suspicion would ever attach to me. And I haven't finished yet.'

'You mean you're going to try to kill Ahmose?'

'Not him, Ahhotep. She is the one who destroyed the Hyksos Empire, and I'm going to destroy her at the height of her glory, so that Egypt will crumble again.'

'You've gone mad, Afghan!'

'On the contrary, I am at last completing the mission with which I was entrusted – and my dead emperor will be the true victor in this war. I have many regrets, my friend, for I have not stopped admiring Ahhotep. I believe that I even fell in love with her the moment I saw her, and that I still love her now. That is why I have spared her so long; too long. But I am a man of honour, like you, and I cannot return to my country until I have fulfilled all my obligations. I am sorry, but I shall have to kill Ahhotep – after I have killed you, my friend.'

Each as swift as the other, the two men snatched up their daggers. Each knew that he had never faced a more difficult opponent. Moving very slowly, eyes locked, they searched for an opening, each man certain that the first blow would be decisive.

Moustache struck first. His dagger only scratched the Afghan's arm, and the Afghan knocked Moustache off balance and threw him down on his back. As he fell, Moustache dropped his weapon. The traitor's blade was at his throat, and blood was already trickling from it.

'It's a pity,' said the Afghan, 'but you shouldn't have searched my things. I liked you and I've been happy fighting beside you.'

Suddenly, he stiffened and let out a muffled cry, as though trying to contain the terrible pain that was taking his life away. Even mortally wounded by the dagger She-Cat had just plunged into his back, the Afghan could have cut Moustache's throat. But he spared his brother in arms and, his eyes already staring into nothingness, collapsed on to his side.

'I forgot to tell you how many pills to take,' She-Cat explained to Moustache. 'Taking too many would have been dangerous.'

On an altar Pharaoh Ahmose laid a silver boat mounted on wheels not unlike those of the war-chariots. This evoked the power and ability to move of Ahhotep's protector, the moon-god.

Like the others, Moustache – whose wound was concealed by a bandage – could not take his eyes off Queen Ahhotep in all her finery and her great beauty. This sixty-year-old woman outshone all the elegant ladies of the court.

Having heard Moustache's story, Ahhotep was at last truly at peace. No further dangers threatened the pharaoh's life.

'Let us bow before the Queen of Freedom,' ordered Ahmose. 'We owe her our lives, and she has brought life back to this land, which we shall rebuild together.'

In the silence that reigned over the great courtyard at Karnak, love of all her fellow-countrymen filled Ahhotep's heart.

The pharaoh turned his mother. 'Never, in all the long history of Egypt, has a queen received a military decoration. Majesty, you shall be the first – and, I hope, the last, since peace has succeeded war through the accomplishment of your name. May this symbol of the unceasing struggle you led against the powers of darkness bear witness to the worship of all your subjects.'

Ahmose decorated Ahhotep with a gold pendant, from which hung three beautifully stylised golden flies.

In the front row, Young Laughter, Way-Finder and Rascal all had the same thought: there was no insect as tenacious or as persistent as the fly. Ahhotep had transformed that idiosyncrasy into a warlike virtue in order to defeat the Hyksos.

'Supreme power ought to return to you, Mother,' whispered the king.

'No, Ahmose. It is your task to found a new dynasty, a new kingdom, and to make the Golden Age live again. As for me, I swore an oath: to withdraw into the temple as soon as our country had been liberated. And that happy day has arrived, my son.'

Radiant with joy, the queen walked towards the shrine where, as the Wife of God, she would henceforth dwell in company with Amon, in the secret realm of his Light.